a CORNERSTONE novel

Until
THEN

KRISTA NOORMAN

BOOKS by KRISTA NOORMAN

The Truth About Drew
Goodbye, Magnolia
Hello, Forever
Until Then
18 Hours To Us

ISBN: 1516847377
ISBN-13: 978-1516847372

For my biggest fan—my Mom.

1

August 1994

"There is NO WAY I'm going to a Christian college!"

The old, rickety table in the kitchen of the tiny two bedroom apartment was covered with brochures and catalogs from Cedarville, Cornerstone, and Grace—three religious colleges in Ohio, Michigan, and Indiana respectively. All were addressed to Miss Michelle Harrison.

"Well, you better get used to the idea." Her mother, Louise, stood across the table from where she sat.

Michelle shoved the papers across the table toward her mother. A few slid over the edge and floated to the floor. She flipped her dark, silky hair over her shoulder and crossed her arms over her chest in defiance.

Mom shot her a warning look.

Her father had been mostly quiet since he arrived with his parents for this special family meeting. "This is important. This is your future, Michelle."

Michelle wished he would have remained quiet. "You didn't have to come all this way, Dad. Mom and I will manage. Just like we have all these years."

Her grandmother piped in at that. "That's no way to talk to your father."

Michelle raised an eyebrow. "And I don't need *your* help either."

"Well, I never," Grandma huffed.

Grandpa shook his head. He was a man of few words, but Michelle could sense his disappointment in her behavior.

"I'll just go to a community college," Michelle stated.

1

"We can't even afford that." Louise reached for the papers and retrieved them from the floor. She looked weary. Michelle couldn't remember a time when her mother hadn't looked that way.

"Well, I'll get a job and pay for it." She was determined to stand her ground, even if it meant working multiple jobs like Mom always had. "I can do this on my own."

"You *could* do that and struggle your way through school." Louise sat across from her and placed the fallen papers with the others. "Or you could accept your grandparents' generous offer to pay for your tuition and not have to worry about the money."

"You guys don't even like me." She picked at the chipping paint on the edge of the table, not making eye contact with her grandparents.

"That's not true." Grandma took two steps closer and laid her fingertips on the edge of the table. "We love you. But you haven't made it easy." She paused with eyebrow raised. "For any of us."

Michelle rolled her eyes. "You're just doing this because you feel guilty."

Grandma's mouth fell open a little. "What do we have to feel guilty about?"

"That your son is such a horrible father."

Dad took a step forward and addressed her sternly. "You need to learn a little respect, young lady."

"Don't yell at her, Robert." Louise glared at her ex-husband like a mama bear protecting her cub.

"Well, maybe if you had done a better job with her, she wouldn't be acting out like this." He poked the bear.

"Are you kidding me? If anyone's to blame, it's you! She needed a father, and you walked out."

Michelle covered her ears as she had always done when she was little. There had never been a shortage of raised voices in their home. It was how they communicated. When he bothered to be there, that is.

Almost since the day she took her first steps, he had been out the door on this business trip or that, rarely spending more than a couple weeks at home at a time. Her mother was a cold, paranoid sort of woman. Not once in all of her childhood could she remember Mom showing affection to Dad. She didn't know if that was how she had always been or if her father's lengthy absences and suspected rendezvous had caused it. She often wondered why they had married in the first place, because there seemed to be no love there.

They divorced when she was six, and she saw him once, maybe twice a year after that. He was a stranger, and he made no real effort to get to know her, which made their visits awkward and, in her opinion, completely unnecessary.

Mom did the best she could, but she struggled to pay the bills, every spare moment consumed by work. No time for her young daughter, who so desperately needed a mother's guidance.

So Michelle was left to figure life out on her own. With a lack of positive female role models, no real girl friends in her life, and the absence of her father, she gravitated toward the company of boys, which inevitably led to boyfriends at an early age. And where her mother was cold and distant, steering clear of men after the sting of divorce, Michelle was the opposite, almost to the extreme. She was overly warm and affectionate, drawn to the opposite sex like a moth to a flame. And the attention she had never received at home was found in the arms of whatever guy would have her.

Michelle squeezed her eyes shut. Harsh insults and rude remarks overwhelmed the small space. Grandma had joined in, slinging opinions of her own. Her grandfather stood quietly in the corner, staying out of it.

"Stop!" Michelle finally cried. "STOP IT!"

The yelling ceased, but tension still hung heavy in the stale air.

Michelle felt a sudden urge to run. She would rather be with Tyler and Eddie than sitting there reliving the fights of her childhood. It was like the worst deja vu moment ever.

Louise gently pushed the papers in Michelle's direction. "Look, I don't care why your grandparents wanna do this. This is your ticket out of this place."

Michelle didn't want out of Chicago. She was happy there. She had a life there. "I'm not leaving my friends," she snapped.

Her mother snorted. "Friends? Those boys are a bad influence, Missy."

She hated being called *Missy*. And she knew exactly what her mother's comment was referring to—a certain party Mom would never let her forget.

Almost two years had passed since that night at Ray's with Tyler and Eddie, her closest guy friends. They were the guys she grew up with, the ones she felt most herself with, the ones who taught her how to play basketball. They also told her all about sex and introduced her to drinking and smoking pot. Eddie was like a brother to her, but Tyler was the one she wanted. She wanted him to look at her the way he looked at all the other girls, not just like one of the guys. Tyler had been with a lot of girls since she had known him, but she longed to be the one he wanted. She wanted to be the one he kissed behind the school during lunch. She wanted her first time to be with him. And that night at Ray's, thanks to many beers, she got what she wanted.

Ray's was always the place to be—the place to hang out and hook up, among other things. The crowd was larger than usual, the noise level higher than it should have been. It was not uncommon for Ray's parties to be broken up by the cops, and Michelle and her friends were usually among the first to bolt when trouble came knocking. But they'd been drunk—very drunk—when she led Tyler up the smoky staircase to one of the bedrooms and clicked the door shut behind them.

"What are you doing?" he had asked when she pushed him back onto the bed.

"What does it look like I'm doing?"

He didn't complain or try to stop her. And it finally happened. She lost her virginity to Tyler.

And then they spent the night together … in jail.

If they hadn't been upstairs when the cops came, they never would have been caught. And if Eddie had warned them sooner, none of them would have. She totally blamed Eddie.

This incident, her continued association with these boys, and her constant sneaking out of the house led to many fights at home. Mom constantly held the party over her head. She even went so far as to forbid her from seeing any of them, but it didn't work.

Sleeping with Tyler didn't work either. She had hoped it would propel her to girlfriend status, but that didn't happen. Instead, he saw them as friends with benefits and got physical with her whenever he was in the mood.

Sadly, she let him.

Her mother walked over and laid a hand on her shoulder. "You'll find new friends. Better friends."

She shrugged her shoulder away. "I don't want new friends, and you can't make me give them up. I'm not a little kid anymore."

"You're sixteen. In my book, that's still a kid."

"Well, your book is old and out of print." Michelle stood, her chair scraping loudly against the dingy linoleum floor. "And I'm almost seventeen."

"Seventeen is not an adult."

"Close enough." She walked to the wall phone, and picked up the handset.

"What do you think you're doing?"

Michelle looked at her mom like she was totally clueless. "I think we're done here. I have a phone call to make."

"Those boys have no say in this." Her mother walked across the kitchen, grabbed the phone from her hand, and slammed it into place. She grabbed Michelle's arm and tugged her toward the table. "And we aren't done talking yet."

"Hey!" Michelle cried. She twisted her arm from Mom's grip and pushed past, knocking her backwards into the wall.

Her mother's eyes widened with anger.

Dad slammed his hands on the table. "Sit down! NOW!"

Michelle flopped down in the nearest chair and rolled her eyes. She knew her dad wasn't there because he actually cared about her or what was going on in her life. He was only there because his parents had summoned him.

Dad pointed at the brochures. "You will apply to these three schools. You can choose which one you wanna go to when you see which ones accept you. If you don't, we'll pick for you."

She crossed her arms again. Despite her rebellious ways, she was smart and got decent grades. She knew she would inevitably be accepted to all three.

"Why these?" She glared at the brochures in disgust.

"Your Uncle Brian is a professor at Cedarville, and Grandpa and Grandma both went to Grace. It's where they met."

Michelle wondered how her dad grew up in such a religious family yet still turned out the way he did. Neither of her parents ever had much to do with God, except maybe the occasional use of His name in vain, and He had never done anything to help their family. It was for this reason that the idea of God and religion seemed pointless to her.

She motioned to the last brochure for Cornerstone College. "And this one?"

"It's another good Christian college, so you have options."

Michelle flipped each catalog over and noticed the very obvious pattern. "All out of state."

"Yes."

"To get me away from my *horrible* friends," she said sarcastically.

"To give you a chance at a better life," her grandmother interjected.

"This sucks." Michelle hated that they were ganging up on her like this. "I love Chicago. It's my home. I don't wanna live anywhere else."

"You're going," her mother demanded.

"Screw you!" The fury bubbled up within her.

"You are out of control, Missy!"

"You can't make me go!"

Her mother's eyes narrowed. "Watch me."

❧ 2 ❧

$\mathcal{M}$ichelle opened the window of her dorm room to let in the fresh, late-summer air. A soft breeze blew in and cleared the stuffiness away. She glanced around and took in the drab cinder block walls, boring tile floor, and pale wood doors of the closets. Cornerstone College—home for the next nine months.

She took a seat at a built-in desk next to the only single bed in the room, which she had claimed with her bags. The other two beds were bunks, and there was no way she was sleeping on a bunk bed. It was bad enough she had to share a room with two complete strangers.

She sighed, still not quite believing she was there. The benefits of having her grandparents pay for a full ride to college far outweighed any argument she could come up with for not going, so she had caved and agreed to their conditions. And she spent her final year of high school acting out in any way possible to let her family know just how unhappy she was about the whole thing.

Why she chose Cornerstone had little to do with the quality of the academics or the look of the campus and everything to do with her family's lack of affiliation with this particular school. She didn't care to go to Grace just because her grandparents met there, and she didn't want to go to Cedarville and risk having Uncle Brian as one of her professors. So Cornerstone it was.

She didn't know how she would survive a month there, let alone four years, with all its rules and strict morals, of which she was in short supply. And she already missed home. Grand Rapids, Michigan was only three hours away from Chicago, but it may as well have been three hundred. She was dropped off by her mom, left without a car, stranded in a strange place.

The door suddenly opened and in walked a pretty girl with sandy blonde hair carrying a laundry basket overflowing with her belongings. A man, woman, and teenaged boy followed carrying boxes and bags.

"Hi," the girl said. "You must be one of my roommates. I'm Maggie."

Michelle smiled weakly. "Michelle."

The man and woman introduced themselves as Patty and Ron James, Maggie's parents, and shook her hand politely.

The teenaged boy hovered nearby with a flirty grin on his face, his strawberry blond hair hanging over one eye. "Hey, I'm Tom."

Maggie smacked him on the arm. "Leave her alone, Tommy."

This made Michelle smile in spite of herself. Being an only child, she had always wondered what it would be like to have a brother or sister to harass.

"I wonder when our other roommate's getting here." Maggie opened the closet doors and checked out the space.

Michelle shrugged. "I just got here about an hour ago myself. No sign of her yet."

Mr. James and Tom left to retrieve the rest of Maggie's things.

"Where are you from, Michelle?" Patty asked.

"Chicago."

"Oh, we love the Windy City," she replied. "Have you always lived there?"

Michelle nodded. "Yep." She didn't really know how to do the whole small talk thing.

Maggie rifled through her pile of things at the foot of the bunk beds. She grabbed a black padded bag from one of the boxes and pulled an expensive looking camera from within.

"Will you take a picture of me and Michelle, Mom?"

Michelle groaned inwardly when Maggie stepped to her side and put an arm around her. She faked a smile.

Ron and Tom returned and stacked a couple more boxes and baskets with the rest.

"I wonder which bed she'll want," Maggie considered.

Michelle sat on the bed she had left her things on. "I say we get first choice since we were here first."

"Sounds good to me," Maggie agreed. She tossed her pillow and some bedding on the bottom bunk. "Hey, we're going to dinner. Do you wanna come along?"

"Oh." Michelle shook her head.

"You're more than welcome to come, Michelle." Patty looked at her with kind, green eyes.

"That's OK. I think I'll stay here and see if the other roommate shows."

"Are you sure?" Maggie's eyes were even greener than her mother's.

Michelle nodded.

"OK. Well, I'll be back in a couple hours, and we can talk more." Michelle cringed at the thought. "OK. Have fun."

They left the door open on their way out.

Michelle rolled onto her stomach and stared out the open door as more students filed through the hallway with their families. Part of her thought she should have gone with Maggie's family. They seemed like nice people, but the idea of more small talk did not sound at all appealing.

Waiting for their other roommate was a good excuse, but she wasn't really going to do that.

The campus was simple yet beautiful, with it's winding sidewalks lined with trees, lovely landscaping, and a picturesque pond. Michelle walked from her dorm, Miller Hall, across the campus to the gymnasium. The doors were open to welcome the students, and the sound of sneakers squeaking on the wood floor greeted her.

Once inside, she discovered a group of guys playing three-on-three basketball. It was the first thing on campus that gave her the slightest feeling of comfort. She stood to the side of the door and watched, itching to grab the ball and join the game.

One of the guys immediately turned her head. He was tall and handsome with nut brown hair and an athletic physique. But he was a terrible shot, hitting the backboard way too high at least half a dozen times. He suddenly lobbed the ball at the basket and completely missed, sending it bouncing in Michelle's direction.

She retrieved the ball and dribbled it in place, glancing his way.

He jogged over to her, and she tossed him the ball.

"Thanks," he said with a grin. "Do you play?"

Michelle flipped her long, dark ponytail over her shoulder and raised an eyebrow in reply. "The real question is ... do you?"

He laughed aloud and returned to the game.

Michelle took a seat on the nearby bleachers. Basketball was her game. She had been playing with the guys since they were kids and had played on the team in junior high and high school. She was good, but never good enough to play first string or dare to dream of a college basketball scholarship. She loved the game, though, and was planning to play on a college intramural team in the spring. In the meantime, she hoped to find some like-minded friends to play with, and these guys definitely looked promising.

When their game ended, the handsome stranger and a couple of his friends approached. He was dribbling the basketball, bouncing it back and forth between his legs, obviously showing off with a little fancy footwork. At least he was good at *that*.

He stilled the basketball and strolled over to her. "Hi again."

"Hey."

"I'm Simon."

"Michelle."

"I would shake your hand, but I'm kinda sweaty."

She laughed.

"These are my roommates, Wes and Sean."

Wes's blond hair was plastered to his forehead with sweat. He brushed it back from his face. "Nice to meet you." He was shorter than the others, but height hadn't kept him from excelling on the court.

Sean wiped his hand on his shorts and held it out to her. "Nice to meet you, Michelle."

She shook Sean's hand. "You, too." He had the bluest eyes she had ever seen, like clear, aquamarine water in some tropical location she would probably never visit.

"Are you a freshman this year?" Simon asked.

"Does it show?" Michelle raised an eyebrow.

"A little. What dorm are you in?"

"Miller. You?"

"We're in Quincer."

"Is this your first year, too, then?" she asked them.

They nodded in reply.

Wes and Sean then excused themselves to go get cleaned up.

As they walked away, Sean glanced back over his shoulder and smiled. "See ya'."

She lifted her hand in a wave. "Yeah. See ya'."

Simon raised a hand to his friends, then turned his attention back to Michelle. "You never answered my question earlier."

"What question is that?"

He tilted his head toward the hoop. "Do you play?"

"I do," she proudly answered. "I was on the team in high school. You?"

"Nah. I play for fun," he replied. "Are you any good?"

Better than you. "I can hold my own." She kept her true thoughts to herself.

Simon suddenly tossed the ball at her, which she caught with lightning fast reflexes. "Prove it."

"OK." She was up for the challenge.

"Play me a game of PIG."

Michelle laughed. "PIG? Really?"

"Come on." He walked backwards toward the court. "You can go first."

She moved to the three-point line and looked him straight in the eye. "This is gonna be a really short game."

⚘ ♡ ⚘

Michelle walked to the dorm with a feeling of satisfaction. She had crushed Simon at multiple games of PIG. He really was a terrible shot. But it felt good to have someone to play ball with again.

When she decided on Cornerstone, she never thought she would meet anyone that she felt as comfortable with as her friends. Simon Walker was a welcome surprise. And not bad to look at either. He was funny and easygoing, like the guys she hung out with back home. Well, not exactly like those guys, but he would do.

"I'll be right back." Michelle left Maggie and Emma in line for food.

"Hey!" Simon greeted her. "Good thing I brought friends." He nodded toward the girls waiting in line.

"I'm gonna have to take a rain check," she told him.

"Your friends can join us, too." He looked across the room at them again.

"My roommates wanna have a girls night and ... bond or whatever." This was probably the first time in her life she had turned down a guy to hang out with girls instead.

"Oh, no problem," Simon said. "I'll catch up with you later then."

"OK. See ya'."

Michelle rejoined the girls in line.

"Who's that guy you were talking to?" Emma asked, her eyes aimed in Simon's direction.

"Simon Walker," she replied. "I met him at the gym today."

Maggie glanced across the room at the guys. "Did you wanna sit with him?"

Michelle shook her head. "No, that's OK."

"Are you sure?"

"Yeah ... let's bond." Michelle almost laughed aloud at her uncharacteristic words.

Emma did her happy clapping again. *Cute as a button.*

The roommates sat for hours munching on cheese fries, chatting, and getting to know each other. Michelle found it to be a lot less painful than she thought it would be.

Maggie gushed about her love of photography. She asked if she could use the two of them as guinea pigs if she needed models for class assignments. Emma delightedly agreed. Michelle not so much.

Maggie also shared about her beloved church youth group, her best friends, Kay and Brooke, and her best guy friend, Ben. Her voice turned soft and sweet when she mentioned him, and Michelle had a feeling there was more to it than Maggie had revealed.

Emma was a PK—Pastor's Kid. She had grown up in the church and seemed to be the most perfect example of a pastor's child that Michelle could have imagined. She came from a big family with lots of siblings, several younger than her, which was one of the reasons she was so drawn to the idea of teaching elementary aged children.

They had filled the shelves with makeup, curling irons, and hair spray. Besides a little lip gloss, Michelle hadn't worn a touch of makeup in her life, and her portion of the closet was drab and minimalistic in comparison to theirs. She had a handful of t-shirts, athletic pants and shorts, a few neutral-colored sweaters and skirts, and some blue jeans. Her clothing took up a small section, while theirs overflowed. It was overwhelming evidence that they came from very different worlds.

She grabbed some fresh clothing and her shower caddy and started in the direction of the communal bathroom at the end of the hall.

"What are you doing tonight?" Maggie asked before Michelle stepped out of the room.

"I thought I'd check out The Skillet."

"Oh, that sounds fun." Maggie's response hung in the air as if awaiting an invitation.

Michelle sighed. "You guys should come along."

Emma clapped her hands happily. "Our first night out together as roomies. I just know we're gonna be the best of friends."

"Girls night!" Maggie announced.

Michelle shook her head and walked to the bathroom. Her biggest concern leading up to college was not about who she might live with, but the fact that she had to go in the first place. She hadn't really thought through how it would be to have roommates or what they might be like. She assumed they wouldn't get along simply because she didn't get along with other girls. She hadn't entertained the idea that they might like her or that she might actually like them, too.

The Skillet was bursting with students snacking on greasy food and pop. Michelle scanned their faces for Simon and spotted him across the room.

He stood and waved to her. His table looked completely crowded with his roommates and several other guys.

Michelle took note of his jeans and green polo. Much better than the sweaty t-shirt and shorts at the gym, although he looked pretty good in those, too.

Simon had taken his defeat like a true gentleman—not something she was used to—and invited her to meet up later at the campus hangout, The Skillet, to celebrate her victory.

She wandered leisurely along the sidewalk and noticed many students still arriving, lugging their stuff into the dorms. As she squeezed past a family carrying boxes and suitcases, she heard chattering girl voices coming from her room. She turned into their doorway to see Maggie talking with a cute, petite blonde.

The third roommate.

"You're back!" Maggie exclaimed. "This is Emma, our other roommate."

"Hi." Michelle gave her the same weak smile she had given Maggie earlier. She was always so uncomfortable around other girls.

The girls rambled on about themselves while Michelle listened. Maggie was from the town of Hastings, an hour south of Cornerstone. She was there to study photography, which explained her fancy camera. Emma was from a town called Bucyrus in Ohio, and she had always dreamed of becoming a teacher, like Anne of Green Gables.

"Who?" Michelle asked.

"You've never read Anne of Green Gables?" Emma asked.

She shook her head. She had never heard of it.

Apparently, Emma and Maggie had both read and loved this series of books, and they went on and on about the movie adaptation, which was their absolute favorite.

Michelle had never been one to open up to complete strangers, especially girls, but she knew she would be living with these two for at least the next nine months, so she gave them the basics—from Chicago, only child, undeclared major.

They accepted her brief background then shared about their families, friends back home, and things they enjoyed.

This was not something Michelle knew how to do. She'd never really had girlfriends, and if this school had permitted it, she would have preferred to live in one of the dorms with the guys.

The guys. She suddenly glanced over at the clock. *Simon.*

Michelle moved to the shared closet and opened the doors to an abundance of colorful shirts, skirts, and dresses. Both of her roommates were so very girly, which was a foreign concept to her.

Michelle was actually enjoying the girls' stories. *So this is bonding.* She even found herself opening up more as time went on. She told them about her love of basketball, the guys back home, and her parents divorce, but she completely skipped over anything relating to her partying ways or what life was really like for her in Chicago.

At the two-hour mark, Maggie excused herself to go back to the room. She was expecting an important phone call that she did not want to miss.

Michelle noticed Emma's gaze wander to the guys' table again. They were still there, talking and laughing with some girls who had joined them.

"Emma?"

Emma turned her attention to Michelle. "What?"

"Do you wanna meet the guys? Is that why you keep looking over there?"

She blushed a little. "Your friend, Simon, is really cute." She couldn't contain her smile.

Michelle wouldn't tell Emma, but she completely agreed. Simon was definitely good-looking.

They tossed their trash in the nearby can and moved in the direction of Simon's table. Michelle was overcome with hesitation. Emma was adorable with a cheerfully sweet personality, and all it would take was an introduction for Simon to instantly fall for her.

"You go first, Michelle," Emma spoke timidly, "since you already know him."

Michelle could tell Emma was nervous and probably had no experience with guys whatsoever. She was the epitome of a good girl.

"He won't bite," Michelle told her.

Emma giggled. "I know that."

Michelle strolled up to the table, and Simon's face lit up when he saw her.

"Hey! You decided to join us after all." He found a couple extra chairs from a nearby table and squeezed them in among the already overcrowded table.

"Who's your friend?" he asked with a smile, his eyes locked with Emma's.

"This is my roommate, Emma." She could tell by the look on his face that he was already smitten.

15

He took his seat again and patted the open chair next to him. "You can sit by me, Emma."

Emma happily sat down, her gaze holding his.

Michelle sighed, knowing she had lost him. She took the empty chair between Emma and Wes.

"Hello again," Wes said. "How was the rest of your day?"

She shrugged her shoulders. "Fine. How 'bout you?"

"Very good. Did you girls get all settled in?"

"Yep. Home sweet home." She faked cheerfulness.

Sean leaned forward and looked around Wes. "I hear you're pretty good with a basketball."

"Pretty good, huh?" *Oh, man, his eyes are so blue.*

"Well, Simon said you're a pretty good shot."

"Ha!" she exclaimed loudly. "Simon got his butt kicked. Did he tell you that?"

"*Ohhh!*" several of the guys exclaimed in unison.

"Hey!" Simon cried. "Nobody's butt was kicked."

Michelle shook her head. "I handed it to you on a platter, Walker."

"Uh-uh! No!" He slapped the table with his palm.

She laughed aloud while the guys continued to tease him. This was more like it. Joking around with the guys. This was what she needed, and it really did feel more like home.

♡

The group stayed until The Skillet closed, then wandered campus, chatting and goofing around. Michelle noticed the extra attention Simon paid to Emma. The two of them walked slightly ahead of the group, their arms brushing, deep in conversation. She tried not to let it bother her. They had all just met, and who knew what the semester held.

Sean suddenly caught up and fell into step with her. "So, I think you're gonna have to show me these mad basketball skills of yours."

"Oh, yeah?" she replied. "You sure you wanna risk it?"

He looked at her curiously.

"I mean, I'm fine kicking your butt, too, if that's what you want." She grinned.

"Oh no. That won't be happening." His bright blue eyes met hers.

"Name the day," she declared.

"Tomorrow afternoon."

"OK." She nodded. "It's your funeral."

"You better give me your number so we can set a time for this funeral." He bumped her arm with his elbow and smiled.

What a flirt. She glanced over at him as they walked. He was taller than her, if only by a few inches. At five foot ten, it wasn't uncommon for guys to be shorter than her, but she liked tall guys. Tall guys with brown hair. Sean's hair was perfect, like waves of dark chocolate, just the right length to bury her fingers in. It looked so soft, and she fought the urge to reach over and touch it.

He looked over at her again. His eyes seemed to change color depending on the light, and they were so icy blue now that they gave her chills, but not because she was the slightest bit cold.

"I don't have a pen, but if you walk me back to the dorm, I'll get one." She gave him a flirty grin.

If things didn't work out with Simon, she could always use a backup.

❧ ♡ ☙

When Michelle and Emma returned to the room near midnight, they found Maggie seated at her desk staring at the telephone. She quickly wiped tears from her cheeks.

Emma went straight across the room and wrapped her arms around Maggie's shoulders. "Maggie, are you OK?"

"I'm fine," Maggie replied. She reached for a tissue and blotted her eyes.

"Ben didn't call, did he?" Emma asked.

Maggie teared up again. "I tried to call him, but his roommate said he was out."

Michelle was uncomfortable around crying girls. She wasn't one to get weepy, especially over boys.

Emma sat on the other desk chair. "Maybe he'll call when he gets back."

"Maybe," Maggie didn't sound convinced. "It's happening just like I was afraid it would. He's forgetting me already."

Emma shook her head. "It's only the first day. He's probably getting settled, too."

"What's so great about this Ben guy?" blurted Michelle. Maybe it wasn't a very sympathetic response to her roommate's sadness, but she never understood girls like Maggie, who wrapped their whole lives up in one guy. "There are plenty of hot guys here. Who cares if he doesn't call. You're not in high school anymore."

Maggie's mouth dropped open and a tear slid down her cheek. She didn't bother to wipe it away.

"Sorry." Michelle hadn't meant to hurt Maggie's feelings with her blunt remarks. Maggie was obviously in love with this Ben guy, but that emotion was not something she was familiar with.

"It's fine."

"So ..." Michelle attempted to make conversation. "He's not just your friend, is he?"

Maggie took a deep breath in and let it out. "He is."

"But you want more." *This* she was familiar with.

Maggie proceeded to share the history of her friendship with Ben from the day he first stepped foot in her church freshman year of high school to the chaste kiss goodbye he had given her days before at their youth group farewell party.

The hour hand on the clock was nearing two when Maggie finally finished her story. Michelle tried not to yawn, but it was a lot of listening. She wasn't used to all this girl talk, but she was trying.

The telephone suddenly rang and the girls jumped.

Michelle and Emma both looked at Maggie, whose eyes were wide.

Ring! Ring!

"Answer it!" Michelle cried.

Maggie fumbled to grab the receiver. "Hello?" Her expression instantly went soft, and she wrapped the spiral cord around her fingers. "Hey, Ben. How are you?"

Emma looked at Michelle with a little smile.

Michelle rolled her eyes. Maggie seemed like a confident girl, but it was obvious, when it came to Ben, she was a mess. Still, she liked Maggie. She was kind and easy to talk to, maybe even capable of having some fun every once in a while. And maybe Michelle needed to be the one to help Maggie get her mind off of Ben.

3

The first week of classes crawled by. Michelle wasn't thrilled about any of the prerequisite biblical classes. She knew this was part of the deal at a Christian college, but she didn't have to like it. The best thing about her Old Testament class was Simon. She was happy to walk in on the first day and find him seated toward the back with Wes. He would definitely make the class easier to endure.

Her schedule wasn't bad, with all but one of her classes scheduled after ten o'clock, but she still had to drag herself out of bed every other morning for chapel—another requirement. It was bad enough students had to find a local church to attend on Sundays.

Michelle wasn't sure she could adhere to all the rules of the school.

She had never had to follow a dress code before. Why, oh why, did she have to wear a skirt to class? She didn't mind showing off her legs, but she was much more comfortable in a t-shirt and jeans. And what difference did it make what she wore? Couldn't she learn just as well in sweatpants?

There was a campus curfew—midnight on weeknights and one o'clock on weekends. She had never had a curfew in her entire life, and she thought this was absurd. They were technically adults now, so why did she feel more like a child than she ever had before?

The list of rules seemed to keep growing.

Worst of all, the campus was bone dry. When someone mentioned a party, it usually meant hanging out in the dorm lounge with pizza and pop. And there wasn't a cigarette in sight, let alone a joint. The guys back home would have laughed their heads off.

She often wondered what the guys were doing. None of them had gone to college after high school. They were working and living at home or getting places of their own. Normal life was happening in Chicago without her, while life at Cornerstone was like being trapped inside a giant Christian bubble.

When she had arrived on campus, everyone seemed just like her—new college students ready to start the next chapter of their lives. But she soon realized how very different they were. There was an overall vibe of goodness around campus. People got together just to discuss the Bible and what God was doing in their lives. And they prayed for everything. Emma began her days reading her Bible, while Maggie ended her days the same way. Michelle went through *her* days pretending to understand what they were all talking about, pretending to be one of them—a believer. But she didn't, and she wasn't.

Most nights when Emma and Maggie fell asleep, Michelle lay wide awake in bed. She found it difficult to sleep without the familiar noises of the city outside her window.

If she were back home, she would have been out with the guys somewhere or crashing on someone's couch. This place was too weird for her. She was lonely and in need of some male companionship. Tyler had never been her boyfriend, but he had been ready and willing for a hookup. And while she lay there night after night thinking about being with him, she realized *that* was the only thing she really missed about him. He was rude and crass and downright mean sometimes. His attention was easily shifted to other girls, and he never cared for her as much as she cared for him. He used her for sex when he wanted it, and treated her like just a friend the rest of the time, which wasn't saying much. He had not once called to see how she was doing since she left Chicago. She couldn't even remember why she had wanted him in the first place.

And then one night, three unexpected words crept into her train of thought.

You deserve better.

It took her by surprise, and she began to wonder what, or who, *better* might be.

Her nighttime thoughts soon began to feature Simon. He was funny, sweet, and so likable, and she loved spending time with him. She fantasized about kissing him and imagined having an actual relationship with a nice guy for a change. But her mind always replayed the way he had looked at Emma at the Skillet that first night. It was different than the way he looked at her—like a friend. She was sick of the guys she wanted looking at her that way.

During the first week, there had been a lot of talk about Celebration On The Grand, an annual end-of-summer festival held downtown along the banks of The Grand River. The biggest draw was the fireworks show on Saturday night, which Simon invited Michelle to attend.

"You should invite your roommates," Simon suggested.

Michelle knew exactly why he wanted her to invite them. "You know, if you wanna ask Emma, you don't need me to do it for you."

Simon put an arm around her and gave her a squeeze. "I'm asking *you*, Chelle, but we've got a bunch of guys going. You'll be outnumbered."

Michelle chuckled. "I think I can handle that."

He laughed aloud. "I have no doubt that you can."

Gah! That laugh. She loved a guy with a great laugh, and his was like music to her ears.

"Come on. It'll be fun."

She didn't care if he had ulterior motives. When he grinned at her with that playful look in his eyes, she couldn't refuse. "All right. I'll ask them."

He smiled and nodded.

On Saturday, Michelle and Emma, along with their next door neighbors, Darcy and Jill, accompanied the guys downtown to the celebration. The city was alive with activity, the streets filled with people enjoying Grand Rapids. Their little group wandered around for a while, walked along the river, got some snacks and drinks, then found a good spot in Ah-Nab-Awen Park, where there was live entertainment before the fireworks.

Emma pulled a blanket out of the bag she was carrying, and Simon helped her spread it out on the grass.

Michelle sat next to Emma toward the front edge of the blanket.

Simon plopped down behind them and scooted over closer to Emma. "How was your first week of classes?"

"Great! I love all of them," Emma gushed. "Every one of my professors is so interesting. How's your photography class?"

Simon's face lit up. "It's awesome. I can already tell I'm gonna learn a lot in there."

"Cool."

"Your roommate's in my class. What's her name again?"

"Maggie," Michelle interjected.

"Where's she tonight?" Simon glanced over at Michelle, then back at Emma.

"She's coming later with a friend of hers from back home," Emma replied.

In truth, Michelle was worried about Maggie. They had left her alone in the room waiting to hear from Ben, and she had a bad feeling about it. She knew plenty of unreliable guys like him, and her gut instinct told her he was not to be trusted.

Michelle glanced around the expansive lawn of the park, which sloped from the Gerald R. Ford Museum on the hill to the river below. The lush green grass was covered with blankets and lawn chairs filled with people enjoying the warm September evening. There were couples holding hands, families and friends, children running around. One little girl ran across in front of them, nearly tripping over Michelle's legs, followed by her concerned and slightly embarrassed father.

"Sorry." He waved as he passed by in pursuit of his daughter.

Michelle watched the man scoop up the little girl and say something into her ear before he blew against her arm, making a loud, slobbery noise. Her wild giggles floated on the wind, and Michelle's mood sank.

The rowdy laughter of a large group of teenagers turned her head. They were hanging out under the nearby trees, joking crudely, and annoying the people seated next to them. One couple was making out rather inappropriately against a tree. They reminded Michelle of her friends in Chicago.

She looked over at Simon and Emma all cozied up together, and she wanted to leave. These weren't her people. They were a whole different species. She wanted to go home. Back to Chicago, where she belonged.

Darcy's booming laughter suddenly grabbed her attention. Michelle looked back at her and Jill, seated on the back edge of the blanket facing Sean, Wes, and several guys from the dorm. The girls were clearly entertained by something one of the guys had said. Darcy flipped her long, blonde tresses over her shoulder flirtatiously. Jill seemed to be the more reserved of the two, giggling demurely while she twisted a fiery red curl around her finger.

Michelle's gaze fell on Sean, who she caught staring at her with those intense, blue eyes of his.

He flashed his perfect pearly whites at her.

She smiled in return, and he moved to stand.

"Hey," he said as he approached.

"Hey."

He pointed at the blanket. "May I?"

"Sure."

He sat behind her, and she shifted sideways, so he wouldn't have to talk to the back of her head.

"How are you?" he asked.

"Good. You?"

"Good."

"Nice night."

"Yeah."

"Kinda crowded."

"I know."

"You look nice."

"Thanks. You, too."

They had perfected the art of economical conversation.

"So ..." He tilted his head a little to the right and grinned at her. "You never called me back."

She cringed, hoping he wouldn't make a big deal of it. "I know. I'm sorry about that." He had called to schedule their basketball game and left a message with Emma. "Things have been pretty busy with registration and classes starting." Honestly, her attention had been focused on Simon, and she had forgotten.

"For me, too." He shrugged his shoulders and laid a hand on hers. "It's fine. You can make it up to me." His fingertips traced softly back and forth across the top of her hand.

"I can do that," she replied with her best come-hither look. If he was going to flirt with her, she was going to give it right back.

When twilight set in, the lawn became more crowded in anticipation of the fireworks. More students from the college surrounded their blanket, and Sean and a few of the guys ran off to get more drinks for everyone.

Emma seemed very antsy, constantly standing and looking around.

"What's the matter?" asked Simon from his place on the blanket.

"I'm worried about Maggie." Emma looked at Michelle with concern. "She should be here by now."

"Why are you so worried?" Simon reached up and grabbed Emma's hand.

Michelle grimaced. She didn't mean to, but it was like an automatic reaction to Simon touching another girl.

"She was supposed to come here with her friend, Ben," Emma explained. "They should have been here forty-five minutes ago."

"I'm sure she's OK." He squeezed her hand reassuringly.

"I want to call her," Emma stated.

Simon stood up next to her. "I'll walk you to a pay phone."

Emma sighed with relief. "Thank you, Simon."

"We'll be right back, Chelle." Simon wound his fingers through Emma's. "Save our place."

She loved it when he called her that, but she didn't love the sight of him walking hand in hand with Emma.

Sean returned to his place on the blanket just then with a Mountain Dew for Michelle and a Pepsi for himself.

"Thanks." Michelle took a sip.

"No problem." He pointed to the empty spot on the blanket. "Where'd they go?"

"To call our roommate, Maggie. She was supposed to meet us, and she's not here yet."

"Oh, I thought maybe they wanted some alone time or something."

Michelle didn't care for that comment, but he made up for it by running his fingers up the side of her arm, leaving little goosebumps in their wake. She lost focus on everything, except that sensation. She forgot about the crowd of people around them. She forgot about

Simon holding Emma's hand. She only had room for one thought at the moment. Sean wanted her. She could tell by the smoldering look in his eyes—a look many guys had given her in the past.

Their eyes locked in a sultry stare. He scooted close behind her and shifted so one leg was on either side of her. She twisted her body to face him and laid her hands on his chest.

"Speaking of alone time," she flirted.

He laughed a little, and she nearly swooned. Another guy with a great laugh. She had hit the jackpot at this college.

She could feel Sean's heart racing beneath her fingertips, his breaths came quicker, and his ice blue eyes were on fire. His gaze shifted to her lips then, and she closed the distance between them, putting him out of his misery. It had been a long time since she'd had a really good kiss. This one fit the bill, for sure.

Her hands slid up around his neck into his dark, wavy hair. It was as soft as she imagined it would be. She pressed herself fully against his solid chest.

Sean's arms wound around her back and held her firmly to him as their kisses grew deeper and more passionate right there in the middle of Ah-Nab-Awen Park.

Oh, he's a good kisser. She'd been in need of some male attention, and that's exactly what he gave her. His full, undivided attention.

"*Ahem.*" The sound of someone's throat clearing interrupted their steamy moment.

Michelle pulled back and looked up to discover Simon standing over them. Her face was on fire, partly from kissing Sean, but also because Simon was the last person on earth she wanted to find her like that.

"Sorry to interrupt." He raised an eyebrow at them and looked extremely amused.

Emma's eyes widened. She said nothing.

Sean kissed the corner of her mouth, then leaned in and whispered, "We're doing that again later."

Her stomach flipped at the tone in his voice and the feel of his breath against her ear, but she was still very aware that Simon and Emma were standing there watching them. She shifted so she was facing the river again and sat straight up.

"Did you get ahold of Maggie?" Michelle stuttered, while Sean's fingertips traced softly up and down her back.

Emma shook her head. "She didn't answer, but I got ahold of Janice, the R.D. She went and knocked on the door and nobody answered, but she thought she heard somebody inside. Possibly crying."

Michelle was furious. "Son of a ..." she paused, remembering the company she was in. "I'm gonna kill Ben."

"Who's Ben?" asked Sean.

"Someone Maggie would be better off without."

It surprised her how protective she felt of Maggie already. If she ever came face to face with this Ben character, they were going to have words. And then she was going to beat the crap out of him.

Simon was kind enough to drive them back early and forego the fireworks. Sean offered, too, but Michelle insisted he stay and enjoy the show.

When the girls opened the door to their room, the lights were out.

"Maybe she went to the fireworks after all." Emma flipped the lights on.

Michelle quickly slapped the light switch off when she noticed their roommate asleep in her bed. She pointed at Maggie then motioned for Emma to follow her into the hall.

"Should we wake her and make sure she's OK?" Emma quietly clicked the door closed behind them.

"Let's let her sleep."

They moved in the direction of the lounge.

"I wish I knew how to find this Ben guy right now." Michelle gritted her teeth. "He needs to be taught a lesson."

"I'm just worried about Maggie. I feel so bad for her."

"I've known guys like him, and I don't care how good a friend she thinks he is, she deserves better."

Emma nodded. "I agree."

They pushed through the door into the lounge, and Michelle was surprised to see Simon still standing in their dorm. He had turned on the charm with a couple girls from the other hall, and they were all giggles, totally falling for it.

He glanced over and spotted them. "Hey, how's Maggie?"

"She's asleep," Emma replied sadly.

"Do you wanna go get ice cream or something?" he asked, all but ignoring the girls he had been talking to. "There's still time until curfew." He winked at Michelle, knowing full well her opinions about the school curfew.

"Sure." Michelle would never say no to more time with Simon.

"I think I'm gonna stay here," Emma replied, "just in case she wakes up and wants to talk."

"Are you sure?" he asked.

"Yeah."

Michelle felt kind of bad. "Do you want me to stay, too?"

"No, you two go ahead."

"OK." She wasn't going to ask twice.

Simon hugged Emma, and a wave of jealousy hit Michelle. He said goodbye to his new friends, who seemed annoyed that he was leaving them so soon, then held the door open for Michelle. They walked along the sidewalk toward his car.

"She's so nice," Simon gushed about Emma.

"Yeah, she is. You like her, don't you?"

"Not as much as you like Sean." He elbowed her.

Michelle blushed, remembering. "Hey!"

"He's a good guy. Plus, he's from your neck of the woods, so you have that in common."

"He's from Chicago?" Sean hadn't told her that, but then they hadn't done much talking.

Simon looked at her curiously. "Yeah. You didn't know?"

She shook her head.

"He's here on a basketball scholarship."

Her eyes widened. "Really?"

"You didn't know that either?"

She shrugged.

"What *do* you know?"

"That he's a good kisser." She grinned behind a look of guilt.

He put his arm around her and pulled her into his side for a hug.

"What am I gonna do with you?"

I can think of a few things.

They drove to the nearest McDonald's for sundaes—hot fudge for Simon and caramel with peanuts for Michelle. She wasn't sure how it began, but they started talking about their hometowns and their families. Michelle found herself opening up to him about her home life, telling him things she had never shared with anyone, and he seemed to be doing the same with her. Two hours passed in the blink of an eye.

"Do you miss California?" She scooped some ice cream and made sure to get a little caramel and peanuts on the spoon.

He shrugged his shoulders. "I miss the ocean sometimes."

"What about your family?"

"Yeah, I miss my mom."

"Not your dad?"

Simon shrugged again. "Let's just say my father has high expectations when it comes to his son." He paused for a scoop of ice cream. "I like living here. My Uncle Pete is cool, and he's been more of a dad to me than my father ever has, really."

"So your uncle lives around here. Is he the reason you chose Cornerstone?"

"That was part of it. I knew I could visit him or stay with him whenever I wanted to. And they have a great photography program here. He recommended it."

"Is he into photography, too?"

"He used to have his own studio."

"Oh, that's very cool."

"Yeah, he's taught me everything he knows. He's been my biggest inspiration. My dream is to someday run my own photography business, maybe have a studio one day."

"You'll totally get there, Simon. I know it."

"Thanks, Chelle. That means a lot." He reached over and squeezed her hand. "So, what about you? Are you missing Chicago yet?"

She pondered that for a second. "You know, I was. But not so much right now." Her lips turned up in a little smile.

He smiled back at her.

"I was missing my friends, mostly. My family, not so much."

"You aren't close with them?"

That was the understatement of the year. "Not at all. I don't really know my dad. He wasn't around much when I was growing up. He traveled a lot for work."

"Sounds like my dad. He didn't travel much, but he worked long hours. The up before dawn, home after dark sorta thing. We don't really get along. He doesn't treat my mom very well."

She felt a special bond with him over this commonality.

"What about your mom?" Simon asked.

"My mom worked all the time. She wasn't there for me like a mom should be. When she *was* there, she wasn't really present. I think she was just too tired to be."

"If she and your dad were both gone so much, who took care of you?"

She shrugged. "I took care of myself. And my friends looked out for me."

"No brothers or sisters?"

"Just me."

"I'm sorry. That must have been rough."

She didn't have a response to that. Life had never seemed particularly rough when she was with her friends, but she could see how someone on the outside would think growing up without parents was totally tragic.

"Do you have any brothers or sisters?" she asked.

He shook his head. "Just me."

She liked that they had yet another thing in common.

"Are your parents still together?" he asked.

"No. Yours?"

"Yeah, they are, actually. Sometimes I don't know why, though. They don't seem to like each other very much. And my dad's never been one to stick around and fix what's wrong. When things got rough in the past, he would just walk out."

"But he came back, right?"

Simon nodded. "Yeah, he always came back."

"You're lucky."

"I guess. I don't know. Sometimes I thought it might be better if he didn't come back. Do you think things would have been better if your dad stayed?"

"I doubt it."

There was a long pause in conversation while they finished off their sundaes, which were more like soup at that point.

Simon pushed his empty sundae cup to the side. "Can I tell you something?" He suddenly looked very serious.

"Anything."

"When we first met that day in the gym, I thought you were really hot."

She raised an eyebrow. "And I'm not hot now?"

"Oh, you are." He gave her a cocky grin.

She laughed and blushed a little.

"But now it's more than that."

She held her breath.

"I've never met someone I feel so comfortable with so quickly. I feel like I can tell you anything, like I've known you for years."

She understood exactly what he meant. "Me, too."

"Really?"

She grinned and nodded, nearly bursting with the anticipation of what he would say next.

"Wow!" He sat back and looked at her in awe. "I've never had a girl best friend before."

And just like that, her hopes of more than friendship with Simon were shattered.

4

$\mathcal{M}$ichelle hadn't worn roller skates since she was ten years old, and now that she was standing atop a set of wheels, she was sure this was a colossal mistake. She rolled slowly onto the floor, pushing forward with her right foot, then her left, until she had a bit of a rhythm going. A very slow rhythm.

Her gaze moved away from her feet to the rink ahead. Emma, who had convinced her to come, took off across the floor like a pro, swerving left and right around slower skaters, followed closely by Simon. They seemed to have a race going on.

Michelle attempted to increase her speed, but her feet suddenly slipped out from under her, an expletive escaping her lips when she hit the floor. Skaters flew past, and she folded herself up and covered her head.

"Are you OK?"

She peeked from behind her arms to see a guy standing over her with hands extended. She took them gladly.

"Are you hurt?" he asked as he helped her to her feet.

She held securely with one hand and rubbed her back side with the other. "I did that on purpose."

He chuckled, then grabbed her other hand and, skating backwards, led her across the floor.

"Oh, I don't know about this." She squeezed his hands so tight she was sure he had lost all circulation.

"Trust me."

She raised her eyebrows at him. "I don't even know you."

31

"Hey, I saved your life back there."

She laughed, then wobbled as he began to move faster. She looked down, mesmerized by the way his feet were moving back and forth, somehow propelling him backwards. This caused her to teeter forward.

"Look up."

Her eyes met his.

"If you keep looking down, we're both gonna fall."

He had hazel eyes like Simon, only deeper, and his hair was a darker brown than Sean's, almost black. He was like a nice mix of the two of them.

"What's that look for?"

She hadn't realized she had a goofy grin on her face, and she shook it off.

He spun using some kind of fancy footwork and was suddenly skating next to her. The motion threw her off balance, and she tumbled onto her left hip taking him with her. They were a jumble of arms and legs, the stranger sprawled across her mid-section.

They couldn't stop laughing.

He helped her up again and guided her off the floor to a bench on the sidelines. "I think we need a break."

She sighed. "I think you're right."

"Do you want something to drink?"

"A Pepsi would be great."

The sweet stranger skated off and returned with two drinks and an order of nachos and cheese. He plopped down beside her on the bench and offered her some chips.

"Thanks." She helped herself.

Emma and Simon skated past just then, and Simon gave Michelle a thumbs-up, like he was giving her his approval or something, which irritated her.

She also spotted Wes and Sean skating not far behind them. Sean's expression showed no sign of approval.

A couple of girls skated by and waved at her new friend.

Her gaze followed the girls. "Are you here with someone?"

"You mean like a date?" he asked.

She nodded.

"Well, that's still to be determined."

Their eyes met again, and the intensity of his stare made butterflies go wild in her stomach.

Her eyes narrowed. "Are you ever gonna tell me your name?"

"Only if you can guess it."

"Seriously?"

He nodded.

"Fine." She chewed the inside of her lip while she tried to come up with a name that fit him. "Carl."

He laughed heartily. "You think I look like a Carl?"

She chuckled.

"OK, then, you must be Carla," he teased.

"You guessed it." She laughed. "Carl and Carla. That's us."

Their flirty guessing game went on for a while. "Carl" eventually tried to get her back onto the skating rink, but she refused to go through that humiliation again. So, they turned in their skates and walked outside to get a little fresh air.

Other than a couple small groups hanging out by their cars, the parking lot was empty. They found a quiet spot near the front corner of the building that was barely illuminated.

"I'm glad we met," he told her. "I wasn't expecting to have any fun tonight."

She raised an eyebrow at him. "That's what you call fun?"

His arms suddenly snaked around her waist. "This is." He pulled her close, covering her lips with his.

It wasn't the soft, sweet kiss she expected after their light banter. No, this kiss was firm and deep and presumptuous. This kiss felt like the ones from the guys back in Chicago. Not that she didn't like it. She did. It simply surprised her.

They kissed until things started heating up between them. It was obvious he wanted her, but she felt uneasy and confused. What had she done or said to make him kiss her this way? Why did it even matter? She liked guys, and guys liked her. So why was she questioning this at all?

She pulled back, out of breath. "I should probably go find my friends soon."

It was the first time she had ever stopped herself from going all the way. Back home, she would not have thought twice about doing it against a brick wall with people walking in and out of the building forty feet away. But here ... something made her stop.

"OK. That's cool." He released her, and they walked toward the door. "Do you happen to know what time it is?"

She shrugged. "I have no idea."

"I need to find a clock."

"Are you late for something?"

"I might be if I don't find a clock," he replied with a wink.

They walked inside, and he checked the time. "I've gotta go, but it was nice meeting you ..." He paused as though he was waiting for her name.

"Michelle." She filled in the blank for him. "My name is Michelle."

"This was fun, Michelle." He had a mischievous glint in his eyes.

"Yes it was ... Carl."

He let out a loud laugh at that. "Maybe I'll see you around."

"Maybe." She watched him walk away, unable to shake the uneasiness.

Michelle scanned the room for her friends. Emma, Jill, and Darcy were seated at a booth in the snack bar.

"Hey!" She sat down and bumped Darcy's hip with hers to get her to scoot over.

"Where have you been?" asked Emma. "With a guy? Simon said you were with a guy." She seemed very excited that Michelle might have met someone.

Michelle grinned. "Maybe."

Then the girls' questions came. What's he like? Is he cute? What did you two talk about? Did he ask for your number? Are you gonna see him again?

As she answered their questions, the grin slowly disappeared from her face. A strange, unsettling emotion came over her, an overwhelming need to hide what had just happened between her and a total stranger. She felt oddly embarrassed, like she had done something wrong. And suddenly, she hoped beyond hope that they would stop asking questions about him.

Simon skated to their table just then. "Come skate with me, Chelle."

Relieved, she took his hand and went to retrieve another pair of skates, pushing the unfamiliar feelings aside and forgetting all about the mystery man.

ॐ ♡ ॐ

On her walk back from chapel Wednesday morning, Michelle spotted Simon with his roommates heading in the direction of their dorm. She jogged along the sidewalk to catch up with them and called his name.

Simon looked over his shoulder just as she jumped onto his back and wrapped her arms and legs around him. He spun around and pretended to stumble toward the pond, threatening to drop her in with the geese.

She screamed, and one of the professors walking nearby reprimanded them.

Simon placed her back on solid ground, the two of them cracking up at themselves. He put an arm around her shoulders.

While they walked, Michelle caught Sean's eye for a moment, and a flash of something resembling anger crossed his face.

"What?" she asked.

"I didn't say anything," he snapped and moved further ahead of them.

Her relationship with Sean, if you could call it that, had not progressed past their kisses in the park. She'd made out with plenty of guys and never seen them again. Heck, she'd done much more than kiss with guys she barely knew. Maybe that wasn't something to be proud of, but it was a fact.

She liked Sean, but it didn't bother her that nothing else had happened between them. They had kissed once, weeks ago. But she wondered if it bothered him, because he was obviously upset with her.

She glanced over at Simon, who simply shrugged his shoulders.

As they approached the dorm, Michelle sped up to Sean's pace. "Hey! Can we talk?"

He let out an exasperated breath. "Fine."

They walked to a nearby bench and sat down.

"Are you mad at me or something?" She searched his face.

His eyes met hers. "You and Simon are embarrassing."

Her forehead creased. "What does that mean?"

He looked away uncomfortably.

"Sean?"

"You're all over each other all the time."

She stopped herself from laughing, but a little giggle managed to escape.

His eyes darted to hers.

"Oh, you're serious? All over each other?" *Only in my dreams.* "Simon and I are just friends."

"Yeah, that's what he said, too."

That was disappointing. "It's true. He likes Emma."

"Among others," Sean replied.

"Well, that may be," she stated, "but I'm not one of them."

He was silent.

She looked him in the eye. "Sean? What's going on?"

"I thought maybe this was going somewhere. You and me." He seemed shy and at a loss for words all of the sudden. "After that night at the park ... well, after we kissed, I thought ... I mean, I wanted ... and then you and Simon ..."

She grinned at him. He was cute when he stumbled over his words.

"Well, you and Simon were together all the time."

He finally got to the point, and he was right. They *had* been inseparable since Celebration On The Grand.

"And then I saw you making out with that guy at the rollerskating place."

Her heart leapt into her throat. "You saw us?"

"Yeah, I left early, and I saw you in the parking lot. You seemed pretty hot and heavy." He stared at the ground, and she was surprised by how dejected he looked.

"He was nobody," she explained.

He glanced her way. "So what does that make me?"

She didn't know what to say. It didn't look good, her making out with a complete stranger after kissing him at Celebration. She could see that now.

"It's fine. You're not into me. I get it."

"But I am," she blurted. She had his attention now. "That guy at the roller rink ... that was a huge mistake. Please believe me. I really do like you, Sean."

He seemed to soften. "I like you, too."

The sweet tone in his voice made her lips curl into a smile.

"So, how 'bout a date then?"

"OK," she replied without hesitation.

"OK?" He seemed a little surprised at her quick response.

"Sure."

He smiled, and her heartbeat picked up the pace.

She leaned in close until their lips were mere millimeters apart. "Then I can show you what all over each other *really* looks like."

He swallowed hard.

She gave him a quick kiss on the cheek and departed with a smile.

It was Michelle's first real date. Never had she been picked up at a set time, never had doors been opened for her, never had she walked hand in hand with a guy. It was sweet. Sean was a total gentleman, and he made her feel special in a way no other guy ever had.

The air was brisk on this October evening, but that didn't stop them from exploring the grounds at Frederik Meijer Gardens, just a short walk from the college. They wandered the paths that wound through the outdoor sculpture park and fell into easy conversation, mostly about basketball.

When they reached the koi pond waterfall, they sat together on a bench and listened to the sound of the water flowing over the rocks. He rested their joined hands on his thigh, softly caressing the back of her hand with his thumb. She glanced over at him, feeling suddenly content in the moment.

"So, you didn't tell me you're from Chicago."

"You didn't ask." He tilted his head.

"I'm from Chicago, too," she revealed. "Where do you live?"

"Oak Brook. How 'bout you?"

Hearing he was from Oak Brook, an affluent suburb, made her embarrassed to admit where she and her mother had lived.

"Um, a few places." She hesitated. "Mostly South Side, around Bridgeport and Douglas."

Sean nodded. "I've never been there."

"I didn't figure." Why would he ever have a reason to visit that part of town? She wondered if he thought less of her now that he knew where she came from.

"Do you miss it?"

"I miss my friends." She thought about her so-called friends for a moment. She hadn't thought about any of them in a while, and not one of them had stayed in touch with her. "Actually, no. I take that back. I thought I'd miss them, but I don't." And she was surprised to find that it was the truth. "I miss the city sometimes. Not the crime, though. A couple places we lived weren't very safe, especially at night."

Sean looked at her with concern. "Well, I'm glad you're here instead of there then."

"Yeah, this place is like the polar opposite of where I grew up."

He laughed, and her heart skipped a beat at the sound.

"How 'bout you?" she asked. "Are you homesick?"

"I miss my family, but I'm happy to be at Cornerstone. I'm here on a basketball scholarship."

"Simon mentioned that."

Sean nodded.

"So, a scholarship. You must be really good then."

He shrugged his shoulders. "I do OK."

"OK? I bet you're better than OK to get a scholarship. I was lucky if my butt ever left the bench."

"Oh, you played in school?"

She nodded. "Yeah, but I wasn't good enough for a fancy scholarship." She elbowed him, which prompted his great laugh again. She was tempted to keep doing it just to hear that sound.

"I'm sure you're better than you're letting on."

"I do OK," she teased.

He elbowed her. "I think I see a little one-on-one in our future."

She raised an eyebrow at his comment, and she thought he actually blushed. She knew he didn't mean it the way it sounded, but the innuendo was out there. No taking it back now.

He laughed nervously. "I mean ... we should ... ya' know, shoot hoops sometime."

She loved the way he stumbled over his words when he was nervous around her. It gave her a heady feeling knowing she affected him so.

"We will," she replied.

꙳ ♡ ꙳

The windows of Sean's maroon, two-door Chevy Corsica were steamy with condensation. After dinner, they took a detour to a nearby secluded parking lot to say goodnight. Another of Michelle's "favorite" college rules was the limit of three seconds for a goodnight kiss at the door. That was simply not going to fly with her.

Sean was the best kisser. Tender and passionate. His hands were strong, yet gentle. Those hands wandered, sliding beneath the back of her shirt, flirting with the clasp of her bra.

So that's how it's gonna be, is it?

She shifted in the passenger seat to get closer. Making out in a vehicle was not exactly easy or comfortable.

He leaned away, breathing heavily, and glanced at the back seat.

Her eyes met his, and she nodded in reply.

"Ladies first."

They took turns climbing between the seats, laughing at their not-so-graceful maneuvers. She tumbled into the back, her right leg somehow twisted up in the seatbelt. He unwound her, then climbed through, only to get his leg wedged between the driver seat and the steering wheel. They couldn't stop laughing, and that laugh of his skyrocketed him from hot to simply irresistible.

When Sean finally made it into the back seat, she moved into his arms, leaning her body into his. Many minutes passed as they kissed, pulses racing, sweat forming on their brows in the close confines of his car.

She paused for a moment to catch her breath and stared into his eyes. They were darker in the center, with tiny lines of white and pale blue swirling throughout the iris, like electricity in one of those plasma globes in science class.

Sean reached out and gently ran his fingertips down the side of her face.

She closed her eyes in response, then shifted her right leg up and over until she straddled his lap.

He went still.

Michelle searched his face. "What?"

When he didn't reply, she leaned in and kissed him again.

He returned the kiss, then rested his forehead against hers, their breaths mingling. "Are you sure about this?" His voice wavered.

"Would I be here if I wasn't?" Her lips brushed his softly as she whispered her reply.

He paused, not moving, like he was working something out in his mind.

Why is he stopping? Did I read him wrong?

"I thought you liked me." Sadness and disappointment ruled the moment. She began to move away, but his hands gripped her hips and held her in place.

"I do. I just ... well, I thought maybe you were a ..." He stopped as if afraid to finish the sentence.

She leaned back to gauge his expression. "A virgin?" She made it sound like a dirty word.

He nodded.

"Are *you*?" She raised a questioning eyebrow at him.

He shook his head no.

"Well, then we don't have a problem now, do we?"

$$\text{\textcmc{γ}} \heartsuit \text{\textcmc{γ}}$$

This wasn't the first time she'd had sex in a car, so why did everything feel different this time?

She should have been happy. Sean was a great guy, and their date had been wonderful. They had so much in common, and she liked him. So much more than she thought she would. He seemed to like her, too, but he had barely spoken to her on their drive back to campus.

He walked her to the dorm and followed the three-second rule when he kissed her at the door. It was probably less than three seconds, in fact—more like a hesitant peck.

She watched him walk away, his head down, shoulders slouched. This wasn't how the night was supposed to go. This wasn't how things had gone with other guys in the past. It had always led to more. So why did this feel like the end?

When she walked into the dorm, nearly missing the one o'clock curfew, Janice, the Resident Director, gave her a look.

"That was close." Janice locked the door behind her.

Michelle didn't respond. Why did she feel like Janice knew exactly what she had done? And why did she feel like she had done something wrong? She had never felt this way before. There was a strange ache in her heart, like at the roller rink, only much stronger. It hurt. So much so that she thought she might actually cry. *What is happening to me?*

She shuffled along to her room, her sneakers scuffing against the carpet with each step.

Her roommates' laughter carried down the hallway, and a loud *"Shhh!"* came from the room across from theirs.

Maggie looked up when she wandered in. "What's wrong? Your date didn't go well?"

Michelle didn't know how to answer that question.

"What happened?" Emma asked. "You can tell us."

She wasn't sure she *could* tell these sweet, innocent girls what she had done with Sean. Because once she told them, they would never look at her the same way again.

"It was fine. I'm just tired."

A week passed without a call from Sean, and these foreign emotions continued to overwhelm her. She was quiet. Her roommates noticed, Simon noticed, even R.D. Janice noticed.

In the college Sunday School class at Calvary Church, someone brought up sexual immorality as an answer to a question Michelle hadn't even heard the teacher ask. She usually tuned out the teachers and pastors, because she didn't understand half of what they were talking about when it came to the Bible. But on this day, she listened. The teacher mentioned repentance of sin, including sexual sins, and God's forgiveness. The word *saved* was used several times. *Saved by grace? Saved from what? Saved from sin?* The confusion only added to the uneasy feelings she'd been dealing with.

It didn't help that Sean sat across the room from her in that very class. She was sure the teacher's words were affecting him, too, because he looked incredibly uncomfortable. She stared at him, hoping he would make eye contact, but as soon as the class ended, he was out the door before she could attempt to catch up to him.

When she returned to the dorm that afternoon, she could no longer contain her emotions. She climbed into bed, hid under the covers, and cried into her pillow.

What is wrong with me? Why won't Sean talk to me? What did I do wrong?

Never had she felt so confused or hurt by a guy. She let it all out until there were no tears left to cry.

When Maggie and Emma arrived after lunch, she tried to pretend to be asleep, but the pile of tissues on the floor gave her away.

The bed sank a little as Maggie sat down next to her.

Emma laid a hand on her shoulder. "What's wrong, Michelle?"

She rolled over to look at them, revealing her puffy, red eyes. Tears filled them again.

"Michelle, what is it?" Maggie's voice was filled with concern.

"I had sex with Sean," she blurted.

Neither girl spoke, and Michelle could have sworn Emma's cheeks matched the fuzzy pink pillow on the end of her bed. The room was dead quiet, except for the hum of the fluorescent lights.

Maggie jumped up to make sure the door was firmly closed.

"Um, did he ... pressure you into it?" Emma stuttered.

Michelle shook her head.

Emma swallowed nervously. She had clearly never had friends who were sexually active before.

"I'm sorry, Emma. I didn't mean to make you uncomfortable."

"You know you could get kicked out of school for this," Emma mumbled.

Michelle knew full well this sort of thing was unacceptable at a Christian college. Premarital sex was against their beliefs, and every student there had signed an agreement to live in accordance with a Christian lifestyle. Although, Michelle had mostly skimmed through that part of the application.

Maggie sat next to Michelle again. "Are you OK? I mean, were you ... safe?" She had trouble getting out the last word.

Michelle nodded. "Yeah, and I'm on the pill."

Emma was clearly fidgeting now.

"We don't have to talk about this." Michelle wiped leftover tears from her cheeks.

"Yes, we do," Maggie replied.

"I'm sorry, Michelle." Emma had tears in her eyes. "I don't know what to say. Maybe I should just let you two talk."

"It's OK, Emma. You don't have to stay if you don't want to."

Emma walked over and hugged her. She took a few steps toward the door, then turned. "I'm gonna pray for you, Michelle."

The last person to say that to her was her grandmother, but it came with only condescension and judgment. It was different coming from Emma. It was honest and kind and the sweetest thing she could have said.

"Thanks, Emma."

Once they were alone, Maggie took a deep breath and let it out. "So, I'm assuming since you're on the pill this isn't your first time."

Michelle shook her head. "But it's never been like this before."

"What do you mean?"

"I've been with some real losers, but Sean is so great. I like him so much. I feel like I should be celebrating or something, but his reaction was not what I expected."

"What did he do?"

"After we ..." She paused, not wanting to say it again, and Maggie motioned for her to continue. "He looked at me, like really looked into my eyes. He looked so sad." The sadness in his eyes had penetrated all the way to her bones. She had never experienced anything like it. Another tear formed and slipped down her cheek. She flicked it away. "I feel like I did something really, really terrible here."

"Maybe Sean feels the same way. Maybe he feels bad that he let it happen."

"Maybe. But he knew I wasn't a virgin. He knew he wasn't forcing me into anything."

"Well, you are both at a Christian college. Maybe he feels guilty about that."

"I don't know." Michelle stared blankly at the poster taped to the wall above Emma's bunk. The text was in the shape of a cross and read "I can do all things through Christ who strengthens me".

"Maybe he's worried about getting kicked out," Maggie speculated.

Michelle's heart wrenched. "His scholarship! If anyone found out, he could lose his basketball scholarship." She felt awful. Maybe that was the reason he hadn't called her. Maybe that's why he was so upset.

Maggie put an arm around her and did her best to give comfort.

Michelle found herself leaning her head on Maggie's shoulder. They sat for a while not saying anything. It was nice, like what she imagined having a sister would be like.

Maggie stood and went to her desk. After rifling through some of her things, she returned with a book. "This is kind of old and worn out, and it's written all over inside with my own notes, but maybe it will help you."

Michelle stared at the cover of a book about dating.

"We studied this book in my youth group a couple years ago. It explains what God says in the Bible about sex. I know the stuff about waiting 'til marriage ... well, it might not apply to you anymore, but there's a lot of good stuff in there about the different kinds of love and the emotional stuff people deal with when they have sex at a young age."

She shook her head. "I don't know." She had barely touched a Bible before stepping foot on Cornerstone's campus. Her Old Testament class was the most in depth she'd ever gotten into it in her life. And all the Christian words and phrases she kept hearing at church confused her even more.

Maggie laid it on Michelle's pillow. "Well, I'll just leave it here for you. You can read it or not. It's up to you."

Michelle looked up at her. "Thank you."

"No problem. Emma and I love you, Michelle. And God loves you, too. You're gonna be OK."

"I don't know about Emma."

"I think she's been pretty sheltered growing up as a pastor's kid. She was just a little shocked."

"Yeah, I seem to have that reaction on people."

As October came to a close, the air turned colder, much like Sean's attitude toward her since their date. She had attempted to contact him on multiple occasions, leaving messages with Simon or Wes, but her calls were never returned. Whenever she got anywhere near him, he would take off in the opposite direction without a word. And it stung.

She couldn't seem to fight off the steady ache in her heart or the memory of the look in Sean's eyes that haunted her thoughts and dreams.

"What is wrong with him?" Michelle asked Simon as they walked to Quincer dorm on Halloween night dressed as a couple of Harlem Globetrotters.

He dribbled the basketball he was carrying. "I don't know, Chelle. He just mopes around. He won't talk about it."

She hoped this party would give her an opportunity to corner Sean and get to the bottom of things.

Simon stopped dribbling and draped his arm across her shoulders, giving her a squeeze.

She smiled up at him.

"Hey, I met your roommate today," Simon declared.

Her nose crinkled up in confusion. "You've already met my roommates."

"Not Maggie." He removed his arm and started dribbling the basketball again. "Not officially."

"She's nice, huh?"

"Ha!" He shook his head.

Michelle looked at him curiously. "She's not nice?"

"Maybe to you, but she does *not* like me."

"Why do you say that?"

"We had to take pictures of each other for photography class today. She wanted *nothing* to do with me."

Michelle snickered. "Well, were you rude to her or something?"

"Hey!" he elbowed her. "Am I ever rude?"

He wasn't. He was fun and outgoing and friends with everyone. She didn't know anyone who didn't like Simon. Well, until now.

"I invited her to the party tonight." He stilled the ball and tucked it under his arm.

She raised an eyebrow. "What about Emma?"

He was quiet for a moment before responding. "I was just being nice."

Michelle thought this was strange. Was something going wrong between them?

"Is Maggie coming then?" she asked. "I thought she already had plans."

He shook his head no. "She told me I should go to the party and hit on you instead."

She could totally picture Maggie saying it, and she laughed. "I love that girl."

Simon rolled his eyes.

She suddenly lunged and stole the ball, dribbling it away from him.

"Hey!" He chased her the rest of the way to the dorm.

The party was alive with disco lights, karaoke, and plenty of pop and snacks to go around. It was tame compared to the parties she'd been to in high school, but everyone was having a great time, and she was beginning to like tame.

The guys' hallways were open and some of the rooms had been decorated like mini haunted houses. Simon led Michelle to their room, which had some streamers hanging in the doorway and fake cobwebs hanging throughout.

"*Oooh.*" She faked a shiver. "I'm *sooo* scared."

Sudden movement across the room caught her eye, and she jumped.

Simon laughed at her. "See. Scary."

Sean turned from where he was seated at his desk. "Oh, sorry. I didn't know you guys were coming down here."

"Sean." His name was her plea.

He avoided eye contact with her.

"Will you please talk to me?"

"I can't right now." He stood, grabbed his keys, and started walking toward the door.

Simon shifted to the side and blocked the doorway.

"Get out of my way, Simon," Sean demanded.

Simon stood his ground. "She's right. You two have got to talk. I can't stand this brooding thing you've got going on. I want my roommate back."

Sean hung his head and exhaled loudly. "Fine."

When Sean locked eyes with her, she was overcome with relief. A little smile crossed her face. Finally, she had his attention.

"We can't talk here," he stated.

"OK," she eagerly replied. "Anywhere you wanna go. Lead the way." She followed him along the hallway and past the party people in the lounge. He held the exterior door for her, and their arms brushed as she walked past him. The cool night air hit her, but she felt only warmth from his nearness.

He led her to the same bench where they had made plans for their date. She was anxious. They were going to talk. She would finally have the answers she had longed for and, hopefully, get rid of the uncertainty she'd been feeling since their night together.

"I don't really know what you want me to say." His tone was colder than ice.

"I want to know what happened."

"What do you mean?" His attention was fixed on the sidewalk in front of them.

"After our date. What changed? I mean, I thought things went so well. I had a great time with you, and I thought you did, too. But something happened, and I think I deserve to know why you're giving me the silent treatment."

He shook his head, clearly struggling to speak.

"Just tell me, Sean," she begged.

"I don't think we should have done what we did in my car."

Her heart sank. "But I thought you wanted to."

"Well, I didn't." He was short with her.

"You should have said something."

"Well, there wasn't a lot of talking going on before you threw yourself at me."

Her mouth dropped open. "Well, I didn't see you fighting me off."

He shot her a look.

"What? It's true. And *you* asked *me* out, remember?"

His expression changed, and she suddenly saw the sadness in his eyes again. "I shouldn't have said that. I'm sorry. That was totally uncalled for."

"Sean, what is going on? I know there's more to it. Is this about your scholarship?"

His eyes darted to hers. "You didn't tell anyone, did you?"

"Just my roommates."

His eyes widened. "Great!"

"They won't say anything. I promise."

He wrung his hands. "They better not."

"*You* didn't tell anyone?" she asked.

He shook his head.

This was a shock to her system. She had never done stuff with a guy and not had him brag about it to every other guy in the Chicagoland area.

Neither of them spoke for several eternally long minutes. The silence was almost too much to take.

When Sean spoke again, she thought she saw his chin quiver a little. "Michelle, I lied to you."

"About what? About liking me? Don't worry about it." It wasn't like she hadn't been in that situation before.

"No." He looked her straight in the eye. "About not being a virgin."

5

$\mathcal{S}$ean was a virgin. Well, he had been. His admission had successfully shifted her thinking about everything. She had never been on the other side of the situation before. The guys she had been with had all been more experienced. She had never been the one to take someone's virginity.

She wasn't sure how to feel. Her emotions were a jumbled mess. A huge blanket of regret smothered her, and she didn't fight it. She hid under it, wallowing in her misery, with no clue what to do next. If she thought about the situation for too long, she felt physically ill, like she might actually toss her cookie dough ice cream.

There was also a part of her that was upset with Sean for lying to her. Had she known the truth, she never would have gone through with it. No matter how great their date had been. But there was no going back now.

Their words played in a loop in her mind for days.

"I'm so sorry, Sean. I don't know what else to say."

"There's nothing left to say. It's my fault, and I can't take it back, no matter how much I want to."

Whenever she remembered his words, she felt a gnawing in the pit of her stomach and a tightness in her chest. She had taken something from him that night, something she could never return.

It was clear to everyone that something was wrong. Michelle's mood was dismal. She barely left her room aside from meals, chapel, and classes. Her roommates continuously invited her to this event or that, but she wasn't in the mood. Not even basketball could entice her to leave the dorm.

Simon tried to cheer her daily with no luck.

Maggie tried to get her to open up, but she couldn't.

She was too ashamed.

Michelle opted to stay at the dorm for the long Thanksgiving weekend rather than going home to Chicago. She would be heading there in a few weeks for winter break, and she didn't see the point. Both Simon and Maggie invited her home with them for the holiday, but she declined.

"I'll be fine," she assured them. "I could use the peace and quiet. Don't worry about me. Really."

They were hesitant to leave her alone after her recent funk, but they didn't push.

Michelle wandered campus, shot hoops in the gym, watched television in the lounge, and listened to music in her room. There were a handful of students still on campus, but for the most part, she was alone with her thoughts.

The dorm was extremely quiet with most everyone gone. It was eerie at times.

Michelle liked being alone in her room for once. She leaned back against her pillow and stared up at the ceiling. These were the first solitary moments she'd had since the day she arrived.

She glanced over at the bookshelf and noticed the dating book Maggie had given her collecting dust. Curiosity got the better of her, and she walked over and grabbed it. Flopping down on her stomach on the bed, she cracked the cover. Maggie wasn't kidding when she'd said it was full of notes. There was barely an empty space left on any of the pages. She had used all of the lines provided for notes and written all over in the margins.

"God made sex to be between a husband and wife. He wants me to experience this kind of love only within marriage." *Only* was underlined a bunch of times.

"There's a big difference between love and lust."

"Agape love is unconditional."

"Even if Ben never loves me back, God is enough."

Oh, Maggie.

She lay there and read the book from cover to cover. There were a lot of things on those pages she wished someone had told her a long time ago. If only she could go back in time and take this book along.

The ache in her heart that had been nagging at her for months hurt worse now. There was nothing left of her to give to a husband someday. She'd already given it all away.

She wished she knew more about what the Bible said. Not only about this, but about ... everything.

The King James Bible her grandparents had given her to take to college was under some textbooks on her desk. She grabbed it and thumbed through a few pages. The only passages she had read so far were those required for her Old Testament class. She approached it as she would any other history class—complete the assigned reading, take notes, pass the tests.

She reached for the dating book again and turned to the back to read more of Maggie's notes. A bookmark slipped from within the pages and fell onto her pillow. It listed several verses from the book of Romans, so Michelle decided to venture into the New Testament.

The first verse she looked up read "For all have sinned and come short of the glory of God." Yeah, according to everything in the dating book and every rule at this college, she was a sinner. A big one!

She flipped back a few chapters and read "But God commendeth His love toward us, in that, while we were yet sinners, Christ died for us." She knew the basics of the story from a couple Easter services with her grandparents as a child and from things she had picked up during chapel. Jesus was God's son. He was hung on a cross, though he was an innocent man, then three days later he miraculously rose from the dead.

She turned a couple pages. "For the wages of sin is death; but the gift of God is eternal life through Jesus Christ our Lord."

What does that mean?

She eagerly flipped to the next verse on the bookmark. "If thou shalt confess with thy mouth the Lord Jesus, and shalt believe in thine heart that God hath raised him from the dead, thou shalt be saved."

This was all news to her. She believed there was a God. She was pretty sure she believed in Heaven and Hell. But the rest of it, the part about being saved and having eternal life by believing in Jesus, she had never heard before. She had too many questions and this little bookmark was not enough. She tried to find more verses, but she had no idea where to look.

Feeling lost and confused, Michelle shuffled down the hallway in search of a little guidance. Clinging to her Bible, she knocked on the door that read "Resident Director".

"Come in," Janice called from within.

Michelle walked in not quite sure where to start.

"Hi, Michelle. How are you?" Janice greeted her cheerfully. She was dressed in a sweatshirt and sweatpants with her thick, brown hair in a loose ponytail atop her head.

"I was wondering if I could ask you some questions."

"Sure. About what?"

Michelle swallowed hard. "About Jesus."

Janice looked pleased. "Of course. What would you like to know?"

They sat together for a long time, maybe hours. Janice had kind eyes and a sweet temperament. She patiently listened and answered all of Michelle's questions, then shared more Bible verses and her own story of coming to know Jesus when she was a teenager.

"I always thought it was enough to just say I believed in God," Janice shared. "I thought you had to live a good life to get to Heaven."

Michelle nodded. "That's what I thought, too. Good people go to Heaven. Bad people go to Hell." She never actually thought she would be going to Heaven anyway with all the bad things she had done in her life so far.

"Being good is important," Janice replied, "but it means nothing if you don't ask Jesus to forgive you of all of your sins and come into your heart and save you. Jesus said, 'I am the way and the truth and the life. No one comes to the Father except through me.'"

"I haven't lived like I should," Michelle admitted. "I don't ..." She was too afraid to say the words aloud. *I don't wanna go to Hell.*

"I'm sorry. I have to ask," Janice interjected. "What made you choose a Christian college if you aren't a Christian?"

"My grandparents are paying for it." She wore a sheepish expression. "My parents couldn't afford college, and they sort of made me choose this place."

Janice nodded sympathetically.

"Am I a lost cause?" Michelle felt distraught over that possibility.

Janice touched her hand. "Why would you say that?"

"I've done some awful things in my life. I haven't been a good person at all. I've hurt people." *Sean.*

"No one is a lost cause, Michelle. God brought you here to this college for a reason, and right now, I truly believe this conversation is part of that reason."

Michelle's throat tightened. "I believe that, too."

Janice squeezed her hand. "I think you already know why you're here, Michelle."

"Yeah, I need to go to confession or whatever."

Janice giggled a little. "Oh, that's Catholics, sweetie. They confess to a priest."

"No, it said in this verse I read that if you confess and believe that God raised Jesus from the dead, then you will be saved."

"I'm sorry. You're right." Janice proceeded to quote the verses in Romans from memory, only a slightly different version. "If you declare with your mouth, 'Jesus is Lord,' and believe in your heart that God raised him from the dead, you will be saved. For it is with your heart that you believe and are justified, and it is with your mouth that you profess your faith and are saved."

"Yeah, that's the one."

Janice looked at her seriously then. "Do you believe that, Michelle?"

Michelle nodded without hesitation.

"God loves you so much, and He wants to have a relationship with you. Are you ready to accept Him?"

Tears pooled in her eyes. "Yes."

A smile spread across Janice's face. "I'll help you pray if you want."

Michelle nodded again, and the tears slipped down her cheeks.

Janice took her hands, bowed her head, and began to pray. "Dear Lord, I know I am a sinner, and I need your forgiveness."

Michelle eagerly repeated every word Janice spoke.

"I believe Jesus died on the cross and took the ultimate penalty for all of my sins."

When she first stepped foot on campus, she never thought she would one day be bowing her head in the R.D.'s room praying for God's forgiveness. Choosing Cornerstone seemed like such a massive decision at the time, but this was bigger. This felt like the most important decision she had ever made in her entire life.

She could barely contain her excitement for the next two days waiting for everyone to return. Some of the students were already getting back to campus, but Michelle's friends wouldn't be there until Sunday evening. She really wished at least one of them would show up early. She missed them all so much. More so now that she had such important news to share.

On Sunday, she made the short walk with Janice to nearby Calvary Church. It was the first time she actually paid attention to what the pastor was saying. Everything he said seemed to be directed at her, and she soaked it all in, even taking notes throughout, which was so not like her.

"All things work together for good to them that love God," Pastor Dobson said. "To them who are called according to His purpose."

She felt different. She had a newfound confidence that everything was going to work out, like God actually cared about her, about where she was, and where she was going. For the first time in her life, she felt truly alive.

That afternoon, a light rapping on the door interrupted her Bible reading, and a girl from a few doors down stuck her head in the room.

"Michelle, there's a guy named Sean here to see you."

Her stomach flipped at the mention of his name. She quickly checked her reflection in the mirror, threw on a little blush and lip gloss, then tried to walk slowly to the lounge so not to seem too eager.

She came through the door to see Sean staring out the big window by the entrance. *Oh, man, he looks good.*

"Hi," she greeted him.

He gave her a weak wave.

"How was your Thanksgiving?" she asked.

"Tense," he replied.

"Oh no. Why?"

He glanced around the room nervously. "Are you hungry?"

She raised her eyebrows in surprise. "I could eat."

Sean took her hand as they walked to the parking lot.

She looked over at him, and when he smiled sweetly at her for the first time in two months, she had a feeling everything was going to be just fine. She had a feeling God was going to work it all out.

He drove onto the highway and headed west, babbling on about the weather and traffic.

She could tell he was nervous, because he was doing that thing where he spoke in a bunch of broken sentences, like he couldn't figure out exactly what it was he wanted to say. It was adorable.

He drove and drove, switching highways, and took the Holland exit.

She noticed a sign for Holland State Park. "I thought we were gonna eat."

"We are."

"Are we gonna have to catch our dinner?"

He laughed at that. It was the best sound in the world.

They had their pick of parking spots when they reached Lake Michigan. There were a handful of die-hard beach lovers out, but it was mostly empty. The weather was a little warmer than average for the end of November—not a full blown Indian summer, but warm enough for a light jacket.

Sean popped the trunk and grabbed a picnic basket and a couple blankets.

"Wow! You came prepared. How did you know I would come with you?"

He shrugged. "I hoped you would."

He took her hand again, and they found a spot on the beach to lay out their blanket. He wrapped the extra blanket around her shoulders and took a seat next to her, digging into the basket of food. He had gone all out with Subway subs and giant chocolate chip cookies for dessert. They ate in comfortable silence.

When they finished, he scooted closer to her and leaned back onto his arms. His chest lifted as he took a deep breath in. "There are some things I need to say to you, Michelle."

She turned to face him and gave him her full attention.

"I'm really sorry for what I did." The words came out as he exhaled. "It was wrong. I didn't … I mean … you deserved more respect than that. I took what I wanted, even though I knew better and—"

"I didn't," she interrupted.

He looked at her, his brow furrowed.

"Up until that day, I didn't think there was anything wrong with what I was doing." Tears threatened. She was not used to all the tears. "But the way you looked at me, I knew you regretted it. I'd never had that happen before. I never felt like it was wrong before. Nobody ever told me it was wrong."

A tear slid down her cheek, and he gently brushed it away.

"I liked you so much," she continued. "And I thought that's what I had to do to get you to like me, too."

He smiled a little, but there was a hint of sadness there. "I liked you so much, too."

His words simultaneously melted and broke her heart. More tears filled her eyes.

"But this isn't all on you." He shook his head. "We were both there. And I'm really the one to blame here."

"You were right. I threw myself at you." She looked down and bit her lower lip, trying to stop the tears.

"I shouldn't have said that." He tilted his head in an attempt to regain her attention.

She glanced his way. "It's the truth, though."

"I could have stopped." He stared out at the lake. "I should have. But we can't take it back."

"I'm so sorry, Sean." Her chin quivered. "I'm sorry I took something from you, something so special that you can't ever get back. Can you ever forgive me for that?"

He reached out and touched her chin, turning her face toward his. "Hey, it's OK. I forgive you."

The tears let loose then, and he wrapped her in his arms. He softly rubbed his hands up and down her back as she cried, and she wanted to stay there forever.

When he eventually released her from his embrace, she wiped her tears on the edge of the blanket.

"Michelle, I shouldn't have lied to you. I shouldn't have misled you like that. I hope you can forgive me, too."

She leaned her head on his shoulder, and he lowered his to rest against hers. "Of course, I can. A few months ago, even a few days ago,

I might not have been able to say that. But if God can forgive me for all the horrible things I've done, then I can forgive you for this."

He lifted his head and looked at her.

A stray tear fell down her cheek, and she shrugged her shoulders and smiled. "I got saved this weekend."

He abruptly hugged her. "That's so awesome, Michelle."

"Thank you."

As he let go, he kissed her on the cheek. "Welcome to the family." He wore a huge smile.

"Huh?"

"The family of Christ. You're one of us now," he said with a wink.

She grinned. "I like that."

Sean grabbed two water bottles and a couple napkins from the picnic basket and handed one of each to Michelle.

"Thanks." She dabbed her eyes with the napkin and crinkled it up.

"You might wanna hold onto that. There's something else I need to tell you." He took a big swig from the water bottle.

She waited for what felt like bad news.

He set the bottle down and cleared his throat. "I'm not coming back after winter break."

"What? Why not?" Her response nearly caught in her throat.

"When I chose Cornerstone for my basketball scholarship, I agreed to represent this school and all they stand for. I agreed to the rules. *All* of the rules."

"Sean." This was worse than anything she could have imagined.

"But I broke one. A big one. And I'm going to speak to the dean this week and admit what I did."

"No. You don't have to do that," she pleaded. "Maggie and Emma will never tell. Nobody else knows about us. And I'll never say a word. I promise."

"Yeah, but *I* will know, and the guilt will eat me alive."

Tears again? She was sure her eyes would be swollen shut by morning at this rate. Desperation, panic, and fear caused a million thoughts to fly through her mind as she tried to concoct a way to keep him there.

"I just wouldn't be able to live with myself." His bottom lip stuck out in an adorable pout.

He truly was a good and honorable guy, and now he was leaving. Just when she was starting to get her own life figured out and things were right between them.

"What will your parents say?" she asked.

"They already know."

"I'm gonna miss you." Her voice was quiet. She couldn't believe he was leaving. Now that the communication lines were open again, she didn't want this to be the end.

He took her face in his hands. "I'm gonna miss you more than you will ever know."

"I wish we could go back and start over at the beginning of the semester, do everything differently."

"Me, too. But maybe it's for the best."

How could him leaving possibly be for the best? Her puzzled expression demanded an explanation.

"Hey, if things had been different, you might not have gotten saved."

"Maybe. But I don't want you to leave."

"I know." He let go of her face and took another sip from the water bottle.

"And you should know this about me. I don't do goodbyes." She cringed as the word left her lips. She could still hear the words her mother spoke every time her father left on another one of his trips. *Say goodbye to your father.* Anxiety began to build inside her just thinking about it. "There were too many of those with my dad when I was growing up, and I just can't handle it."

"Well, we don't have to say it." He put his arm around her shoulders. "We'll just say ... until then."

She looked at him sadly. "Until when?"

"Until the next time we see each other."

"What if that never happens?" Her heart broke a little at the thought.

"It will." He spoke with confidence. "Even if it's not in our lifetime, we'll see each other one day in Heaven."

She breathed out, exasperated. "That sounds morbid."

"It's not morbid. It's eternity together with God. Sounds pretty good to me."

"I hope we don't have to wait that long." She smiled at him.

"Me, too."

They stayed to watch the sunset, then Sean returned her to the dorm.

"Thanks for coming out with me tonight." He hugged her tightly against him, and she never wanted him to let go. "Pray for me, OK?"

"I will." His meeting with the dean was sure to be scary and uncomfortable.

His arms loosened, and he pulled back just enough to place a soft, tender kiss on her lips.

Her stomach flipped at the contact.

"Three-second rule!" cried Jill and Darcy from their dorm room window, which had a front row seat to the door.

Michelle and Sean laughed. It felt wonderful to laugh with him again.

He leaned in and gave her one more three-second kiss.

"Rule breaker," she whispered.

He grinned at that. "Goodnight."

"Night."

Michelle floated into the dorm and down the hallway, where she was tackled by her roommates. They dragged her into the room and slammed the door.

"Did we just see you with Sean?" Maggie asked.

"What happened?" Emma had made such an effort to support her, despite how uncomfortable she was about Michelle and Sean's night together.

Michelle didn't know where to start. "I have so much to tell you, but before I do, I want to hear about your Thanksgiving holidays."

"No way!" Maggie cried. "We're not letting you off the hook."

Michelle laughed, and the phone started ringing. She lunged for it, beating them to the receiver. "Hello?"

"Hey, Chelle. I'm back!" Simon announced.

"So you are. How was your flight?"

"Good. How was your holiday in the dorm? Miserable without me, right?"

"Absolutely miserable." Her tone held a hint of sarcasm, and she rolled her eyes at her roommates.

"Is that Simon?" Emma whispered.

"Yeah, it's him."

"Hey, are your roommates back yet?" he asked.

"Yeah, they're both here. Do you wanna talk—"

"No," Simon cut her off. "I wanna talk to you."

"Okaaay." *Weird.*

Simon's end of the line was silent.

"Did you have turkey and stuffing? A good home-cooked meal?" she asked.

"Home-cooked?" He laughed. "We had it catered in."

While Simon shared the details of their dinner and house full of guests, Michelle noticed Emma brush a tear from her cheek. She was subtle about it, turning away and casually wiping as she stretched her arms above her head, but Michelle caught a glint of light reflected on the tear. Something was going on between Emma and Simon. She was sure of it.

Simon finished his story. "I don't wanna interrupt your girl time. Just wanted to hear your voice. I'll see ya' tomorrow."

"OK."

"Night, Chelle." And he hung up.

Michelle slowly turned to face Emma, who looked as if she might burst into tears at any moment.

"I'm gonna go get ready for bed." Emma pouted as she gathered her toiletries.

"Emma, what's wrong?" Michelle asked.

"Nothing."

"You can talk to us, Em," Maggie assured her. "You know that."

"Simon never called me."

"Oh, I'm sure he was just busy with his family." Michelle defended him. "Plus, it's long distance to call from California."

"I guess. It's just ... he said he'd call. He hasn't been returning any of my calls lately. Not since ..." Her words trailed off.

"Not since what?" Michelle asked.

"It's nothing. Never mind."

Michelle looked at Maggie, who shook her head in disgust.

"I don't know how you can be friends with him. He's such a jerk." Maggie turned her attention to Emma. "He's a guy, Em. Sometimes they don't call when they say they will. Ben does that to me all the time. It's annoying, but I think it's just a guy thing."

Michelle knew the conversation would somehow be steered back to Ben. Maggie had a one-track mind. But Michelle didn't want to hear about Ben tonight. She wanted to comfort Emma. And she wanted to share her important news with her friends. She wanted to tell them she was a Christian now, just like them.

But then Emma asked Maggie if she saw Ben much at Thanksgiving, and Maggie spent the next who-knows-how-long gushing about him. She was talking fast and bursting with excitement. "We went to church together this morning, and he put his arm around me. The whole weekend felt just like old times."

By the time Maggie finished her stories, Emma seemed to forget the fact that Simon had blown her off. Michelle was more than a little curious to know why Simon chose not to speak to Emma earlier.

It also seemed to slip their minds that Michelle and Sean had been seen kissing by the front door. She tried not to be hurt that what happened in her life didn't seem as important as theirs. But it did hurt. For once in her life, she had real girlfriends. She had let them into her heart, but she doubted that she was truly accepted into theirs. Like because of the things she had done before, she wasn't worthy of true friendship status or something.

Suddenly, she didn't feel much like sharing after all.

Simon's reaction to the news of her salvation was a bear hug and a simple "good for you", which was kind of a letdown. She thought everyone would be as happy for her as Janice and Sean had been. Simon was her best friend. At least he claimed to be. He, of all people, should be taking her out to celebrate.

She knew Simon was a Christian, yet he didn't seem to be very focused on that part of his life. When she asked to hear the story of how he got saved, he told her he barely remembered it. It was at his church's Vacation Bible School when he was five.

"I prayed with one of the leaders, and that was it," he told her.

That *was* it. *That* was the moment his life had changed. Yet he acted like it was no big deal. Maybe it was because he made the decision at such a young age. Maybe growing up surrounded by Christians and going to church every week had become just another routine and had made him complacent.

"Did you hear about Sean leaving school?" he asked during their walk to chapel.

"Yeah." She hung her head, partly because she was sad about Sean, but also because she had expected more of a reaction to her news, not a change of subject.

"Did he tell you why?"

Simon's eyes were on her, and she swallowed hard. "Personal reasons," she managed, throwing in a shrug to make it seem like she didn't know anything more.

Simon shook his head. "Yeah, that's what he told me, too. Must be something serious. Why else would he leave and give up his scholarship?"

She shrugged again, relieved that Sean had not confessed to his roommates. There was no way she was telling Simon the real reason. She didn't want him to ever know she had been intimate with Sean or any other guy for that matter.

Simon suddenly wrapped an arm around her shoulders. "Don't be sad. You still have me." He squeezed her to him and kissed the top of her head.

"Yes, I do." She smiled up at him. "Hey, what is going on with you and Emma?"

"What do you mean?" He made a face, then tried to act casual about it.

She stopped walking. "Come on, Simon. Spill."

He lowered his arm and closed his eyes, his nose wrinkled up, and he cringed. "She won't let me kiss her." He peeked out from behind one eye then the other, awaiting her reaction.

"What is that face for?"

"I thought you might punch me."

"Why would I punch you?" She laughed at his crazy behavior.

"Because I don't think I can be in a relationship with someone like that, and it makes me sound like a terrible person when I say that out loud."

"You *are* terrible," she replied. "Emma is the sweetest."

He groaned. "I know she is, but she doesn't wanna kiss *anyone*. Not until her wedding day."

"Really?" Michelle had never heard of such a thing. "That's so nice. Saving all of herself for her future husband. I like her even more now."

"Thanks a lot."

She laughed again.

"I can't help it." He leaned in close, his lips inches from hers. "I like to kiss."

She raised an eyebrow and pushed him away, knowing he was just joking around. "You really are a jerk, Simon."

"I know."

୫ଚ ♡ ঙଙ

On the way to lunch, Michelle and her roommates ran into Janice on the sidewalk outside the dorm. They made small talk about Thanksgiving, then Janice turned to Michelle.

"I was hoping to run into you, Michelle. I've got a couple books for you, and I wondered if you'd like to get together and have a Bible study with me."

Michelle could not contain her smile. "That sounds great. Thank you so much, Janice."

"No problem. Stop by my room later, and we'll make a plan."

"Awesome. I will."

Janice waved as she walked on. "Have a great day, ladies."

Emma and Maggie gave Michelle strange looks as they started walking again.

"What was that all about?" Maggie asked.

Better now than never. "Oh, I got saved on Friday," she replied nonchalantly.

"What?" Emma screeched. "Are you serious?"

A huge smile spread across Michelle's face.

Maggie embraced her. "Why didn't you tell us last night?"

"I don't know." She couldn't tell Maggie that all her talk of Ben was the reason she hadn't felt up to sharing. "It just didn't feel like the right time."

"Oh my goodness." Emma grabbed hold of them, her eyes brimming with tears. "There's never a wrong time for news like this. I'm so happy for you, Michelle."

The warmth and support from her roommates surprised her. This was the sort of reaction she wished Simon had given her. The girls were both overjoyed that she had come to know Christ, especially Emma, who admitted she had been afraid for Michelle's soul.

Shortly after midnight, there was a loud commotion in the hallway outside their room.

"Candlelight!" Someone knocked loudly on their door. "Candlelight!" The cries and knocking moved to the next door, then the next, and so on to the end of the hall.

Emma clapped her hands together. "Our first candlelight."

Maggie looked excited.

Michelle felt indifferent.

Candlelights were a long-standing and beloved tradition at Cornerstone, a unique way for couples to announce their recent engagement to the rest of the students on campus.

The girls filtered out of their room and made their way to the lounge, where everyone was seated in a circle waiting to learn the identity of the bride-to-be. Janice emerged from her room carrying a long, tapered candle with a ribbon tied around it, and the song "Everything I Do" by Bryan Adams started playing on the boom box in the corner. Janice handed the candle to one of the girls in the circle, who admired the sparkling engagement ring that was hanging from the ribbon before passing it on around the circle. As the candle moved from girl to girl, the anticipation grew. Who would blow out the candle? Who was the bride-to-be?

When it reached Darcy, she pretended to blow it out, then passed it on to Jill, which made everyone laugh.

After several trips around the circle, Joanna, one of the girls from the other hallway, puffed it out, and the room erupted with applause and congratulations. She took a seat in the center, and spent some time answering questions about how she and her fiancé met, how long they had been together, and how they got engaged. Then her roommate prayed for her and their future marriage.

Michelle wasn't one to get mushy over sentimental things, but after experiencing the candlelight ceremony, she thought it was a lovely tradition.

The girls of the dorm then lined up outside to form a human tunnel. Joanna ran through and on toward the pole at the center of campus, where her fiancé was waiting at the end of a tunnel of guys. They embraced and shared a tender kiss, after which, he climbed the pole and rang the bell at the top, proclaiming their engagement to the entire campus and anyone else within earshot.

Once he slid down the pole, the crowd of guys grabbed hold and hoisted him above their heads. They carried him across the yard and hurled him into the slimy pond. He climbed out not-so-gracefully and planted another kiss on Joanna's lips.

It seemed to Michelle that the groom got the short end of the stick in all of this.

"That was so romantic." Emma swooned as they walked back to the dorm.

"I don't know," Michelle said. "Why would anyone wanna get married at our age?"

"They're in love," Maggie replied. "They wanna start their life together."

"Yeah, well, I don't know if I ever wanna get married." Part of that comment was influenced by her parents' broken marriage, the other part by the fact that, although she knew God had forgiven her for her past, she still felt like she had nothing left to give. "And I sure wouldn't want my fiancé thrown into the pond with all the goose crap. Who would wanna kiss him after that?"

They all laughed.

Michelle wasn't sure when the bench next to Quincer had become theirs, but when Sean called the next day and asked her to meet him at the bench, she knew exactly which one he was talking about.

"How did it go?" She sat next to him and greeted him with a hug.

He seemed calm, like a weight had been lifted from his shoulders. "Awkward. Uncomfortable. About what I expected under the circumstances."

"Are you OK?"

"I am. I really am."

Sean relayed the events of the meeting beginning with the dean, who commended him for coming forward to admit his wrongdoing and for voluntarily stepping away from the team and the college. The most difficult part was facing his basketball coach.

"Coach got real quiet for a long time. At least it seemed like a long time. That room was so quiet, you could have heard a pin drop in there."

"Oh, man. That must have been intense."

Sean nodded. "He was pretty disappointed, because he said I was such a great asset to the team. But he said the most important thing is that I admitted what I did and apologized and asked God's forgiveness for it. And he told me he was proud of me for doing the right thing."

Michelle reached over and took his hand. "I'm proud of you, too."

He smiled at her.

"Even though I got you into this whole mess." She frowned.

His eyes narrowed. "Hey, I told you about that."

She scoffed at his comment.

"Besides, that doesn't matter anymore. That was before. That was the old you."

"You're right." She smiled from ear to ear.

He gazed at her. "You have the most beautiful smile."

The color rushed to her cheeks. "Um ... thanks. So do you."

He smiled back at her, and they both laughed nervously.

"So, then what happened?" Michelle asked.

He looked at her with concern. "They asked me if it was with another student."

She got a sick feeling in the pit of her stomach. "So I guess I'm out, too, then." *Grandpa and Grandma are gonna kill me.*

"I told them no."

Michelle wasn't sure whether to hit him or hug him. "You shouldn't have lied for me, Sean. I should be kicked out of here for what I did to you."

"Look at all the good this place has done for you already. I wasn't gonna take that away from you. You need to be here right now."

Sean relayed the rest of the conversation, including the final words the coach had left him with. "No matter what your past looks like, God promises His children a future, and I know He has an amazing one planned for you."

She thought it was incredibly fitting, not just in Sean's situation, but in her own life as well.

6

$\mathcal{A}$s Michelle approached the dorm after dinner one chilly evening, she heard Maggie's voice, only high-pitched and much louder than usual.

"You're a complete jerk flaunting your date in front of her." Maggie stood near the front door, arms crossed over her chest, not wearing her winter coat.

Simon and Andi, a girl from the other hallway in their dorm, stood across the sidewalk from her.

"Maybe I should go." Andi started to walk away.

"How 'bout I meet you at the Skillet when I'm done with ... this." He gave Maggie the evil eye, and Andi nodded and walked on.

"You totally broke Emma's heart, Simon," Maggie cried, her breath visible in the cold air. Soft, fluffy snowflakes began to fall from the sky.

"Hey!" He held his hands up in defense. "We were never exclusive. She can go out with whoever she wants to."

"*Oooh*," she groaned. "I hate it when guys say that."

Michelle approached slowly, not wanting to get into the middle of it. She had never seen Maggie so angry.

"So that's all you have to say for yourself then?"

"There's nothing more to say," Simon stated.

Maggie shook her head in disgust. "Be man enough to tell her it's over. Don't just blow her off."

"I handled things how I thought they should be handled."

"Well, you thought wrong."

"Whatever!" He looked exasperated.

"There is such a thing as common decency, but I'd say you're sorely lacking."

He stepped closer, and she took a step back. They glared at each other, the tension crackling between them.

Michelle saw Simon's eyes dip to Maggie's lips for just a moment, and a jealous burn instantly hit her in the gut.

He glanced in Michelle's direction. "Back me up here, Chelle."

She swallowed her jealousy. "I'm not getting involved."

Maggie spun and marched to the door.

"Hey!" he hollered after her.

"Stay away from my friends!" she yelled, disappearing into the dorm.

He ran his fingers through his hair as Michelle approached. "That girl is so frustrating."

"Well, you did break Emma's heart," Michelle informed him. "She's been crying for days."

Simon's shoulders sank. "What am I supposed to do?"

"Learn better communication in your dating relationships." She took a page from Maggie's dating book. "Make your intentions clear from the start. Don't lead people on. Be honest when you want to break up."

"Hey!"

She laughed at the look of surprise on his face.

The surprise quickly turned to sadness. "Do you think I should have told her I wasn't OK with the no kissing thing?"

"Yes!" She laughed again, this time at the absurdity of his question. "Of course you should have told her."

"I feel bad now."

"You should."

"I thought you were on my side." He was adorable when he pouted.

She stepped closer and grabbed hold of his upper arms. *Sigh.* She nearly forgot what she was going to say.

"I'm always on your side, Simon. But I'm not gonna sugarcoat things."

He nodded and pulled her in for a hug.

She closed her eyes and soaked in his warmth as the snow fell around them.

"Thanks, Chelle."

Back in the room, Maggie was still fuming, but Michelle could tell she was trying to keep it under wraps for Emma's sake.

"So, I talked to my parents tonight, and I'm transferring to Cedarville," Emma announced.

"Emma, no!" Maggie dropped into the nearest desk chair.

"Are you sure about this?" Michelle asked.

"I'm homesick," Emma explained. "Cedarville's only two hours from home, and I was already accepted there. I'm taking next semester off, and I'll start again in the fall."

"You're not leaving because of Simon, are you?" Michelle asked.

Maggie cringed a little at the mention of his name.

Emma shrugged and wouldn't make eye contact.

So she was.

"You can't let a guy change your entire life's path," Maggie declared.

Michelle winced. She wanted to help convince Emma to stay, but she had no place giving her any sort of advice. After all, it was her fault that Sean had to change his life's path.

"That's only part of it," Emma explained. "I feel like I'm missing so much back home. My brother, Josh, is a senior, and he's about to start his last season of basketball. My sister, Hannah, started sixth grade this year, and she's having a rough time with it. She needs me for all that pre-teen drama. And my big sister, Molly, is getting married in the spring. I'm missing out on all the planning and stuff. I hate missing that." She sat up tall as if to display her resolve. "If I go to Cedarville, I can be home more often. I just know it's the right decision for me."

Oh, what it must be like to belong to such a large, loving family as Emma's. Michelle had always secretly wished for a brother or sister. At least then she would have had someone to go through her terrible childhood with. She could only imagine what it was like to leave a family like Emma's and live so far away.

"If you're sure, then I'm happy for you." Maggie hugged her. "But I will miss you so much."

"Me, too." Michelle joined in the hug.

"I *am* sure," Emma replied. "I've been praying about it a lot, and I truly believe this is what God wants me to do."

🌿 ♡ 🌿

Time was speeding toward Sean's impending farewell faster than a bullet train. Michelle spent every free moment with him that she could, but the end of the semester arrived too quickly. On their final weekend, they walked to Calvary Church with Simon for the annual Festival of Lights Christmas program. The night felt extra special because she was sharing it with her two favorite guys in the world.

When they arrived, they were each given a candle for later in the program. They found a seat in the balcony, and Michelle settled in next to Sean, who kept his arm around her the entire time.

The church was all decked out with twinkly lights, pine wreaths and garland, and pretty red bows. The actors, dressed in Victorian Christmas garb, performed a drama depicting the Christmas story with such talent, and the choir sang gloriously. Michelle had never cared much for traditional Christmas carols, but hearing them now that she was a believer made her appreciate them in a whole new way.

When the program came to a close, the house lights dimmed. Several of the actors walked the aisles and lit the candles of those seated on the end of each row. One by one, people lit the candle of the person seated next to them as the congregation sang "Silent Night" a cappella. Michelle watched as the light spread across the rows and illuminated whole sections. And soon the light was passed throughout the balcony and down their row.

Sean held his candle out to light hers and leaned close to her ear. "It's your first real Christmas."

She smiled at him. "You're right. It is."

When all the candles were lit, it was truly a sight to behold—a wonderful reminder that Jesus birth brought so much light to the world on a silent night so long ago. It was the most beautiful thing Michelle had ever experienced.

As they walked back from the church, Michelle couldn't help but think of the girl she had been only four months before. She never wanted to come to this school in the first place, yet now, she couldn't imagine leaving. She didn't want to go back to Chicago for winter break. Home was cold and unfeeling. She wanted to stay in their warm, safe bubble forever.

"You're quiet, Chelle," Simon commented as his arm came to rest across her shoulders.

She wrapped her arms around his waist and hugged him as they walked. "I'm gonna miss you, that's all."

"Break's only a month," Simon stated.

She gazed sadly at Sean, who gave her a knowing look. It would be only a month until she would see Simon, but God knows if she would ever see Sean again. And they were down to less than a week.

Emma's family arrived on Thursday to pack her things. It was bittersweet. They had only just gotten to know each other, and now she was leaving. It was clear that Maggie had formed a closer bond with Emma than she had. They were both a mess of tears.

"Call me every day," Maggie said.

"I will." Emma sniffled.

"Tell me everything about Cedarville."

"I will."

They hugged and cried some more.

Emma turned to Michelle and smiled as she wiped away her tears. "I'm so glad we got to be roommates, Michelle."

Michelle got choked up. "So am I."

Emma hugged her and held on extra long. "I'll be praying for you."

"Thank you, Emma. I'll be praying for you, too."

The girls grabbed the last of Emma's bags and helped carry them to her family's station wagon. When everything was loaded, Emma walked toward the passenger door.

"Emma!" Michelle called out.

Emma turned to her.

"Thanks for being my friend." She wasn't sure why she felt such a strong need to say it.

Emma walked to her and hugged her again. "I love you, Michelle. No matter what."

That wasn't something she was used to hearing. She squeezed Emma tightly. "I love you, too."

Michelle and Maggie stood together on the sidewalk and watched their sweet roommate drive away, waving as the car turned the corner and disappeared from sight.

"This is so sad," Maggie murmured. "I can't believe she's gone. Promise me you're coming back next semester."

Michelle laughed. "Yes, I'm coming back. I wouldn't desert you like that."

"Good."

Maggie put an arm around her as they walked, and Michelle did the same.

"It's my two favorite girls," a voice called from behind them.

Michelle grinned over her shoulder at Simon.

Maggie did not.

"I came to say goodbye."

"And good riddance." Maggie headed off toward the dorm.

Michelle tried her best to hold in a laugh.

Simon was not amused. "I was just trying to be nice. What do I have to do with her?"

"Just leave her alone."

He closed the distance between them and hugged her.

She rested her head against his shoulder and inhaled his fresh-from-the-shower scent. His hair was still slightly damp. "Did you just get up? It's the middle of the afternoon?"

He snickered. "Some of the guys threw me in the pond."

"*Brrr!* Did you get hypothermia?"

"Almost. Be glad I showered or you would not wanna hug me right now."

She laughed. The aroma of his soap was much better than that of the geese that normally resided in the pond.

"When do you leave?" he asked as he let go.

"Tomorrow morning." She stuck her bottom lip out.

"I'm heading to my uncle's lake house in a few."

"*Ooh*, a lake house. That sounds fancy."

He shook his head. "Don't get too excited. It's just a little house on Algonquin Lake in Hastings."

"Hastings?" Michelle raised an eyebrow. "Like Hastings that's an hour from here?"

He looked at her curiously. "Yeah. You know it?"

Michelle pursed her lips. "Maggie's from Hastings."

"Nuh-uh." Simon's mouth dropped open.

She nodded. "She is."

He grinned deviously. "Maybe she needs a ride home."

"Don't even think about it."

Guys weren't normally allowed in the girls dorm hallways, but moving days were always an exception to the rule. While Michelle was packing a few things into her suitcase, a voice from behind startled her.

"Is Maggie around?"

She turned and came face to face with the mystery guy from the roller rink. The blow dryer she'd been holding slipped from her fingers and landed on her foot. "*Ah!*" she cried out in pain.

"Are you OK?" He rushed toward her.

She held her hand out to stop him and retrieved the dryer. "I'm fine." She was in shock that he was standing in her dorm room.

Recognition suddenly flickered in his eyes. "Hey, it's you."

"Uh ... hi."

"Are you Maggie's roommate?"

"One and the same."

"Michelle, right?"

She nodded, surprised he remembered her name after their brief encounter.

"Small world." He laid a hand on his chest. "I'm Ben."

Michelle's stomach dropped. *This is Ben? Maggie's Ben?* Michelle had no words. Of all the guys at the roller rink that night, *he* had to be the one she made out with?

"Do you know where she is?"

"Uh, she's in the bathroom," she stuttered.

"OK. Well, I'm giving her a ride home." He glanced at the pile of things by the bed. "Is this her stuff?"

"Yeah, but I'm not sure if she has everything packed up yet."

"I can wait." He stood quietly in the doorway.

Michelle didn't know what to do or say. She couldn't believe her horrible luck. If Maggie ever found out about them, she would be crushed.

She glanced over at Ben and caught him checking out her backside.

He looked away as if he knew he'd been busted, and anger began to bubble up within her.

She turned to face him. "Maggie's an amazing person and a good friend."

He nodded in agreement. "She is. She's the best."

Michelle thought for a moment. "I don't like to see my friends get hurt."

"Neither do I." He looked at her searchingly.

Her eyebrow raised.

"Look, we had no idea we both knew Maggie when we met. And she's my friend, not my girlfriend, so we did nothing wrong."

"But you know how she feels about you," Michelle stated.

He shrugged his shoulders indifferently. "I'm more interested in how *you* feel about me."

"Really?" Her sarcasm was unmistakable.

"Hey, I had fun with you that night." His gaze intensified. "And I know you had a good time, too."

Michelle chewed on the inside of her bottom lip as she remembered their intimate make out session. At the time, it had been exactly what she wanted, but that was the old Michelle. Now, she felt only shame. And the fact that he completely disregarded Maggie's feelings made her anger boil over. Her eyes narrowed, but just as she was about to rip into him, Maggie breezed into the room.

"Ben!" Maggie threw her arms around his neck. "You're here!"

He gave her a quick hug. "Hey, Magnolia. You ready to go?" His eyes were still locked with Michelle's.

"Just about." Maggie scurried around the room gathering her bags, never noticing the tension or the stare down between her friends. "This is my roommate, Michelle."

"Nice to meet you, Michelle." Ben continued to stare at her.

Michelle shook her head and rolled her eyes. "Why Magnolia?" she asked Maggie.

"Oh, that's just what Ben calls me sometimes." Maggie had the same smile on her face she always got when she talked about him.

"It's a high school thing," he added in a patronizing tone. "Guess you had to be there."

Ben finally turned his attention to Maggie when she began handing him things.

Maggie hugged Michelle, then grabbed her last couple bags. "Merry Christmas. See you next month."

"Merry Christmas. Call me if you need me." She watched Maggie exit the room with a bag over each arm.

Ben looked back over his shoulder. "Bye, Michelle."

Michelle was more sure than ever that Ben was no good for Maggie. But how could she tell her without breaking her heart? Or worse, without losing her friendship?

After Maggie's departure, there was only one person left to see before she headed off to Chicago. Knowing she would be back and see her friends again in a month gave her some comfort. But Sean ... this might be the last time she ever saw him. She didn't know what to do with that or with the guilt and sadness that still weighed heavy on her heart. Sean might not blame her for his leaving, but she couldn't help but feel responsible.

As she finished packing the last of her clothes in her suitcase, there came a soft knocking on her already wide open door.

She glanced up at Sean's smiling face. Her heart leapt.

"Hey." He took a couple steps toward her.

"Hey." Her sadness was impossible to hide.

"So, I'm about to head out." He tilted his head toward the hallway, then took another step.

She softly chewed on the corner of her lip.

Another step. "And I wanted to say—"

She launched herself forward and wrapped her arms around his waist. "Don't say it. Please, don't say it."

His arms enfolded her, and he kissed the top of her head. "I'm gonna miss you so much." He leaned back and looked at her, his arms still locked around her. "I was thinking ... we both live in Chicago. Maybe we can see each other while you're home on break."

"Yes!" She knew she was smiling like a lovestruck fool, but she didn't care. "Yes! That is the best idea ever!" She squeezed him tightly, which elicited his wonderful laugh. When she pulled back and looked at him again, the right side of his mouth curved up a little. He smiled at her in a way that seemed reserved just for her.

She smiled sweetly in return.

He gazed into her eyes, adoration swimming in a sea of blue, and her heart soared. Emotions she had never experienced welled up inside her. Emotions she thought might be the closest thing to love she had ever felt in her life.

He leaned closer, the warmth of his breath caressing her face. Their noses brushed, and her lips parted.

"Until then," he whispered.

"Until then," she whispered back as his lips softly met hers.

7

*Y*ou miss me, don't you?" Sean asked at the start of every phone conversation.

"You know the answer to that," she always replied.

"How's Michigan?"

"It would be better if you were here. How's Northwestern?"

"It's great. Very different than Cornerstone, but I like it."

They talked about classes, new people he had met, the lovely campus in Evanston, and her recent choice to major in psychology. He liked his new roommates. She liked having only one roommate. Not that she didn't miss Emma, but the extra space was nice. He liked being close to home. She wished he was closer to her.

Their plans to get together over winter break had been thwarted by his parents, who did not approve of Michelle. They never came right out and said it in so many words, but she knew they had probably figured out she was the one he had been with. She understood. She had ruined their son's plans. If she were them, she probably wouldn't have let him spend time with the likes of her either. Even if she *had* found Jesus along the way.

"We'll see each other," Sean said on the phone one day.

"There's always Spring Break."

"What? You don't have plans to go to Florida with the girls for Spring Break?" He chuckled.

"*You* are my Spring Break plans," she responded sweetly.

"*Mmm.* I like the sound of that."

Long distance calls weren't cheap, especially three-hour-long conversations. So when they couldn't afford to talk on the phone, they wrote letters to each other. Michelle looked forward to her daily walks to the mail room. Every other day, there was a card or letter from Sean. She had never been much of a writer, but she found herself scribbling page after page of the happenings around campus and the things she was learning in her classes and in chapel. Sometimes their letters crossed in the mail, because she was too anxious to wait for his next one before she sent hers.

With every letter, they opened up to each other about what had happened between them and how they felt about the whole thing.

"When I came home to Chicago, I was angry at myself for being so weak when it came to you and not standing strong in my beliefs. And I questioned everything and went through the long list of what ifs. I wondered if I had done the right thing, leaving Grand Rapids and transferring to Northwestern. I still wonder that. Because I miss you. I hate being so far away from you."

When he said things like this, her heart melted.

"I wonder a lot, too," she wrote. "I wish you had transferred somewhere closer so we could see each other, because I miss you. It's totally my fault all of this happened, and I don't think I can say sorry enough. I care so much about you, Sean. I wish things had turned out differently."

The next correspondence from Sean was a card with a sweet sentiment about never having regrets and always seeing the good in every situation. He filled the blank side of the card with words of his own.

"You know I do not blame you for what happened. I take full responsibility for my part in it. If I could go back and do it all over again, I'm not sure I would change a thing, because I don't regret you. Not one bit. And I don't question what came after. I stand by my decision to go to the dean. I will never question that, because I know it was the right thing to do. I can't help but regret leaving you, though."

Michelle read the card probably a hundred times over the next few days. She went to Meijer one-hour photo, made a copy of a picture Maggie had taken of the two of them, and sent it off to him with a simple note. "I don't regret you either."

In the following week's letter, Sean declared he was coming to visit on a very special day that was all about hearts and flowers.

Michelle immediately marked her calendar with a giant red heart over February the fourteenth.

But the night before, she returned to the room to find a note from Maggie telling her Sean had called to let her know he wasn't coming after all. She called him back, but there was no answer.

A belated Valentine card arrived a few days later. "Michelle, I'm so sorry I didn't make it over to see you. I hope you had a good Valentine's Day. I was thinking about you every moment." Above the *i* in her name, he had drawn a little heart, which brought a smile to her face.

Over the next two months, the frequency of Sean's letters began to dwindle. Michelle continued to write him every few days, letting him know what was happening and how much she missed him. His letters were brief. He had a big course load and was playing some intramural basketball, which took up more of his time. She understood, but she found herself hating the walk to the mail room, because she didn't know whether she would be happy at the sight of a letter or crushed when the mailbox was empty again.

"I'm sure you're busy," she wrote one night. "I know classes can be time-consuming and difficult, but I hate not hearing from you. I want to know how you are and what's going on there. I tried calling, but you're never there. The silence on your end is making me feel like something is wrong."

Two weeks later came Sean's reply. She practically yanked the door off the little mailbox when she saw his return address. The small envelope was torn open in a matter of moments. She was anxious for his words.

"I'm sorry I haven't written lately. I've been really busy. Classes are killing me, but I'm loving intramurals. Hope life at Cornerstone is treating you well. Sean."

She leaned back against the wall of mailboxes and stared at the single sheet of paper. *That's it?* She flipped the paper over hoping for more, but that was definitely all he had written. Tears stung her eyes, and she walked as fast as she could back to her dorm room before she completely lost it. She burst through the door, wadded up his note, and tossed it at the picture of the two of them she had framed on her desk. The tears came then and didn't stop. She climbed into her bed and cried herself to sleep.

80

One of her arms felt colder than the other. It was so cold that it stung, like touching an ice cube or snow, and her eyes flew open. Maggie stood over her holding a pint of Ben & Jerry's ice cream in one hand and two spoons in the other.

Michelle sat up and rubbed her puffy eyes.

"I saw Sean's letter on the floor. Are you OK?"

"That was no letter," Michelle declared. "That was a brush off."

Maggie climbed onto the bed and sat cross-legged facing her. "I've got the remedy." She handed Michelle one of the spoons, and they dug into the Chocolate Chip Cookie Dough.

"I just don't get it." Michelle spoke with the spoon in her mouth. "I thought things were so good between us. I thought this was going somewhere."

"Guys suck!" Maggie exclaimed.

"They really do." Michelle took another very large scoop of ice cream and gobbled it down, then looked at Maggie. "Maybe he met someone."

"Don't think like that."

"I can't help it. It's the only thing that makes any sense."

Maggie held out the pint of ice cream again.

Michelle laughed a little and took another scoop. "This was a good idea."

Maggie nodded as she devoured her own scoop.

"Should I write him back?"

"I don't know."

"Because there are a lot of things I'd like to say to him right about now."

"Maybe you should take a day or two and think about it."

"What I really wanna do is grab that phone and call him." Michelle nodded her head in the direction of the telephone. "I want answers."

"You should. You deserve to know what's going on."

"I do deserve that. I'm gonna do it." She climbed off the bed and lifted the phone to her ear, dialing Sean's number while taking deep breaths in and out.

It rang several times before an answering machine picked up.

She dropped the phone onto the base, and plopped down in the desk chair. "Machine."

"I'm sorry, Chelle."

"I wish I could talk to him face to face. I just wanna know what happened."

On a bright, shiny May afternoon, Michelle walked along the sidewalk next to Simon. The breeze blew warm against her face, and the birds chirped as they darted between tree branches. Summer was on its way, yet her mood remained as somber as a midwinter's day.

"You're not *you* lately, Chelle," Simon told her. "Where's that smile I love so much?"

She gave him a weak smile.

"That was pitiful." He put his arm around her shoulders and pulled her into him. "Smile! It's a beautiful day. And you're with me."

She did smile at that.

"There's my girl." He kissed her on the top of the head and kept his arm around her as they walked, leading them in the direction of the mail room.

Michelle's love affair with the mailbox was a thing of the past. There had been no more letters from Sean, and she never wrote him back. If he wasn't man enough to be honest with her and admit it was over, then he wasn't worth it after all. It broke her heart, but she was trying to move past it.

She walked to her box and opened it. Empty. *Of course.*

Simon had three pieces of mail. A large, cream-colored envelope with an Evanston, Illinois return address caught her eye.

"What's that?" She pointed at it.

He slid his finger under the seal and opened the flap, removing a thick card with fancy calligraphy from within. He read aloud, "The pleasure of your company is requested at the wedding of Lindsay Marie Bishop and Sean Aaron Davis on the fourteenth of June ..." His voice trailed off. "What the?"

Michelle thought she was having an out-of-body experience. Did he just read that right? Sean was getting married? Her body sank to the floor as her heart sank to the depths of despair. This girl, Lindsay, was obviously the reason he had stopped writing. Tears sprung to her eyes, and she was visibly trembling.

Simon dropped to the floor next to her and wrapped her up in his arms. "I'm so sorry, Chelle. I know how much you cared about him."

She pushed against his chest and scrambled to her feet, brushing the tears from her cheeks. "I'm fine. I've known it was over for a while now. It's no big deal." Her instinct was to push the pain aside as she always had when her dad left her. "I'll talk to you later." Her feet carried her quickly from the building. Simon called out her name, but she ignored him and made a beeline for the gym. She grabbed a basketball and proceeded to sink it over and over through the hoop, hoping it would help take her mind off the pain and heartbreak. It didn't. The more shots she took, the more it reminded her of Sean and his scholarship and all that had happened between them.

"This really sucks, God," she mumbled to herself. "Thanks a lot."

8

While this day was filled with plenty of pomp, Michelle found herself unhappy with the circumstances. She had worked hard for four years to get to graduation, and here she stood with degree in hand, yet uncertainty clouded her future. She was supposed to have a plan by the time she earned her degree. Things were supposed to fall into place now. So why did she feel no closer to any real direction than when she first arrived on campus?

She truly believed God had led her to Cornerstone, but there had been many times when she felt completely lost. Everyone around her seemed to know exactly where they were headed, but Michelle bounced back and forth between majors. By the end of freshman year, she settled on psychology, but before junior year, her major had changed to business, then back again. Her grandparents became concerned that she was taking unnecessary classes and urged her to pick one thing.

"Just get any degree," they had said. "You can always do something different than your chosen major, but having a degree will help you get a job."

In the end, she settled on psychology, but she had no idea what to do with it.

She knew God had a plan, but it eluded her.

As "Pomp and Circumstance" played, she walked arm in arm down the aisle with Maggie.

"We did it," Maggie whispered. "I'm so proud of us."

"Me, too."

They filtered out into the foyer of Calvary Church with the rest of the graduates to wait for their families. Michelle watched as the last of those in gowns exited, those with last names in the *W*'s.

Simon's eyes met hers and he raised his degree high in the air as he maneuvered through the crowd to get to her.

"Congratulations!" he cried, as he scooped her up and swung her around.

She laughed.

"Can you believe it? We actually graduated." He flipped open the cover of his degree and showed her.

"I know. They gave us actual degrees, and now what? We just go out into the world? What were they thinking?"

"I think they've made a huge mistake. In your case anyway." He winked.

"Hey!" She punched him playfully on the arm.

"Congratulations, Maggie." Simon glanced over at her.

Maggie smirked. "Thanks. You, too." Her eyes scanned the room, no doubt looking for her family and ... "Ben!" she exclaimed.

Ben pushed through the crowds to get to her, wrapped his arms around her waist, and kissed her firmly on the lips. "Congratulations, honey."

Maggie beamed with happiness.

Michelle felt like gagging.

Simon looked annoyed. He hugged Michelle again. "I'm gonna go find my family, OK?"

"OK."

"I'll catch up with you in a bit."

Michelle watched him walk away, then turned back to Maggie and Ben.

Watching them over the past eight months had been difficult. In the fall, Ben began to call almost every day and started showing up at their apartment often. Maggie would return home from seeing him with this blissful, dreamy look on her face. By Christmas, they were officially a couple.

It was difficult not to be jealous, not to want what Maggie had—a happy family life, a budding photography career, and happily ever after with the guy she had always loved.

Michelle wondered if she would ever have any of it.

Her family life had only become more complicated over the past couple years when, out of the blue, her father called to inform her that he had remarried and his new wife was pregnant. She suddenly had a step-mother and a baby sister on the way. That baby sister, Ava, was now a year old, and they had still never met. Michelle wasn't sure why her dad had bothered to tell her since he made no effort to include her in his new life.

The news of Dad's marriage seemed to trigger something in her mother. Louise had never dated after the divorce, which always made Michelle wonder if her mom hoped for a reconciliation someday. But when Robert married, it seemed to give her the nudge she needed to get back out there. She started dating a man from work, Marvin, who had been interested in her over the years.

It was strange having parents who were dating and having babies. *Shouldn't that be me?*

Louise joined her daughter in the church foyer. "Congratulations."

Marvin followed close behind. "Good job, Michelle." He was a nice man—kind of loud and a little rough around the edges, but he made her mom happy.

"Thanks, Marv." Michelle looked over at her mother, who looked as if she might cry. "Mom, what is it?"

Louise shook her head and dismissed her with a wave.

Michelle stepped closer and gave her a hug.

Her mother spoke quietly in her ear. "I'm so proud of you."

Michelle couldn't remember her mother ever saying those words to her. They tugged at a place deep inside her heart, a place that longed for the special mother-daughter relationship she had seen between Maggie and her mom.

"Thank you, Mom. I love you."

Louise let go of her then and straightened, smoothing her shirt over her dress pants, as if the time for serious emotion had passed. "Love you, too."

The distance expanded between them again.

Maggie's family gathered around, and they exchanged introductions and pleasantries.

Louise had never been very good at getting to know new people, so it was no surprise to Michelle when she and Marv left soon after.

At least they came. Dad certainly couldn't bother himself to show up.

"You girls have worked so hard for this." Maggie's mother hugged Michelle. "I'm very proud of you both."

"Thank you, Mrs. James," Michelle said.

"Oh, sweetie, you know after all these years you can call me Patty."

"I know."

Ron scooped his daughter up in his arms. "I love you, Magpie."

"Daddy." Maggie closed her eyes as she held onto her father.

"I'm proud of you, baby girl."

Michelle's heart ached. No matter how much she despised her father, something inside still wanted the kind of connection Maggie and her dad shared.

"Congratulations, Michelle." Ron took his turn hugging her next, and she fought hard to keep from breaking down.

"Thank you," she managed.

He let go and turned his attention back to his family.

A tear slid down Michelle's cheek before she could catch it.

"Hey, you," a familiar voice called from behind.

She turned to see the friendly face of Janice, her former R.D.

"Oh, sweet girl, I hope those are tears of joy."

Michelle could no longer contain her tears, and she leaned into Janice's open arms and let them fall.

"Let's talk." Janice led her to a seat in a quiet corner of the auditorium, where they could speak privately. "What's going on?"

"My dad didn't show." Michelle sniffled.

"I'm so sorry, sweetie."

"I didn't really expect him to come, but I sent him and Bitsy or Betsy or whatever his new wife's name is an invitation anyway." More tears began to fall. "I don't know why I'm so upset. I guess because Maggie's dad was hugging her and telling her how proud he was of her."

Janice put an arm around Michelle's shoulder and gave her a squeeze. "It's all right to be upset, Michelle. You don't have to be strong all the time, ya' know? God sees your heart. He knows how you're hurting. You can give it all to Him."

"I know I can. I know that. I just didn't expect to feel like this. It's not like my dad's ever been there for any of the important events in my life. But it feels different now. I guess because I'm different now."

"Can I pray for you?"

Michelle nodded, and her sweet friend and mentor prayed her through the sadness and disappointment. Janice had been a constant in her life ever since the night she wandered into her room asking about Jesus. She could always count on Janice to listen, give an encouraging word, and be her prayer warrior.

"Thanks, Jan." Michelle gave her a hug.

"You bet. Are you ready to go or do you need a few minutes?"

"A few minutes would be good."

"All right." Janice stood. "I'll see ya' later. Love you, girl."

Michelle closed her eyes. Just a few minutes of quiet before she went in search of her grandparents. She bowed her head and focused on her breathing. And in the calm of the moment, she could almost hear her Heavenly Father whispering these words to her.

I'm proud of you, baby girl.

"Where have you been?" This was the greeting she received from her grandmother, who stared at her stone-faced as she walked into the foyer.

"Nice to see you, too, Grandma."

Her silver-haired grandfather wore almost the same expression as his wife.

"We've been looking for you for twenty minutes," Grandma stated.

Michelle didn't know what to say. "I'm sorry. I was talking with a friend."

"Well, we came all this way to see the results of our investment. The least you can do is give us a little of your time and respect."

"I do respect you guys," Michelle assured them, "but I'm not an investment. I'm your granddaughter."

"We know that, Michelle," Grandpa said. "Grandma just meant—"

"I know what she meant." Michelle tried not to lose it all over again.

"I didn't mean anything by it," Grandma insisted. "Don't blow this out of proportion."

Being around them always reminded her of Dad. It was easy to see where he got the quick temper and permanent scowl.

"You got me out of Chicago, away from my reckless life, and I will always be grateful to you for that." Michelle tried to let the love of Jesus shine through. "Thank you."

Grandpa seemed taken aback by her kindness and Grandma more so.

"Well, I ..." Grandma stuttered. "We were happy to help."

"It was the least we could do." Grandpa's lips turned up in a little smile.

Michelle couldn't remember the last time she'd seen him smile, if ever. She thought about his words. *The least we could do.*

"Because of Dad?" Michelle asked.

Her grandparents didn't reply.

"It was really nice of him to show up today." Her words dripped with sarcasm.

"Avey's sick. He couldn't get away," Grandma explained.

Michelle got an uneasy feeling at the mention of her baby sister. She shook her head. "You don't have to make excuses for him, Grandma."

Grandma reached into her purse then and retrieved an envelope. "This is for you. From your dad."

Michelle stared at the card in Grandma's hand. She wasn't sure whether to take it or run for the hills.

"Well, go on. Take it." Grandma practically shoved it at her.

The envelope felt as heavy as a brick in her hands. Not because there was anything substantial within, but because of the weight of emotion that overcame her as she held it.

"Open it," Grandma ordered.

"Maybe I should wait until I get home."

"Fine," she grumbled. "Do what you want."

But she was too curious to see what it said, so she slid her finger under the closure. *"Ow!" A paper cut? Really?*

She pulled the card out and was greeted with a generic picture of a graduation cap next to a vase of flowers with "Congratulations, Graduate" across the top. She cracked open the card, which read "All the best for your future." His name was scribbled beneath. Not "Dad", but his full name, like he was signing a contract or something. Her heart sank, and tears filled her eyes again.

"What's the matter?" Grandma asked.

Michelle took a deep breath and, just then, spotted Simon walking toward them. "Thank you for coming. And thanks again for all you did for me and my college education, but I have to go." She shoved the card back into Grandma's purse and walked around her toward her best friend.

Grandma called after her, but she couldn't stay there with them anymore.

Simon's smile was the most welcome sight. The tears were still hanging in her eyes when she met him.

"Chelle, what's wrong?" He held his arms out to her.

She walked into him, wrapping her arms around his waist.

He kissed the top of her head and held her comfortingly.

She brushed the tears away and looked up at him. "Can we get out of here?"

"Heck, yeah! Let's party!"

Simon's Uncle Pete lived in a modest house on Algonquin Lake. It was a simple, white, two-story with a couple bedrooms and a bath. The yard was large and nicely landscaped, with plenty of frontage along the water. There was a picnic table, a bonfire circle, and an old wooden dock with a pontoon boat in the lake.

Michelle sat on a bench beside the bonfire guzzling Mountain Dew after Mountain Dew. If it had been beer in her cup, she would have been very drunk by now. But those days were long gone. Even so, she wished there was something that could take the pain away. How many times had she prayed for God to heal the hurt her father had caused her? How many hours had she spent talking with Janice about that very thing? Always when she thought she had moved past it, something would happen to bring it to the forefront of her mind again. Seeing that card with the canned message and formal signature had done the job.

She glanced toward the lake and sighed. The water shimmered in vibrant pinks and oranges that faded into a deep blue as the last light of day reflected across its surface.

"You know you're supposed to be celebrating, right?" Simon dropped beside her on the bench and took a bite of hot dog, mustard leaking out the bottom of the bun and sliding down his chin.

She couldn't help but grin. "You are the biggest slob."

He wiped the mustard from his chin with the back of his hand and smiled at her with a chunk of bun sticking out of his mouth.

Now she was smiling.

The sound of splashing water caused them both to turn their heads as a dozen partygoers jumped off the dock. Their jubilant cries echoed across the small lake.

"They are crazy." She shivered thinking about how cold the water probably was at this time of year.

Simon inhaled the rest of his hot dog and grabbed Michelle's hand as he stood. "Come on."

"What are you doing? No! I don't really feel like taking a polar bear dip."

He tugged at her arm. "It's not *that* cold. Let's do it. This is our night."

She smiled up at him, but he didn't give her a chance to reply. He pulled her to standing, grabbed her around the waist, and threw her over his shoulder.

"Simon!" She pounded on his back, but she wasn't actually mad. She loved every minute of it.

He marched to the dock. "Are you ready?"

"Put me down," she demanded.

"One ... two ..."

"Simon!"

He didn't reach "three" before he tossed her into the lake and jumped in after her.

"Oh my gosh! It *is* cold." His teeth chattered.

She couldn't stop laughing. Simon always seemed to have a way of bringing her out of her funks. Whether it was with a joke or a hug or some kind of distraction, he was her ever-present source of joy.

She swam to him and grabbed his head, trying her best to dunk him, but he was too strong.

He swiftly turned the tables and dunked her instead.

Michelle coughed and spit water in his face when she surfaced.

"Thanks a lot, jerk." She hacked up more water, then put on a show with more coughing.

"I'm sorry, Chelle." He swam closer to make sure she was all right.

She let out a loud exaggerated cough before she propelled herself upward, pushing his head under the water on her way down.

He grabbed her waist as he came up and spit a fountain of water in her face.

"*Ack!*" She wrapped her arms around his neck and hugged him.

Their laughter carried across the water.

His hands slipped around her back, holding her to him. "Feel better now?"

"Much." She needed this—the closeness. She wanted to be held. But she and Simon were friends and, despite the fact that they had been like two peas in a pod for the past four years, there had never been talk of anything more than that. Not since the night at McDonald's when he called her his best friend for the first time. Their relationship was so much stronger than it had been that night, and she wondered if it was time to let him know how she felt about him. How she'd always felt about him.

Simon's lips brushed against her temple then, and it gave her just the encouragement she needed. She nuzzled his neck and lifted her legs, wrapping them around his waist.

The muscles in his back tensed, and he loosened his grip on her, letting the water flow between them.

She immediately dropped her legs and floated back away from him, too embarrassed to make eye contact.

He let out a slow breath, but said nothing.

The silence was killing her, and she gave in and glanced over at him.

Those hazel eyes of his were following the ripples his hands were sending out across the surface of the water.

She had to break the tension. This was too much. She splashed him.

His eyes met hers, and he grinned.

She splashed him again, which started a full-on splashing war.

Tension broken.

❧ ♡ ❧

A couple weeks later, the familiar tune of *The X-Files* theme song filled Michelle and Maggie's apartment as Michelle dumped a bag of microwave popcorn into a gigantic bowl.

"It's starting," Simon cried from his place on the couch.

"Hold your horses." She carried the bowl across the room to him.

He snatched it from her hands, spilling a handful of popcorn in the process.

"Hey!" She plopped down on the couch next to him.

"Season finale time," he declared.

She grinned at him and shook her head.

They watched in silence as Mulder was hospitalized by a reaction to a strange, possibly extra-terrestrial artifact, and Scully ran off to find out more.

Michelle glanced over at Simon, who was intensely watching the television and crunching the half-popped kernels left in the bottom of the bowl. They really were like an old married couple sometimes—having dinner together most nights, watching their favorite television shows, staying in more than they ever went out.

Maggie often said, "Why don't you two just start dating and get it over with."

Simon dated plenty. He always seemed to be going out with someone new, never settling down with any one girl. It bothered her, but when he would tell her he had a date, she never took it seriously. Probably because *he* didn't take it that seriously.

Michelle could have dated, too, but she chose not to. There was a part of her that was fearful. The life of a new Christian had not been without its struggles. She knew her past was her past, but she also knew what she was capable of when it came to guys, and she was afraid of making a mistake again. Her mind returned to the bonfire, the way she had wrapped herself around Simon in such an intimate way, and her cheeks warmed as the embarrassment and humiliation hit her all over again. There had never been anything but friendship between them. *What was I thinking?*

Except she knew what she was thinking, and she thought about it a lot. She couldn't help wondering what it would be like to be closer to Simon—physically. And he was her biggest hesitation when it came to dating. She was holding onto hope that one day he would finally see what was right in front of his eyes.

At a commercial break, Simon grabbed her knee and squeezed playfully.

She grabbed his and did the same, squeezing as hard as she could.

The click of a key in the door did not hinder their attacks.

"*Aaah!*" Michelle cried.

Simon laughed. "Say 'uncle'."

"Never!" She cringed.

Maggie came through the door and tossed her purse and keys on the kitchen counter.

"Say it!" he ordered.

She winced as he squeezed harder, knowing she would probably have a bruise on her thigh by morning.

"Uncle! Uncle!" she finally conceded.

He smirked proudly, then stood and walked to the kitchen.

"Hey, Canon." Simon greeted Maggie with the nickname he had given her during one of their many photography classes. He was very proud of his Nikon camera. Maggie's preferred brand was Canon, hence the nickname.

"Hi," she replied with an edge of annoyance in her voice. She did not appreciate the nickname.

"Where's your boyfriend tonight?" he asked.

"Working."

He helped himself to a refill of iced tea and returned to the couch for more Mulder and Scully.

Michelle noticed Simon's gaze follow Maggie into her bedroom.

"She's extra friendly tonight," he remarked.

Michelle shrugged.

Maggie still did *not* like Simon. She hadn't let him off the hook for the way he broke Emma's heart freshman year. Poor Simon, God love him, tried his hardest to win her over with his friendly teasing, but she would have none of it. The more she snubbed him, the more it seemed to bother him. Michelle wished he would just let it go, but he never did.

Simon soon became absorbed in alien artifacts and conspiracy theories again, but Michelle's mind wandered. She couldn't help it when she was sitting so close to him. She shifted and grabbed the throw blanket from the back of the couch. Simon snatched a corner and pulled it across the both of them, stretching his arm across the empty spot where the blanket had been. Michelle leaned her head against his chest, and he lowered his arm to her shoulders. She found it impossible to focus on what Skinner was telling Scully or on Krycek's evildoings. All she could think about was the warmth of Simon's arm and the faint smell of his cologne.

It seemed everyone she knew was either in a serious relationship, engaged, or married. Everyone was finishing college and settling down. And she wanted that. After all this time not dating, she wanted it so badly.

At episode's end, Simon and Michelle looked at each other with wide eyes, having been left with a whopper of a cliffhanger.

"Whoa!" he exclaimed.

She nodded, her chin resting on his chest.

Their eyes held, and the mood slowly shifted.

Simon's gaze fell to her lips, and her heart skipped a beat.

She tentatively laid her hand on his chest and slid it ever so slowly to rest on the side of his neck, scared she might spook him.

He tilted his head toward her, leaning closer and closer, still staring at her mouth.

She licked her lips, and his eyes met hers.

His breath was coming quicker as he moved in. He had barely brushed his lips against hers when the sound of Maggie's door opening caused him to jerk his head away. He watched her walk into the kitchen and grab a drink from the fridge.

Michelle glanced over at her, and she gave them half a smile, then disappeared into her room again.

Simon chuckled nervously. "Sorry about that." He lowered his arm and shifted her off of his chest.

She sat up straight and clasped her hands together in her lap. "You don't have to be sorry, Simon." She wished she could tell what he was thinking, but he was unreadable.

He stared down at his knees for a few seconds, then looked straight into her eyes. "You're my best friend, Chelle. Let's not go there."

Her heart felt heavy. Not at all what she wanted to hear. "But what if I want to?"

Simon shook his head. "I really don't wanna mess this up. I couldn't bear losing your friendship if things didn't work out."

She nodded sadly.

"I think I'm gonna go," he spoke softly. "Are we OK?"

"Yeah." She smiled a little.

"Are you sure?" He laid his hand over hers and squeezed.

"We're OK," she assured him. "Now, get outta here."

He stood and kissed her on the top of the head, then left with a casual wave, the door softly clicking behind him.

Michelle sat staring at the door for several long minutes, her heart still racing. It was the closest they had ever come to taking their friendship to the next level.

But maybe he was right. He was like family to her at this point, more than her actual family ever was, and she didn't want to risk losing that. Not ever.

But that almost kiss moment had given her a glimmer of hope she would cling to for dear life.

9

"We're engaged!" Maggie announced as she burst through the apartment door with Ben following close behind.

"No way!" Michelle looked up from her spot at the kitchen table and dropped her fork of lasagna with a *clink*.

Maggie walked toward her with outstretched hand, beaming as bright as the marquise cut diamond on her ring finger.

Michelle checked out the rock. "Wow! It's beautiful."

"Already?" Simon asked from his place across the table. "Isn't that a little fast?"

Maggie shot him a dirty look.

"When you're with the right person, you just know," Ben piped in.

Simon looked over at Michelle and rolled his eyes.

The animosity between Simon and Ben was palpable. From day one, the two of them had never gotten along. Maggie's dislike of Simon may have rubbed off on Ben, because he never gave the guy a chance. And Michelle could almost feel Simon tense up whenever Ben walked into the room.

Michelle stood and hugged Maggie. "Congratulations, Mags. It's what you've always wanted."

Maggie squeezed her tightly. "I know. God's timing, right?"

"Right." Michelle had learned a lot over the past four years about God's timing, but she still struggled to understand why things happened the way they did sometimes. She wrestled with letting go of control and letting go of her past, which haunted her.

She released her hold on Maggie and reluctantly hugged Ben. "Congratulations."

"Thanks, Michelle." Ben grinned at her when they parted, then took Maggie's hand.

Michelle still did not trust Ben. No matter how happy he seemed with Maggie, he reminded her too much of the guys she had known in high school. She wanted it to work out for Maggie's sake. She wanted to believe he had grown up and changed in the last four years, but she still saw him as the guy she made out with at the roller rink, the guy who constantly broke her roommate's heart. Even now, she still held her breath a little whenever Maggie left with him, afraid her roommate might come home brokenhearted again.

"We should celebrate," Michelle declared, trying to be supportive. "Wanna go get some dessert or something?"

Maggie glanced over at Ben. They seemed to have an unspoken conversation going on with their eyes. "We're gonna go share the good news with our parents, but I had to come tell you."

"I'm glad you did. Have fun, you two."

When the newly engaged couple had gone, Michelle looked over at Simon, who was sulking. "I'm happy for her. She's been waiting a long time for this."

Simon didn't respond.

"I knew they wouldn't wait too long to get engaged," she continued. "They've known each other since high school."

"Yeah, well, she can do much better." He sounded bitter.

"You don't even know him, Simon."

"I've been around him enough to know he's not good enough for her."

"What does *that* mean?" She completely agreed, but she wanted to know why he felt so strongly about it.

"Nothing."

"I really wanna know."

"Whatever." He stood suddenly and left his half-eaten plate of food behind.

"That's such a copout. What's your problem with him?"

"Just a feeling."

"Oh, come on. It's gotta be more than that. You seriously don't like him, and I wanna know why."

Simon turned to face her. "I don't like the way he looks at you."

"What?" Michelle eyes widened in surprise.

"I'm not kidding. He's always checking you out when Maggie's not looking."

Michelle stomach churned nervously, remembering the night at the roller rink.

"That guy is hot for you, so I don't know why he's asking Maggie to marry him."

"Because he loves her." It came out as more of a question than a statement.

"Well, he sure doesn't act like a man in love with his fiancée."

She didn't know what to say. He was right, of course. She already knew it, and he had seen it. If only Maggie could see it, too.

"I'm gonna go."

"Simon."

He walked to her and hugged her close. "Sorry. Just forget what I said. I'm exhausted from shooting that wedding last night. I hope Maggie will be very happy. You can tell her I said that."

She soaked in his warmth. She liked that Simon was bothered by the way Ben looked at her. Was he jealous? She wished she knew.

"Are you gonna go to Uncle Pete's with me next weekend for Fourth of July?" He continued to hold her.

"Of course." She spoke into his neck.

"Good." He kissed the top of her head, then walked to the door. "I'll call you tomorrow."

"OK. Goodnight."

"Night."

❧ ♡ ☙

Michelle scanned the church pews for Janice. Their usual pew was taken, and she had no idea if Janice was even there. In a church of Calvary's size, it wasn't always easy to find people. Just as she was about to head upstairs to the balcony seating, she spotted Janice on the opposite side of the sanctuary seated in the middle of a row talking with a nice-looking guy. There was just enough room for her to squeeze in if she hurried over.

She greeted Janice with a wave.

"Oh, hi!"

"Is there room for me?"

"Sure. Sure." Janice scooted closer to the guy and made a little extra room.

Michelle apologized as she crawled past the half a dozen people on the end. She couldn't help but bump into their legs, and she accidentally stepped on one man's toes. "Sorry."

"Hey, how are you?" Janice asked as Michelle took her seat.

"Pretty good. How are you?"

Janice had the same happy expression on her face that she always seemed to have. "I'm alive and praising God for it." Her positivity made Michelle smile. "This is my cousin, Jeremy." She motioned to the young man sitting next to her.

"Nice to meet you." Jeremy held his hand out to Michelle.

Michelle shook it. "You, too."

"Jeremy's going to Cornerstone. He'll be a junior in the fall." Janice had a peculiar look in her eyes, like she was up to something.

"Oh, you look kind of familiar," Michelle said. "I'm sure I saw you around campus."

Jeremy laughed a little. "Probably not, since I'm a transfer student."

"Oh." She chuckled. "Well, you still look familiar."

"I have that kind of face, I guess."

When he smiled at her, she realized what was so familiar about him. He looked a little like Sean with his dark hair, the shape of his face, and blue eyes. His eyes weren't as blue as Sean's, though. Nobody's eyes were as blue as Sean's.

The music began to play, and they stood for the opening worship songs.

Janice elbowed her and subtly tilted her head in Jeremy's direction. She had that look in her eyes again.

Michelle suddenly understood. Janice was trying to find her a man. She gave her friend a disapproving look.

Janice shrugged. "Worth a try," she whispered.

Michelle giggled.

"So, how did your interview go?" Janice asked.

"I got the job."

"You did? That's awesome!" Janice hugged her. "I've been praying you would."

"It's not the dream job or anything, but it's a place to start, I guess."

"What's the job again?"

"Customer relations at an investment firm."

"That sounds important."

Michelle shook her head. "It's not. I'm a glorified receptionist."

Janice patted her on the hand. "God can use you in whatever job he sees fit to give you."

If only she had a clear vision of what she was supposed to be doing with her life, maybe she wouldn't second-guess every decision. Day after day, the all-important degree with Bachelor of Arts Psychology printed in bold script stared at her from its place on the corner of her desk. It taunted her. Especially now that she had been hired at this new job. Receptionist? Really? Four long years to end up answering phone calls and taking messages?

Everyone seemed to have grand plans and great jobs lined up. Simon was now working with a photographer in Grand Rapids, learning the business firsthand. Maggie was second shooting weddings with some area photographers and had started making plans to open her own photography business back in her hometown. Wes landed a job as an assistant youth pastor at a church in Ohio, fairly close to Emma, who would soon be graduating from Cedarville with her teaching degree.

Even Sean had a great job. Oh, how the thought of him still scattered butterflies around in her stomach. She tried not to think of him anymore. After Sean married that girl, he went to work for his father-in-law's construction company, and now lived happily in the suburbs somewhere. At least that's what Simon had told her. So it seemed that God had worked everything out for him, too.

It felt like she was the only one without a real purpose.

"What is God's purpose for your life?" Pastor Dobson's words suddenly captured Michelle's full attention. "For the next few weeks, that is exactly what we'll be talking about."

Michelle smiled to herself. God's timing really was so perfect.

❧ 10 ❧

On a warm July evening, Ben's parents threw an engagement party for their son and his new fiancée at their home on Gun Lake. They had a nicely landscaped yard with a huge patio area perfect for hosting parties. Strings of bare, round bulbs hung between the trees and under the patio roof, illuminating the tables set up with food. The yard was overflowing with people, many from their church. There was so much happiness over this impending union.

Maggie led Michelle around, introducing her to this person and that. "This is Michelle, my maid of honor."

When it came to Maggie's bridal party, she had plenty of close friends to choose from. Michelle had never been in a wedding before, and being chosen as maid of honor over Maggie's best friends, Kay and Brooke, was an unexpected, yet pleasant surprise. The maid of honor title made her feel truly important.

"I can't believe you and Ben are getting married." Kay embraced Maggie, then glanced over at Michelle. "You would not believe what a huge crush our girl had on Ben back in high school."

"Oh, I believe it." Michelle laughed.

"Are you happy?" Brooke asked the bride-to-be.

Maggie was beaming. "So happy."

"Where's that fiancé of yours?" asked Kay. "I haven't seen him in forever."

Maggie glanced around the yard. "He's mingling somewhere."

"I'll go find him," Michelle offered. "You girls stay here and catch up."

She wandered along the perimeter of the yard, scanning the small groups of guests, until she spotted Ben standing amidst a group of girls. Michelle took note of the way Ben hung closer to one of them, resting his hand on her lower back as they talked. They all seemed to hang on his every word and cracked up laughing as she approached their group.

Ben dropped his hand as soon as he spotted Michelle.

"Your fiancée is looking for you," she announced.

"Ok. Tell her I'll be right there."

"Aren't you gonna introduce me to your friends?" Michelle put him on the spot.

"Oh, yeah. Of course. This is Maggie's roommate, Michelle. She's the maid of honor." He didn't bother to tell Michelle who the girls were.

She shook her head as she walked across the yard.

When she returned to Maggie, a thirty-something couple had joined their little group.

"Michelle, this is Pastor Jon, my high school youth pastor, and his wife, Fran."

"Nice to meet you." Michelle shook their hands.

"P.J. is marrying us," Maggie announced with glee just as Ben arrived.

"Ben." Pastor Jon extended his hand.

"Hey, P.J." Ben shook his hand.

Pastor Jon grabbed his forearm and pulled him forward, twisting his arm around behind his back.

Ben cried out in pain.

Michelle stepped back in surprise and glanced over at Maggie, who was laughing with the rest of the group.

Noticing Michelle's confused expression, Maggie moved over and put an arm around her. "Don't worry. They're always like this."

Pastor Jon twisted harder, but Ben fought back, whirling his body in the opposite direction. The men stumbled toward Maggie and Michelle, who separated just in time to avoid being hit. The guys wrestled across the yard until they were just behind Michelle again. The girls had gone back to chatting amongst themselves, but Michelle watched the wrestlers. As Pastor Jon finally let up on Ben, he kept a grip on his hand and patted him on the back. Then she heard him say in a quiet voice, "If you do anything to hurt her, you're gonna have to answer to me."

As the party continued on after sunset, Michelle grew more comfortable with Maggie's friends. They were a wonderful, close-knit group, this church family of hers, and she envied the unity they all shared. She knew it was wrong to be jealous, but she couldn't help feeling sad for having grown up where she did, how she did. If only she'd had a supportive group like this, things in her life might have been very different.

Despite the happy mood of the party, Michelle didn't feel much like celebrating. She couldn't stop thinking about making out with Ben at rollerskating freshman year. She kept remembering Simon telling her that Ben was always checking her out. And she didn't like the way Ben's hand had been on that girl's back or the guilty way he had dropped it when she walked up.

She glanced across the yard and saw Ben once again with the same group of girls. Maggie told her they were some of his friends from high school and college. The girls all seemed to be there with other guys, but that didn't stop Ben from flirting with them—especially that one girl in particular.

Maggie didn't seem to notice, or maybe she didn't want to notice.

Michelle wished she could give Ben the benefit of the doubt, because Maggie was completely in love with him. She knew that. And she wanted to be happy for them, but she had a very bad feeling.

Toward the end of the night, that bad feeling was confirmed.

While Maggie and her friends were off singing old favorite youth group songs together, Michelle noticed Ben standing with the girl he'd had his hand on just outside the glow of the patio lights. He leaned close and said something to her, then guided her around to the unlit side of the house.

Nuh-uh. No way!

Michelle moved quietly across the lawn so as not to draw attention to herself. She walked toward the dark side of the house and rounded the corner. Nobody was there, so she moved stealthily along the edge and peeked around the next corner just in time to see Ben leaning in close, about to make his move, his lips millimeters from the girl's.

Michelle cleared her throat, and they both jumped.

"At your engagement party, Ben. Really? That's classy."

"It's not what it looks like."

"Save it." She was fuming.

"Ben was just being a good friend," the girl declared.

Michelle stared at her stone-faced.

"Her dad just died," Ben explained.

She glared at him.

He glared back.

"I'm ... gonna go." The girl scurried away with her head down. "Thanks again, Ben."

"Seriously? A dead father. That's the story you're going with?"

"It's not a story. Her dad *did* die."

"And you had to be the one to comfort her, did ya'?"

"She's one of my oldest friends, and she needed to talk."

"Didn't look like talking to me."

"Knock it off, Michelle."

Her mouth dropped open. "Hey, you're in the wrong here. Not me."

He took a few steps closer. "I didn't do anything."

"Only because I interrupted you."

"Hey!" He grabbed her by the arm. "Don't go telling Maggie stories."

Michelle gritted her teeth and squeezed her hands into fists. More than anything, she wanted to punch him in the face, but she didn't want to ruin the night for Maggie. She would wait until tomorrow to tell her what she had seen.

"I'm not kidding, Michelle. Don't say anything."

"Or what?"

"I know you never told her what happened between us at the skating rink. I don't think she'd be too happy to hear about that after all this time. Her fiancé and her maid of honor? How do you think she would feel about that?"

She didn't know what to say.

Ben leaned in close and kissed her on the cheek. "Enjoy the party," he said smugly.

Michelle despised him at that moment, and she knew his type all too well. She wondered how many other girls he had taken into dark corners during his relationship with Maggie.

Oh, dear sweet Maggie.

❧ 11 ❧

$\mathcal{T}$he last place Michelle ever thought she would be on her twenty-second birthday was standing in a dressing room trying on wedding gowns, but that's exactly where she found herself. Maggie had roped her into modeling for a photo shoot at a new bridal boutique in downtown Grand Rapids in the hopes of building up her photography portfolio.

Michelle slid the dressing room curtain to the side and walked out into the bridal shop, where two of Maggie's photographer friends were already waiting in wedding gowns.

"Michelle, you look beautiful." Maggie motioned for her to step up onto a pedestal surrounded by mirrors.

She moved into place and looked at her reflection. The dress wasn't her style with it's long lace sleeves and beaded detail, but she did feel pretty.

Maggie walked over and handed her a bouquet of flowers, then lifted the train of the dress, letting it fall smoothly behind her. "OK, turn slowly toward me."

Michelle did as Maggie requested, and the train twisted slightly as she turned.

"Perfect!" Maggie declared, raising her camera and snapping a few photos. She paused and peeked up at Michelle. "Try not to look so miserable."

"Sorry." Michelle smiled weakly. "I told you I wouldn't be very good at this."

"What are you talking about? You're gorgeous." Maggie looked through her camera viewfinder again.

Truth be told, Michelle had only agreed to the photo shoot because she felt guilty for never telling Maggie what she had seen at the engagement party. She was too afraid of what might happen if Maggie ever found out she kissed Ben. And maybe she had been wrong. Maybe he *was* just comforting a grieving friend. She seriously doubted that, but she wasn't willing to risk losing Maggie over it.

The three girls took turns posing in several gowns each, and Michelle could see how happy the whole thing made Maggie. She was totally in her element all afternoon.

When it was time for Michelle's last dress change, she took the gown handed to her and walked into the changing room. She heard the chime on the door signal someone entering the shop, though it was supposed to be closed for the photo shoot.

As she walked out into the room again, she spotted Simon standing next to Maggie, talking with one of the other girls. He glanced up and caught sight of her, and his mouth dropped open a little.

"Hey," Michelle greeted him as she took her place on the pedestal again.

"Chelle ..." Simon seemed awestruck. He couldn't find words.

She looked at herself in the mirror. Now *this* dress was totally her—strapless and smooth with a fitted waist and a little poof to the tea-length skirt. With its satin striped border, it reminded her of the "bell dress" Julia Roberts wore in the movie *Runaway Bride*—only shorter.

Her eyes met Simon's again. He was staring at her in a way she had never seen before, and she liked it. A lot.

"You look amazing."

Her cheeks warmed, and her stomach was doing somersaults.

"Seriously. You've never looked so beautiful," he gushed.

She tried to act casual. "Thanks."

He had a goofy look on his face, until the click of Maggie's camera shutter pulled his attention in her direction. Then it was all questions about photography and what lenses she was using and what settings were best for the lighting.

"I'm working here, Simon," Maggie declared, obviously annoyed.

Michelle was secretly pleased by her reaction.

Simon watched silently while Maggie photographed a few final pictures of the models. When she wrapped the session, Simon walked over to Michelle and hugged her.

"Careful of the dress," she ordered with a smile.

He took her hands in his and stepped back. "Look at you. Wow!"

"Simon." She had never felt so shy before, and she let go and spun around to distract from it. The skirt lifted and fell softly around her. It made her feel truly beautiful. And after seeing the look on Simon's face, she was glad she had decided to help Maggie out.

"You should wear that to dinner tonight."

"Are we going to dinner? I thought we were just doing pizza and a movie."

"It's your birthday, and I'm taking you out. Is that OK?"

"Sure. Just let me get changed."

"OK. I've actually got an errand to run first. Can I come back and get you in like fifteen minutes?"

"Sure."

He leaned in and gave her a quick peck on the lips and that charming smile of his, then headed out the door.

Michelle went to the changing room and reluctantly removed the dress. She reached up and touched her bottom lip. She knew Simon meant the kiss as nothing more than friendship, but her lips were tingling from the contact. She hung the dress on the hanger and stared at it longingly. She had never been the kind of girl to dream of her future wedding, plan it out to the tiniest detail, or pretend to be a bride when she was a little girl. That just wasn't her. Marriage had never really been for her. But if she *were* ever to get married one day, if it was in God's plan, this was just the dress she would choose. And for the first time in her life, she daydreamed about her wedding. She imagined Simon waiting at the end of the aisle, looking at her exactly the way he had earlier, and she wanted that moment to be real someday.

When she emerged from the dressing room, Maggie was helping the store owner take care of the gowns. Michelle held the dress out to Maggie, but when she grabbed for it, Michelle pulled it back teasingly.

"I knew you liked that one. It's gorgeous on you, Chelle." Maggie smiled.

"It really is pretty." She released it to Maggie, who put it back on the display rack. "Someday maybe."

"Maybe someday soon." Maggie winked.

"I doubt that."

Maggie slid some dresses to the side, and she suddenly gasped. "*Oooh,* look at this one." It was lacy, long, and flowing. It looked like Maggie.

"Try it on."

"No, I couldn't. I haven't even started dress shopping yet."

"Now's as good a time as any," Michelle insisted.

Maggie giggled. "OK." She snatched the dress and ran off to the changing room.

A few minutes later, Simon returned to the shop with a small bouquet of flowers in hand. "Hey, are you ready to go?"

Michelle held up her index finger as Maggie emerged from the dressing room.

"What do you think?" Maggie lifted the skirt a little as she walked. "Does it look good?"

"*So* good," Michelle replied.

Maggie stepped up on the pedestal. Her mouth fell open slightly as she saw her reflection in the mirrors, and tears began to well up in her eyes. "This is it. *This* is the one."

Michelle was about to respond when she glanced over at Simon. The look he gave her earlier paled in comparison to the way he was looking at Maggie now. She couldn't believe what she was seeing, and her heart began to ache.

How long had Simon been harboring feelings for Maggie? And why had she never noticed? She thought of Simon's reaction to the news of Maggie's engagement, how much her dismissive attitude always got to him, the longing in his eyes when he looked at her, and the sweet tone in his voice when he called her Canon. Michelle hadn't been completely blind to the truth. She had seen glimpses, but she ignored them all, because she had loved Simon Walker from the moment she met him.

Simon suddenly noticed Michelle watching him, and he nervously cleared his throat. "Happy birthday, Chelle." He handed her the flowers. "These are for you."

This sweet moment was completely ruined by the nagging jealousy in the pit of her stomach. "Thank you, Simon. They're beautiful," she managed.

"Shall we go?"

"Let's."

❧ 12 ❦

ichelle never imagined she would have to wait five years to wear the bridesmaid dress that hung in her closet. Maggie and Ben should have been married already, but Ben dragged his feet for three years before setting a date. It didn't surprise Michelle at all given what she knew about him, but she felt horrible for her sweet roommate.

Living with Maggie during that time had been miserable. She became a sad, paranoid, stressed-out version of herself. And Ben's nasty habit of blowing her off back in college carried over into their engagement. He constantly stood her up, but always with an excuse. None of them were good, but Maggie forgave him every time. The closer they got to the wedding, the more times Michelle walked in the apartment and found Maggie crying on the phone with Ben or just plain crying. It didn't seem like the happy time it was supposed to be.

Guilt nagged at Michelle daily. She wished she had been honest years ago about what she saw at the engagement party. Maybe then Maggie wouldn't be in this situation. Ben was no good. That was a fact. But what could she do? Maggie was determined to marry him in two months time.

Simon had his own opinions about the wedding, and they became more and more frequent as the big day neared.

"Ben is such a jerk," he would say. "Maggie deserves so much better."

She suspected he had other reasons for not wanting Maggie to marry Ben, but she knew he would never reveal them to her.

One night, after finding Maggie in tears again, Michelle could stand it no more.

"Maggie, please don't be upset at me for asking this, but do you really want to marry Ben?"

A look of shock crossed Maggie's face. "Why are you asking me that? You know how much I love him."

"Yeah, but *why* do you love him?"

"That's a stupid question."

Michelle shook her head. "No, it's not. It's a valid one."

Maggie sat speechless.

"Brides should be happy. This is supposed to be a celebration."

"There's a lot to do with the wedding coming up and with work. We're both just a little stressed."

"A little?"

Maggie stood from where she sat at the kitchen table and walked to the refrigerator.

"I don't mean to upset you or hurt your feelings. I just want you to be happy, Mags, and you don't seem very happy. You haven't for a long time."

The refrigerator door slammed shut.

"You know you're allowed to change your mind. You don't have to go through with the wedding."

"I *am* happy with Ben," Maggie snapped, "and we are getting married on June twenty-sixth."

After that conversation, tensions were high at the apartment. Maggie barely spoke to Michelle, which made the invitation from her grandparents to come for a visit the perfect escape. Michelle was on edge as she drove toward their house near Springfield. She knew getting away from the apartment was a good idea, but part of her worried that Maggie would be even more upset if she walked out and shirked her maid of honor duties. The bridal shower hosted by her and the other bridesmaids was only a week away, and she had also promised to help address wedding invitations.

She wasn't looking forward to this visit with her grandparents. Not that she didn't love them for all they had done for her, but every conversation centered around her career. They thought she was overqualified for her receptionist job, which they were right about.

Even when she got promoted to office manager, they still weren't satisfied. They were quick to tell her how much they wished she would use the degree they had paid for to get a better job.

She wished for things, too. She wished they had been more than just financially supportive. She wished they had given her encouragement rather than criticism.

As she neared their street, she prayed that maybe this visit would be different.

The garage door on their light blue, ranch-style home was wide open when she arrived. Their Buick was inside, and an unfamiliar SUV sat in the driveway. She entered the house through the breezeway, dropping her bags just inside the door.

"Hello?" The house was silent, but she heard muffled voices coming from outside. She walked through to the back door of the garage and stopped dead in her tracks.

On a shiny new swing set in her grandparents' yard was a giggly little girl with chestnut brown ringlets.

"Higher, Daddy," the little girl cried.

Michelle's heart tightened in her chest at the sight of her father.

"Hold on tight, Ava." Robert pulled back on the chains and let go.

Ava giggled and let out a gleeful shriek.

A strong urge to flee overwhelmed her. She wanted to sneak out, grab her bags, and drive away before anyone saw her. This was not at all what she had expected.

"Michelle." Grandma spotted her.

Darn it!

"Come sit with us. Have a glass of iced tea."

Michelle hesitantly walked into the back yard. Her father looked over at her and waved.

She walked on without a response and sat next to her grandmother, who handed her a glass of tea.

"How was your drive?" Grandma asked.

"Fine." She was mad, fuming really.

"Is something wrong?" Grandma was clueless as ever.

"Why didn't you tell me Dad was gonna be here?" she asked quietly.

"He just showed up this morning. We didn't know he was coming."

Michelle didn't know whether to believe her or not. She glanced across the yard.

"I thought you'd be happy to see Avey."

Michelle turned her eyes on Grandma. "Why would you think that?"

"Because she's your little sister."

"I've never even met her before."

Grandma's mouth dropped open.

Did Grandma really not know that? Does she really not know her own son by now? This was a huge mistake.

Michelle crossed her arms. Before her stood this man, who was supposed to take care of her and love her and push *her* on the swing, but he had never done a single one of those things. He barely seemed to notice her presence. She watched him lift Ava and swing her around. Ava laughed and wrapped her arms around his neck. He squeezed her and kissed her on the cheek, and all Michelle wanted at that moment was to curl up in a ball and die.

As Robert carried Ava across the yard in her direction, Michelle's heart began to race.

"Hello, Michelle. How are you?"

"Fine."

"Ava, say hello to your big sister, Michelle."

Ava's eyes grew as big as saucers. She looked back and forth between Dad and Michelle.

Michelle stared at the adorable little girl, not quite sure what to say to her.

Ava wiggled out of Robert's arms and walked over to Michelle. "Hi."

"Hi."

"You're my sister," Ava declared.

Michelle nodded. "I know."

Ava suddenly climbed into her lap and ran her little hand over Michelle's long, brown waves. "You're pretty."

"So are you," Michelle replied, touching one of her sister's ringlets.

Ava wrapped her arms around Michelle's neck in a hug. "I've never had a sister before."

Michelle's heart turned to mush. "Neither have I." She held tightly to Ava and breathed in the smell of her strawberry-scented kid shampoo. Her eyes stung as tears threatened.

And just as quickly as their conversation began, Ava jumped down and ran back to play on the swings again.

Michelle glanced over at her father, who was watching his little daughter lovingly, and the jealousy burned within her. *What's wrong with me? Why doesn't he love me like he loves Ava? Why am I never enough? For anyone?*

As the afternoon wore on, her father carried on long conversations with his parents and doted on Ava the whole time, but barely said two words to her.

When Grandma got up to begin preparing dinner, Michelle followed her into the kitchen. She could no longer take the torture. "I'm sorry, Grandma. I can't stay."

"But you just got here. I thought you were staying for the whole weekend. We were planning to go to Easter service. We can take Ava to the Easter egg hunt."

"Well, you can still take her, but I have to go."

Grandma looked at her with disapproval. "You should be here with your family."

The tears burned Michelle's eyes again. "Do you have any idea how hard this was for me?"

Her grandmother looked at her in confusion.

"I can't sit here and watch Dad and Ava together. It's too much."

The back door opened and in walked her father. She could tell by the expression on his face that he had heard her.

"Great!" Michelle glared at her dad. "You know what, I'm just gonna say it. You suck." It was a juvenile thing to say, but her teenage side started creeping in. All the things she had never had the guts to say to him when she was that age were about to burst out. "Would it have hurt you to spend a little time with me when I was Ava's age? Would it have been so hard to push me on a swing or teach me how to ride a bike? Or buy me a bike for that matter?" Tears streamed down her face now. "You were never there for me. How could you just leave me? How could you do that?"

"Michelle."

She wouldn't let him speak. "And then you just broke Mom's heart and got yourself a new wife and a new daughter. You act like I don't exist. Well, I do! I exist, Dad. I exist!" She was yelling now.

Ava shuffled in behind their father and stared up at Michelle.

"I was your daughter long before Ava was, but you never treated me like you treat her. You never loved me like you love her."

"That's not true," her dad replied.

"Are you kidding me? I don't think you've ever hugged me once in my life. How do you think that made me feel?"

Dad hung his head.

"Worthless. That's how I felt. That's how I feel. That's how *you* make me feel."

Her dad looked up and took a step toward her.

She held her hand out to stop him. "That little girl standing behind you doesn't even know me. She's six years old, and we're meeting for the first time, and that's *your* fault."

"You know where we live, Michelle."

A laugh escaped her. *Unbelievable.*

She turned swiftly and hugged her grandmother.

"Please stay," Grandma whispered.

"I can't."

She walked over and hugged Grandpa, then grabbed her bags from where they still sat just inside the door.

A little shuffle of footsteps followed her, and her heart broke at the sound.

"Michelle." Ava's tiny voice was sad.

Michelle dropped her bags and turned around, crouching down to Ava's level.

"Are you going home?"

She nodded her reply.

"Bye, Michelle." Ava hugged her so sweetly.

She squeezed her eyes closed and did her best to swallow her sobs as she held her little sister tightly.

Ava let go and wiped tears from Michelle's cheeks. "Don't be sad."

Michelle forced half a smile.

"I love you, big sister." Ava had the most adorable smile.

Michelle kissed her on the top of the head as she stood, then grabbed her bags and walked out of the house.

When Michelle arrived home that night, she was surprised to see Simon's car in front of the building. She got an uneasy feeling as she climbed the stairs to their apartment, afraid of what she might find. Simon was seated on a stool at the kitchen bar, while Maggie stood across the counter from him.

"Hey, Chelle," he greeted her.

"You're back early. How was your trip?" Maggie's words seemed forced, like she wasn't over their previous conversation.

Michelle eyed them suspiciously. "Fine." She carried her bags into her bedroom and threw them down with a loud *thud*.

Simon followed her and laid his hands on her shoulders. "What's wrong?"

She shook him off. "What are you doing here?"

"I came to see you."

"You knew I was going to Illinois."

He shrugged his shoulders. "I forgot."

Unlikely.

"Why are you back early?" he asked.

"It's a long story, and I don't really feel like talking about it."

"OK."

"What were you and Maggie doing?"

"Talking wedding photography."

"What? You weren't trying to convince her to call off her wedding?" she asked sarcastically.

A sly grin crossed his face. "That's a good idea. Someone should do that."

He said it as a joke, but Michelle was not in the mood. She knew there was truth in his remarks.

"Can you just go?"

He was taken aback by her abruptness. "Uh ... yeah. OK."

"I'll call you tomorrow."

"All right." He shuffled out of her room.

She hadn't meant to be so rude. It had been a very long day. She turned to follow him and apologize, but through the bedroom door she saw him walk over to Maggie in the kitchen and put his arm around her.

"Goodnight, Canon."

The sweet tone in his voice unleashed the green-eyed monster within.

On the morning of Maggie's bridal shower brunch, as Michelle prepared the final decorations and food, Simon hovered about the apartment. He was fidgeting and looking genuinely bothered. Michelle was already in a bad mood because Maggie still wasn't speaking to her, and his presence wasn't helping matters.

"Maggie and her mom will be here any minute, and the guests will be arriving soon. You *have* to go."

"She can't marry him," he blurted out.

"Simon, stop!"

He looked her in the eyes. "I'm serious."

She had heard all of his reasons over the years, but now she wanted the truth. She stopped what she was doing and rested her hands on her hips. "Why not, Simon?"

He didn't reply.

"Why not?" She needed to hear it.

"She can do better than that jerk."

She let out an exasperated sigh. "You're a coward."

"What do you want from me?"

"Just be honest with me, Simon." She had seen it in his eyes. That day she had seen them fighting outside the dorm about Emma. The day he walked into the bridal shop and saw Maggie in her wedding dress. The countless times she had seen him gazing at Maggie at the apartment.

"I don't know what you want me to say."

"It bothers you that Maggie hates you."

He stared at her.

"It bothers you that she won't give you the time of day."

Still nothing.

"It bothers you that she's marrying Ben."

"Of course it does."

"Why?" She already knew the answer.

"Michelle," he seemed to be pleading for her not to make him reply.

"Say it!" she cried.

"Fine! I care about her, OK?" His eyes dropped away from hers. "I care about her," he admitted softly.

Michelle cringed at the way he said *care*, because she suspected that *care* really meant *love*, and it broke her heart.

The bridal shower was small and personal, just the mothers, grandmothers, and bridesmaids. Michelle could barely concentrate after her conversation with Simon. She certainly didn't feel like celebrating Maggie's upcoming wedding, but she put on a happy face and made nice, pleasant conversation as best as she could.

Horrible thoughts filled her mind. She knew Ben was a cheater, but she wanted Maggie to marry him anyway so she would never have Simon. A part of her even hoped Ben would cheat on Maggie so her happily ever after fantasy wouldn't come true. Why did Maggie get her dream guy *and* Simon's love? She knew deep down that she needed to pray and ignore these thoughts, but at the moment, she didn't care. *Why doesn't Simon want me? What is wrong with me? When will it finally be my turn?*

When the games had been played and the food eaten, Michelle went about cleaning up, while Maggie hugged all of her guests and thanked them for coming.

"Thank you for all your hard work putting this together, Michelle." Patty gave her a hug. "I'm so glad my daughter has such a wonderful friend."

Michelle faked a smile, just as she had been all day.

While Maggie, Patty, and Ben's mother carried some of the boxes to their cars, the groom-to-be appeared at the door.

"Hey, Michelle." He sauntered in with his usual flirty grin.

She busied herself putting away leftover food and ignored him.

He stood on the other side of the kitchen bar and started covering one of the bowls.

"I got it," she snapped.

He raised his hands in defense. "Sorry."

She lowered her head. "I'm sorry. I didn't mean to snap. I'm just having a day."

"Did the party not go well?"

"Oh no, the party was great. You guys made out like bandits." She pointed to the large pile of gifts by the door.

He moved around to her side of the counter.

She glanced over at him.

"Are you OK?" He seemed genuinely concerned, and walked over and laid a hand on her shoulder.

Tears suddenly burned her eyes. She did not expect it, and she definitely did not want to cry in front of him. She turned away for a moment.

He suddenly took hold of her arm and pulled her in for a hug.

It was unexpected, but not completely unwelcome. She felt very alone, and she let him hold her for a few moments.

He rubbed his hand comfortingly up and down her back.

She pulled away and wiped her tears. "Sorry."

"You gonna be all right?" he asked.

"Yeah." She waved him off. "I'm fine."

He brushed a runaway tear from her cheek, and it made her stomach flip.

She chewed nervously on her lip.

"You know I'm here if you ever need to talk. You're like a sister to Maggie, and that makes us family."

It was the nicest he had been to her in a very long time, but the way he looked at her was not without a little edge of flirtation. She was still reeling from her conversation with Simon earlier, so she decided to keep this little moment with Ben to herself.

Maggie returned with the mothers and greeted her fiancé with a kiss. It annoyed Michelle immensely, and annoyance turned to anger when the four of them gathered the last of the boxes and left. No hug from Maggie. No thank you for all she had done for the bridal shower. Nothing.

I care about her.

The words echoed in her mind as she stood under the steaming shower that evening. Not even a five-mile run could shake them.

Michelle emerged from her room a while later to find Maggie working on her laptop at the kitchen table. She shuffled around the apartment slamming cupboards and doors in her wake. She kept thinking about all that had happened over the past week—the tension between her and Maggie, the conversation with Simon, the disastrous run-in with her father. Part of her wished her dad had tried to stop her or made some effort to talk to her before she left. But he hadn't. He didn't care enough to do that. *Care.* There was that word again. Her thoughts returned to Simon, and she slammed the refrigerator door, bottles clinking and rattling within.

"What is with you?" Maggie asked.

"Nothing," she grumbled.

"Is it Simon?" Maggie looked at her with a raised eyebrow.

Michelle gave her a dirty look.

"Why are you looking at me like that?"

"I don't wanna get into it with you," she snapped.

Maggie stood. "What does *that* mean?"

"You are *so* clueless," Michelle blurted.

Maggie's mouth dropped open.

"About so many things." Michelle couldn't help herself.

"What are you even talking about?" Maggie stared dumbfounded.

"It's so unfair." She had never felt so angry in all the time she had known Maggie.

"What is?"

Michelle nearly confessed it all right then and there. She wanted to burst Maggie's happy little bubble. She wanted to tell her that Ben was probably the biggest cheater on the planet, but she couldn't bring herself to say it. And she couldn't tell her that Simon cared for her and didn't want her to marry Ben. She never wanted Maggie to know that. Ever.

"I have to get out of here." She grabbed her purse and bolted out the door, knowing full well where she was headed.

Michelle was shaking. Jealousy had taken over the sane part of her mind. She stood at the door to Ben's apartment, wishing she hadn't just knocked. *What am I doing?* She started to walk away until she heard his voice.

"Michelle?" He looked surprised to see her. "Is everything OK?"

"Yes. No ... I'm sorry. I shouldn't have come here."

"You look like you need to talk." Ben opened the door further to let her inside.

She paused. *Turn around and walk away, Michelle. Do not step foot inside his apartment.* But she ignored the voice in her head.

Ben laid his hand on her lower back to usher her in. "You're shaking. Come here and sit down." He led her to the couch. "Can I get you something to drink?"

She shook her head no, and he joined her on the couch.

Michelle had no idea what to say or how to explain why she was there. She couldn't tell him what Simon had said about Maggie. She couldn't tell him that she was insanely jealous. She couldn't tell him the real reason that she had driven to his apartment. Because now that she was sitting there next to him, she knew how incredibly juvenile and wrong it was. It was the stuff of high school revenge and rivalry, which she'd had plenty of experience with back in Chicago. But she wasn't a teenager anymore. She was twenty-six years old, and she knew better.

Ben suddenly laid his hand on hers, and all thoughts of right and wrong flew out the window. "You can talk to me, Michelle."

She turned her hand over under his, and his fingertips moved back and forth across her palm.

It had been so long since she felt that old familiar flutter in her stomach, and the warmth moving throughout her body made her pulse race.

This is so wrong.

But it felt very right.

"I don't wanna talk," she admitted.

His fingertips left her palm and caressed the inside of her arm from wrist to elbow.

Her breath caught, and her lips fell open.

Ben took this as his opportunity to swoop in. His lips were on hers, and his fingertips moved further up her arm, over her shoulders to her chin. He turned her head to gain a better angle and kissed her deeper.

They kissed and kissed like the night at the roller rink, and she felt wanted, something Simon would never feel for her. *Simon*. Her heart ached. His words echoed in her mind—*I care about her*—and she leaned back on Ben's couch and pulled him on top of her.

This didn't seem to surprise Ben in the least. He kissed her cheek, her ear, her neck, everywhere skin was visible.

She knew she should stop him. She genuinely despised him. And this would inevitably lead to a place she didn't want it to go, a place from her past that God had forgiven her for, a place she should save for her future husband.

She choked back a sob. She just wanted to stop hurting. She needed to feel like someone wanted her.

When Ben had kissed all the visible places, he grabbed the bottom of her shirt and tugged it up, giving himself access to more. And she didn't stop him. She didn't stop him from doing whatever he wanted that night.

"You're not gonna tell Maggie, are you?" Ben asked when he walked her to her car.

"You need to tell her," Michelle replied.

"What? No way!"

"And you need to end things with her." The words flew out of Michelle's mouth before she knew what she was saying. And she meant them. Despite the fact that she and Maggie weren't in a great place at the moment and might never be friends again once she found out about tonight's tryst, Michelle *did* love her and wanted the very best for her. And Ben was not it.

"That is *not* happening."

"Why are you with her, Ben?"

He gave her a puzzled look. "Because I love her."

A laugh escaped. "No, you don't. You love yourself."

"Shut up, Michelle."

"You love that she loves you so much," Michelle continued. "You love that she's so loyal to you, and she would never, ever cheat on you."

"You don't know what you're talking about."

"You love that she's a good person, because you are most certainly not."

"Hey!"

"I'm sure you wanna be, and maybe you feel like a good person when you're with her. But you don't love her. You love the idea of her." *Wow! The psychology degree is really coming in handy tonight.*

"You're no saint, Michelle."

"I never claimed to be."

"I know about all the guys you've been with."

This comment stung. It hurt that Maggie had told Ben about her past, but she pushed it aside. "Do you even *want* to get married, Ben?"

"Well, it's a little late to change my mind now." He snickered.

She shook her head in disgust. "No, it's not."

"I'm not gonna do that to her so close to the wedding."

"So you'd rather just go through with it even though it's not what you want? Do you have any idea how wrong that is? Marriage is not something to take lightly. If you don't wanna marry Maggie, don't marry her."

"I never said I didn't wanna marry her. I just don't know if I'm ready to marry her right now."

"Ben, it's been five years. If you aren't ready by now, that should tell you something."

"I don't wanna hurt her."

"She's gonna be more hurt if you marry her and it doesn't work out."

He stared off across the parking lot.

"If you don't end things, I'm telling her what just happened."

His head whipped in her direction. "You wouldn't."

"Watch me."

"How could you do that to your best friend?"

She was shaking again. This time from fear. "How could I not?"

123

She snuck quietly into the apartment. It was very late, and she knew Maggie was asleep. She felt sick for what she had done with Ben. When she thought about his hands on her, she thought she might be physically ill. *Oh, God, what have I done?*

Her gut suddenly lurched, and she ran to the bathroom. The contents of her stomach emptied into the toilet. She tried to hurl as quietly as she could so she wouldn't wake Maggie. Good thing Maggie usually slept like a rock.

When she finished, she lay on the cold bathroom floor and sobbed her heart out. Not only had she slept with her best friend's fiancé, she had committed a sin, one that she swore she would never take part in again.

Lord, I'm the lowest of the low. I have no excuse for the disgusting person I am right now. How can I ever face Maggie again after what I've done? Please forgive me. I don't deserve it, but, God, please forgive me.

Her stomach tightened again. She didn't think anything was left in there. She was wrong.

Michelle could barely look at Maggie in the morning. She shuffled into the kitchen near noon with wet hair from her shower. Maggie was seated at the kitchen bar editing photos on her laptop.

"Good morning, sleepyhead." Maggie glanced over at the clock. "Well, almost afternoon now."

Michelle nodded.

Maggie turned in her seat. "I'm really sorry, Michelle. I'm sorry I got so upset with you. I know you just want me to be happy. And I'm sorry I didn't tell you how much I loved my bridal shower. I don't like fighting with you, and I don't wanna do it anymore."

Tears began to sting Michelle's eyes as Maggie stood from the bar stool, walked over, and hugged her.

"I'm sorry if it was my fault that you ran out of here last night. I hope you can forgive me."

Michelle pulled away and gave Maggie a weak smile. It was all the reply she could give at the moment. She walked to the refrigerator and opened the door just in time to hide the tears that slid down her cheeks.

"Where were you? I went to bed after midnight, and you weren't back yet."

Michelle brushed the tears away and grabbed the jug of milk. "I just needed to clear my head."

"Do you wanna talk about it?" Maggie asked.

Michelle looked at her sweet roommate, who was completely oblivious to all that was going on around her and so blindly in love with the wrong guy. Her heart ached for Maggie, and she almost spilled the beans. She almost came right out with it. But she knew that if she told, she would lose Maggie's friendship forever, and that scared her more than anything.

"I'm here for you if you need me. You know that, right?"

Michelle fought back tears again. She gave Maggie a nod, then turned to get a bowl of cereal, so she wouldn't have to look into her friend's kind, faithful eyes. The time would come in the very near future when the truth would be revealed, and Maggie would no longer be there for her. So she remained silent to delay the inevitable as long as possible.

The door opened, and in walked Ben with a smile on his face.

Maggie glanced up at him and smiled.

He walked over, put his arm around her, and kissed her forehead. "Good morning, Magnolia."

Michelle cringed at the nickname Ben so often called Maggie.

"Morning. I'm almost finished," Maggie explained.

Ben looked over his shoulder at Michelle, who glared at him.

He rolled his eyes, which infuriated her.

"What are your plans for today?" Michelle asked Maggie.

Maggie clicked twice, then closed the laptop. "We're spending the day looking at houses."

"Houses?" The question popped out of her mouth with surprise. "I thought you were renting an apartment."

"We're just looking," Maggie replied with a happy grin. "But we need to find a place between here and Hastings, so I don't have to travel so far to my shop every day."

"A house, though?" Michelle was hit with a wave of nausea. "That's a huge commitment." She directed her last comment at Ben.

Maggie looked at her strangely. "So is marriage. We're thinking about our future." She laughed a little at Michelle as she gathered her purse, camera, and a folder with a realty company logo on the front. "I'll take pictures and show you tonight."

Ben took Maggie's hand, and they walked out the door together, leaving Michelle crying into her Cocoa Puffs.

❧ ♡ ❧

Michelle almost couldn't bring herself to step foot in church that weekend, but she made herself go. She was sure Janice could tell exactly what she had done just by the look on her face. Maybe she shouldn't have gone after all. She was a bundle of nerves sitting in the pew listening to the sermon.

"Asaph was a priest, who became envious of others and their prosperity, specifically nonbelievers. He saw the way they thrived, their many belongings, the way situations always seemed to go their way, and he was jealous. He saw believers as the ones who constantly struggled in life, and his faith began to falter."

Michelle felt like the entire message was pointed directly at her. The sermon focused heavily on envy, how it distorts thinking and turns things dark and twisted. She was extremely uncomfortable as she listened to the pastor talk about not letting jealousy get into your heart, because it makes people do things they wouldn't normally do.

Her mind flashed to the other night on Ben's couch, and her stomach clenched.

"Asaph sensed something was wrong inside him, so he went to the sanctuary. He didn't want to. He was weak in his faith, but he made himself go to the place of worship anyway." Pastor stepped from behind the podium and stood on the edge of the steps. "So many times when a believer is dealing with a crisis of faith, they step away from the church, when church is exactly the place they need to be to get through it. I encourage you to seek out a pastor or a spiritual friend or a mentor to help if any of you are going through such a crisis right now."

Michelle glanced over at Janice, her dear friend. She just couldn't do it. She couldn't tell Janice what she had done.

Pastor concluded the sermon with the rest of Asaph's story. "Asaph realized he had been mistaken, that he was the one who truly had everything because of God's goodness and grace. His crisis of faith was over. He had learned his lesson, and he was more committed to God than ever."

Psalm 73:26, an important verse from Asaph's story, displayed on the large screen at the front of the church. "My flesh and my heart may fail, but God is the strength of my heart and my portion forever."

Michelle's throat began to tighten, and she knew she was about to lose it. She had failed God big time. The shame and conviction poured over her.

"I have to go," she whispered to Janice, and she raced out during the closing songs. She couldn't get out of there fast enough.

🙖13🙔

$\mathcal{J}$'m telling her tonight." Michelle spoke sternly into the phone.

A month had passed since her indiscretion with Ben, and he continued to make excuse after excuse to avoid ending things with Maggie.

"Just give me a little more time," he begged.

"You're *out* of time. She finished addressing the wedding invitations today."

He groaned.

Michelle had to stop this wedding, but she was terrified of the moment when everything would be out in the open. Not only because of what Maggie would think of her, but also what Simon would think.

"Ben? Did you hear me?"

"Fine! I'll do it!" There was a long pause. "She'll never forgive you for this, ya' know?"

Michelle knew. "I don't care. I love her, and I'm not letting you ruin her life."

He hung up on her.

🙖♡🙔

Michelle paced the apartment all evening long. She declined Simon's invitation to go to a movie, so she would be there when Maggie returned. It wouldn't be pretty, but she knew she had to face the music.

The second hand on the clock ticked by slower than molasses. Cleaning the kitchen didn't make the time move any faster. Clicking through the television channels only agitated her. The apartment was a little dusty, so she went to work on that.

While dusting the bookcase, she noticed the dating book Maggie had given her. She pulled it from the shelf and sat down on the couch, flipping open the cover. The first page had Maggie's name written on it with doodles in the corners. She flipped through the pages and read some of Maggie's original notes. One thing she had jotted in a margin was "God loves me more than any man ever will. HE is all I need." She prayed Maggie would remember it and hold onto that truth in the days ahead.

The minutes crawled by. Eleven o'clock. Twelve o'clock. One o'clock. *Where is she?*

At one-thirty in the morning, the telephone rang, and she sprang from where she had fallen asleep on the couch.

"Hello?"

"It's done." Ben stated, then abruptly hung up.

꙾ ♡ ꙾

Patty James called in the morning to let Michelle know about the breakup and that Maggie would be staying with them for a few days. After what she had done, she was surprised to get the call. She didn't think Maggie would ever speak to her again, let alone care whether or not she knew about the breakup.

"She needs you, Michelle," Patty implored.

"She does?"

"Of course. She needs her best friend with her right now."

At that moment, Michelle knew. Ben had broken up with Maggie, but he hadn't come clean with her about their night together. She assumed Ben would spin it in a way that made her the one to blame. *Why would he not tell her?* Maybe he was afraid confessing would bring up questions about other girls he had cheated with. Maybe he was just too much of a coward. She knew she would probably never understand.

"Can I ask? What was Ben's reason for breaking up with her?"

"He's not ready to settle down," Patty replied sadly. "Better now than after the wedding."

"Yeah."

Michelle now found herself in a bit of a conundrum. She had to tell Maggie the truth, but should she wait until Maggie got through the shock of the breakup or tell her now? It would cause more pain at first, but better to hurt all at once than to let her heal and rip the wound open again.

Her decision was made, and she was a trembling mess for the entire drive to Maggie's parents' home. *Lord, please help me do this.*

When she arrived, there were several cars in the driveway. The men of the family were seated in the living room with their close friend, Dave, whom she recognized from Maggie's engagement party.

"Hey, Michelle." Maggie's brother was normally a cheerful guy, but the tone of his greeting was dismal.

"Hey, Tom. How is she?"

"It's not good, I'm afraid."

"They're upstairs in Maggie's old room," Ron informed her. "Go on up."

"OK. Thanks, Mr. James."

Michelle could hear weeping sounds as she ascended the stairs. She stepped slowly, afraid of what she would find. Maggie had cried in front of her many times before, but this was different. These were gut-wrenching, agonizing cries. She tried to hold back tears of her own to put on a strong face for her friend.

Patty lay on the bed, holding her sobbing daughter. Dave's wife, Vi, sat on the other side of the bed, running her fingers softly through Maggie's hair. They both glanced over at Michelle with sorrowful looks as she entered the room.

Michelle had never heard anything like Maggie's cries in her life. They were from the depths of her soul, and with each grief-stricken cry, Michelle's resolve to confess the truth weakened. She couldn't do it. Not now. She couldn't subject her friend to more pain than she was already feeling. She would just have to live with what she had done and do her best to support Maggie through this difficult time.

As much as she hurt for Maggie, she knew she had done the right thing making Ben end the relationship. Maggie needed someone who would be faithful to her, someone who would adore her, someone worthy of her love. She was a child of God, a daughter of the King of Kings, and she deserved to be treated as such.

❧ 14 ❧

The apartment was quiet and lonely for weeks, while Maggie stayed with her parents. The week that would have been the wedding and honeymoon, they took her away to a cabin on Lake Michigan to keep her mind off of it. Michelle understood Maggie's need to be close to family after the breakup, but she missed her roommate. And she couldn't shake the feeling that things would never be the same again.

When Maggie finally returned to the apartment, she arrived with a moving van.

"I found an apartment in Hastings," Maggie announced. "I'm so sorry to desert you, Chelle, but I have to get out of Grand Rapids. I can't be here anymore. I just need to follow through with my plans to move closer to the shop and focus on my work right now."

Michelle was surprised, but she had been right. Everything was changing.

As the James family packed Maggie's belongings and loaded the moving van, Michelle felt a nudge deep inside to come clean to Maggie. It was strong, but she fought hard to ignore it. Seeing Maggie in such excruciating pain had been more terrible than she could have imagined, and she never wanted to see her friend suffer like that again. She thought through the possible outcomes and convinced herself that telling Maggie now, all these weeks later, would only set back the healing process.

Her true hesitation, though she would never admit it—not even to herself—was that she was afraid. Afraid Maggie would never forgive her. Afraid she would lose one of the best friends she had ever had in her life. Afraid that what she had believed about herself for so long might be true. She wasn't worthy—of friendship, of happiness, of love.

When the final boxes had been loaded, Maggie and Michelle stood in their apartment together for the final time.

Maggie sighed and looked over at Michelle. "I'm so thankful God brought you to Cornerstone against your will."

Michelle laughed at that. "Me, too."

"Your friendship has been so important to me, Michelle. I hope you know that."

There were no words to tell Maggie just how much she meant to her. She chewed the inside of her cheek, fighting back tears, and once again, fighting the urge to tell her everything.

"I'm gonna miss you." Maggie stepped to her then and hugged her. "I love you, Chelle."

"I love you, too. I can't believe I'm not gonna see you every day."

"I know." Maggie sucked in a deep breath as she stepped back, clearly fighting tears herself. "We'll talk all the time, though, OK? It will be all good."

"Yeah. All good."

Maggie retrieved her keys from her purse and removed the apartment key from the ring. She laid it on the counter and stared at it.

"You were my first *girl* friend," Michelle said.

Maggie turned to look at her.

"Before you and Emma, I never had any friends that were girls."

"Really? You never told me that before."

Michelle shrugged. "I couldn't have asked for a better friend than you." She only wished she had been a better friend to Maggie.

Maggie's tears fell now, which caused a few to slide down Michelle's cheeks as well. This was much harder than Michelle thought it would be.

"OK. I gotta go, or I'll change my mind." Maggie hugged Michelle one last time and walked to the door.

"See ya', Mags."

Maggie looked back over her shoulder. "See ya', Chelle."

In that moment, Michelle wished they could go back to their college days and start all over together in the dorm. Life seemed to get more difficult as the years went by, and this growing up thing kind of sucked.

For the first time in her life, Michelle lived alone.

❧ 15 ❧

"Do you have plans on Saturday?" Simon asked on the phone one night.

"Saturday is Valentine's Day," Michelle replied.

"Yes, I know. I wanna take my best girl out to dinner."

She grinned into the phone. "I'd like that."

She missed Simon. Had it really been three months since she last saw him?

Things had definitely changed in the past five years. Simon was a busy, in-demand wedding photographer now, and the days of hanging out every week were long gone. She was looking forward to catching up with him at dinner.

"I'll be working with my uncle all day. Can you meet me in Hastings?" Simon asked.

"Sure. Maybe at the coffee shop there."

"Sounds good. We can get dinner, and I can show you the new studio."

Simon had been working hard for the past two months, helping his Uncle Pete revive the photography studio he had owned in the eighties. It just so happened the new studio was only blocks away from Maggie's photography shop. Michelle wasn't sure how Maggie felt about that, but given her dislike for Simon, she probably wasn't too thrilled.

She and Maggie rarely saw each other anymore—a few times a year maybe. Maggie was a busy wedding photographer, just like Simon, and her work took up most of her free time. It saddened Michelle that they had drifted apart after Maggie's move, but time and distance had a way of changing things.

❧ ♡ ☙

On Valentine's evening, Michelle traveled to the small town of Hastings and parked in front of the local coffee shop, State Grounds. Just across the street sat Maggie's shop, Magnolia Photography. She had hoped to pop by for a quick visit, but the shop was dark.

Michelle checked her reflection in the rearview mirror and ran her fingers through her freshly-cut, shoulder-length hair. She applied a little extra lip gloss, squeezed her cheeks to add some color, and sighed. It was all for Simon, but would he even notice?

When she opened the door to the quaint coffee shop, she was hit with the wonderful aroma of coffee beans. She was elated to find Maggie sitting on a cozy leather couch just inside the door.

"Maggieee!" she cried.

Maggie was startled. "Michelle?" She jumped up as soon as she realized who it was. "Oh my goodness! What are you doing in Hastings?"

"Can't I just stop by and visit my roomie?"

They sat together on the couch.

"Of course. It's been way too long." Maggie tucked her legs up under her.

"It's good to see you," Michelle said. Maggie looked beautiful, as usual, but her eyes appeared tired.

"You, too. You look great." She grinned. "How's Jeremy? Any big plans tonight?"

Michelle shrugged. "I have no idea how he is. We aren't seeing each other anymore."

Two years was a long time to stay in a relationship that was going nowhere, but that's exactly what Michelle had done. Jeremy was nice and treated her well. He was respectful and loved God. He had filled a void left in her life when Simon became too busy to spend time with her.

Their relationship began at a singles party at church, which Janice had convinced her to attend. Those parties were usually so awkward, but Michelle was happy to see a familiar face—Janice's cousin, Jeremy. They had met briefly years before and had seen each other at church on occasion. They spent the entire party shooting hoops and talking about basketball.

Things progressed slowly from there, with coffee every once in a while, a movie now and then, sometimes dinner. This went on for about six months, before he asked her to officially be his girlfriend.

If Michelle had been completely honest with herself, she would have admitted that the real reason she was attracted to him was how much he reminded her of Sean. It was a lame reason to go out with someone. They had absolutely nothing in common besides basketball, and she never felt the same kind of connection she had with Sean.

Jeremy was an accountant—a numbers guy, at least that's how he always described himself. She could barely keep her checkbook balanced. He didn't care for television much, especially *The X-Files* reruns she loved to watch. And when they kissed, there was no spark. None whatsoever.

Yet she stayed with him. Partly because she was lonely, and partly because she panicked when she hit the big 3-0. She became anxious to find someone and settle down, afraid she never would.

Not the best reasons to stay in a relationship.

When their second anniversary approached and he began to talk about their future together, she knew it wasn't right. She didn't love him like he loved her, so she ended it.

"Oh, Chelle," Maggie said sadly. "I'm so sorry."

"It's no big deal, Mags." She dismissed it casually. "We've been broken up for a few months now."

Maggie looked a little shocked. "I guess it's been longer than I thought since we last talked. Are you seeing anyone new?"

"Not really." Michelle paused. She wanted to mention going out with Simon, but she didn't want to spoil their conversation. She opened her purse to find some cash instead. "How 'bout you? Any big Valentines plans?"

"Just me and Billy." Maggie nodded toward the goateed man with the hipster glasses standing behind the counter. He looked over at her and grinned.

"Friend of yours?" Michelle asked.

"He and his sister own the place," Maggie explained.

"Ah." Michelle laid her purse next to Maggie. "Be right back." She walked to the counter and ordered a latte from Billy.

While she waited, she glanced over at Maggie, who was staring out the window at the people passing by. She looked deep in thought, and Michelle wondered how she was really doing. As far as she knew, Maggie had not dated anyone since Ben. This worried her, because Maggie was so capable of love. She hoped and prayed that one day her friend would find happiness with a wonderful guy.

Michelle returned to the couch and sat facing Maggie. "So, what's it like having another studio right down the street from yours?" She took a sip of her coffee.

Maggie tensed up at the mention. "It's nice that he wants to help his uncle and everything, but what about his studio in Grand Rapids? Who's taking care of that?"

"Oh, he hired someone as his office manager. Some pretty young thing just out of college." She had never met Simon's new assistant, Anna, but he had described her as a blonde bombshell. "And he travels back and forth," Michelle continued. "He works some days here, some days there."

Maggie rolled her eyes. "Well, he should just stay out of Hastings and leave me alone."

"So you've seen him," Michelle remarked.

Maggie nodded.

"*Hmmm*, I'm sensing a little bitterness."

"The thing is, he's everywhere in this little town. And I can't seem to get through an entire week without him bringing up his darn proposal."

Michelle got a nervous feeling in her stomach. "What proposal?"

The bells on the door jingled.

Maggie scrunched her nose at Michelle. "Speak of the devil," she whispered.

"Oh, sorry," Michelle spoke quietly as she stood. "Did I forget to mention that I asked him to meet me here? We're going to dinner."

Simon greeted Michelle with a bear hug and a quick kiss on the lips. "You ready to go?" he asked.

Michelle pointed in her friend's direction. "Coffee with Maggie."

Maggie held up her hand and shook her head. "Oh, no, that's OK. Don't let me keep you."

Simon glanced over at Maggie. "Coffee sounds great." He walked to the counter.

"I guess we'll have to finish our conversation later." Michelle nodded in Simon's direction. "You're welcome to come out with us tonight. It'll be like our old college days."

"Oh, please, no," Maggie replied.

Michelle took another sip of her coffee, amused by her friend's response. Maggie obviously still couldn't stand Simon, and that gave Michelle feelings of satisfaction and relief.

Simon returned to the table and took the seat closest to Michelle. He gave her knee a squeeze. "Long time no see."

Michelle grabbed his knee and squeezed back as hard as she could.

He squeezed harder.

She cried out. "*Ow!* Uncle! Uncle!"

"Well," Maggie spoke as she stood. "That's enough of a college flashback for me." She tucked the magazine she had been reading into her bag and slid on her coat.

"Hot date tonight, Canon?" He had a look in his eye that Michelle recognized—a flirtatious look she'd seen him give many girls in the past. She hated that he was looking at Maggie that way, and tried her best to ignore it.

Maggie gave him a sarcastic smirk, which pleased Michelle.

"Come with us, Maggie." Michelle repeated her invitation. "Simon will pay."

He grabbed her knee once more. "What am I paying for?"

"Our dinner." She smacked his hand off.

Maggie leaned over and hugged Michelle. "You guys have a nice time. We'll get together again soon and finish that conversation."

"You bet." Michelle gave her a final squeeze and kissed her on the cheek. "Call me."

Michelle glanced over at Simon, whose gaze was fixed on Maggie as she walked out.

"So," she said.

He turned his attention to her. "So ... dinner first or studio?"

"Studio!"

The night with Simon was wonderful. It was like old times. They walked down the street to Walker's Photography arm in arm. He showed her their portrait studio, which was nearly ready for its big grand opening. They had dinner at a nice restaurant in town called County Seat and talked and laughed and caught up. He told her all about his recent weddings and funny things that had happened on the job. She told him how proud she was of him. It was the perfect Valentine's Day.

After dinner, they stayed in the booth at County Seat and had dessert.

"I'm glad we did this." Simon devoured a piece of cheesecake. "I miss hanging out with you, Chelle."

"Me, too." She gave him a sweet smile. "So, what is this proposal Maggie was talking about?" Ever since Maggie had mentioned it, she had been dying of curiosity.

"It's nothing. Pete and I just thought we could refer wedding clients to each other that fit our photography styles. Like if somebody came into our studio asking about candid wedding photography, we could refer them to Maggie 'cause that's more her style. And I asked if she would send us the clients that want more formal photography, which is my style."

"That sounds like a good idea."

"I know! That's what *I* said." He seemed a little worked up. "She didn't see it that way."

"Why not?"

"Because she hates me."

Michelle almost laughed out loud at the pouty look on his face, but she held it in because he seemed pretty bothered by the whole thing.

"She doesn't hate you."

"Whatever." He shook his head.

"Maybe she's just worried about losing clients. Did you think of that?"

He was quiet.

"She's had this little town all to herself for quite a while now, and you swooped right in with your new studio. She's gotta feel threatened."

"Yeah, I guess."

Michelle gave him a look. "Be nice, Simon. You know she's been through a lot."

He nodded. She thought she saw a hint of something behind his eyes, but she couldn't read him.

"You really are the best friend, Chelle. I don't know what I would do without you."

She reached across the table and took his hand. "Well, you'll never have to find out."

He grinned and took both of her hands in his.

At first, it was innocent, but then he began to trace little figure eights on the back of her hand.

Her heart was racing as she watched his face.

He didn't look at her, only at their hands.

"Simon." She had to know what was going on in that head of his.

He looked up at her.

"What are you doing?"

"I don't know."

He seemed confused, and it made her smile.

"We should go," he said.

"OK."

He helped her with her coat, and they headed out into the cold. Michelle slid her arm through his as they walked along, snow crunching under their feet.

"I've been meaning to ask you something." Simon looked at her curiously. "What ever happened with you and Jeremy?"

She hadn't expected him to ask that.

"I thought things were getting serious between you two. You were together for a long time."

"I know."

"Why did you break up?"

"Something was just missing in our relationship. I think I knew it early on, but I was lonely, and I stayed with him for all the wrong reasons."

They arrived at Michelle's car, and she looked over at him. "Honestly, I never felt half as much for him as I feel for you."

His mouth dropped open a bit at her admission.

139

She hugged him then, and he held her tightly against him. They stayed that way for several minutes. The night air was chilly, but she didn't feel the least bit cold.

When she started to let go, he kept his arms around her and rested his forehead against hers.

She was unsure what he was thinking, but something in her decided to make the first move and worry about the rest later. She moved her hands from around his waist up to his chest. He didn't move away, so she angled closer and pressed her lips to his.

Simon kissed her back.

Even the softest touch of Simon's lips on hers felt amazing. It was like static electricity—every hair standing on end, goosebumps running over her entire body. This moment she had been imagining for so long met her every expectation.

She tilted her head and increased the pressure, wanting more.

He suddenly jerked away. "I'm sorry." He dropped his arms and took a small step backwards. "We can't do this."

Her shoulders sagged. *Not again.*

"Haven't you ever thought about what it would be like?" she asked. "Us together? Because I think about it all the time."

"Chelle." His eyes pleaded with her.

"We know each other better than anyone else," she continued. "What would be more perfect than for us to be together?"

He took her face in his hands and placed a gentle kiss on her cheek, then leaned his forehead to hers again. He exhaled slowly, his warm breath falling on her lips. "I don't wanna risk our friendship. If anything ever went wrong between us—"

"But what if it doesn't? What if we're meant to be together?"

His thumbs brushed softly against her cheeks. "Just give me a little time to think about it, OK?"

She was disappointed, but she tried to be understanding. It was a big step for them, not to be taken lightly.

On her drive home, she mulled over what had happened and analyzed the whole thing to death. Simon had kissed her. Yes, she had been the one to initiate the kiss, but Simon had actually made the first move—holding her hands in the restaurant the way he had, holding onto her after their hug, leaning his forehead to hers so intimately. It seemed like he didn't want to let her go, like he wanted to be close to her. And he had kissed her back, which gave her hope.

At the end of the month, he would be attending a photography conference in Vegas. Maybe a little time away would help him realize that she was right about them. Maybe when he got back, he would be ready to talk. Dating a friend was not without its risks, but wasn't it worth it to give their relationship a chance?

When she turned into her parking spot at the apartment, her cell phone suddenly beeped, signaling a text message.

"Thanks for the dessert." It was from Maggie.

Michelle was confused. She opened her phone and sent a quick reply. "What dessert?"

No response came back right away, so she went inside. She had no idea what Maggie was talking about.

A few minutes later, a message appeared. "The cheesecake."

She was still confused, but she had a sickening feeling she knew where the cheesecake had come from.

"What cheesecake?" she typed hesitantly.

Another response. "The cheesecake you had Simon drop off for me. Thanks, Chelle."

Her heart sank.

"You're welcome," she lied.

And she knew what Simon's answer would be when he got back. It was what his answer always was.

Just friends.

141

At ten o'clock at night on the last day of February, there was a sudden knock at her door. Michelle wasn't expecting anyone, so she cautiously peeked through the peephole to see who it was. *Simon?*

She opened the door and was about to ask how the photography conference went, when he took her face in his hands and kissed her.

Her heart skipped a beat or ten. This kiss was so much better than their first, because he was the one to initiate it this time.

She leaned away to look at him, wondering what he was thinking.

His hands dropped to his sides, and he searched her face. He looked completely unsure if he should have done that.

One corner of her mouth raised up.

He smiled at her and slid his arms around her waist, drawing her to him, kissing her again.

She felt *this* kiss all the way to her toes.

Stepping back into the apartment, she pulled him with her. He kicked the door shut behind him, and they laughed, breaking their kiss.

She stroked the side of his neck. "I thought you didn't wanna risk our friendship." She raised an eyebrow at him.

His hazel eyes were alight with something new—a look he had never given her before. "I changed my mind."

Was it attraction? Passion? Love? All she knew for sure was that she never wanted him to stop looking at her like that. Ever.

❦ 16 ❧

$\mathcal{B}$eing with Simon was fun and crazy and intoxicating. She couldn't get enough of him. She had always wondered what it would be like if they ever got together. Would it change their friendship? Would it mess things up? But the past two months had been wonderful.

Simon went out of his way to include her in his busy photography schedule. They spent most weekday evenings together since he worked weddings on weekends. She went with him and Uncle Pete to the big Grand Opening of the photography studio in Hastings. He even invited her to join him for a photographer event at Rose's, a quaint little restaurant on the shores of Reeds Lake.

They settled in at a table near the back with a group of Simon's fellow photographers. He introduced her to several people, so many that she couldn't remember all their names. She didn't care much. She was with Simon, and that was all that really mattered to her.

"Hey, Chelle," said a familiar voice.

Simon's whole body tensed up next to her, and she turned to see Maggie standing beside their table with a lovely brunette. Michelle stood and greeted her with a hug.

"How are you?" Maggie asked.

"Really good." She smiled and raised her eyebrows up and down.

Simon was looking anywhere but at them.

"You and Simon?" Maggie whispered, and glanced in Simon's direction.

Michelle smiled happily and took her seat next to Simon again. She leaned in and kissed him on the cheek.

He turned and gave her a soft kiss on the lips, then looked straight at Maggie.

Michelle looked over at Maggie, who glanced at her friend.

"We're gonna go get a drink," the friend said, and they walked to some empty seats at a nearby table.

"Who's that with Maggie?" Michelle asked.

"Her assistant, Sarah. She's dating Maggie's brother, Tom."

Simon had mentioned Tom quite a bit during the past couple months. Ever since Uncle Pete had moved permanently to Hastings, Simon had been spending a lot of time with Tom, and they had become good friends. She still thought of Tom as the flirty teenaged kid who hit on her their first day of college. Michelle was happy that Simon had found a friend in Tom, but she didn't like that he was in such close proximity to Maggie. Something was going on there. She sensed an uncomfortable vibe between them. There was something strange about the way he tensed at the sound of her voice and the way he looked at her after he kissed Michelle. It sort of felt like … well, like he was trying to rub it in Maggie's face. And that did not sit well with her at all.

The photographers were all very passionate about their craft. Michelle listened to them talk for a couple hours about weddings and photography and everything that surrounded their businesses. It was interesting, but it left Michelle with the old familiar feelings of confusion and uncertainty. They all knew what they wanted to do with their lives. She wished she could figure out what to do with hers. What was her purpose? Where was her joy? She sure hadn't found it working ten years in a boring office. The only thing that made her happy these days was Simon.

After a delicious dinner, they moved along the hallway toward the exit. Jamie and Shannon, two photographers who had been seated at their table, walked ahead of them with Maggie and Sarah.

"Girl! I have not seen you in months," Jamie said to Maggie. "You need to fill us in on what happened in Vegas."

"What do you mean?" Maggie replied.

"We saw you and Simon kissing at the party, then you just took off. We need details!"

Michelle gasped and stopped in her tracks. She looked over at Simon in shock.

He glanced at her, guilt written all over his face.

"You kissed Maggie?" The entire room spun around her, as Maggie and her friends rushed out the door.

His shoulders sank, and he looked down at the floor.

"Simon?"

He took her arm and led her from the restaurant.

"Answer me!" she demanded as they walked across the parking lot.

"Let's talk somewhere else."

She was fuming. *He kissed Maggie?* She couldn't believe it. Maggie hated Simon. *How could this happen?*

They climbed into Simon's car, and she turned to face him.

"You better start talking," she demanded.

"Calm down."

"I will *not* calm down until you tell me the truth."

"It happened at my party the last night of the conference." He paused.

"OK?"

He let out a breath. "We were drunk."

She raised an eyebrow. "That's it?"

"What?"

"That's it? You were drunk, and you kissed?"

"That's what happened."

"Maggie was drunk? I highly doubt that." Michelle was fairly certain Maggie had never touched a drop of alcohol in her life.

"Well, *I* was. I don't know about her."

"I want more of the story. How did it happen? Where were you? What were you doing?" The old familiar jealousy kicked into high gear.

He fidgeted in his seat. "We were dancing, and the song turned slow. I kissed her, but she didn't kiss me back. Then she left, I guess."

Michelle didn't know what to say or whether to believe him at all. Her mind was racing a mile a minute, but it suddenly came to a screeching halt when she was struck with a horrible thought—one that she could not easily dismiss.

"She's not the reason ... I mean, that's not why you had a change of heart about us is it?"

"No!" he replied a little too quickly. "Chelle, that's ridiculous."

"Is it? Because it was after Vegas that you came to see me." She felt sick to her stomach. "Maggie turned you down, then you just suddenly changed your mind and wanted to be with me?"

He reached across the space between them and took her hand.

She looked out the window at a passing car.

"Michelle, look at me."

She did.

"I do wanna be with you, and it has nothing to do with what happened in Vegas."

As he drove them to his apartment, she stared out the window. More than anything, she wanted to believe him. He had never lied to her before, but she had a feeling he wasn't telling her the whole truth this time. She thought about the events leading up to this night and tried to piece everything together to fit with what Simon had told her. She reached the same conclusion every time. If Maggie hadn't rejected him in Vegas, they probably wouldn't be together right now.

For some reason, her mind wandered to high school basketball, to sitting on the bench, barely getting to play the game she loved. She had *that* feeling again—that second string, watching from the sidelines, never gonna be first choice feeling.

🌿 17 🌿

Since the events at Rose's, things had felt strained between them. She wasn't sure if Simon was purposely avoiding her or not, but things seemed to be going south fast. More of his time was taken up by work as the most popular month for weddings kicked off.

Michelle received multiple messages from Maggie wanting to explain about Vegas, but she didn't want to hear it. Simon and Maggie had kissed. It didn't matter that the kiss happened before she and Simon got together. They had kissed. And all the old jealousy was back in full force. She couldn't control it. Perfect Maggie, with her perfect family and perfect photography business, who always seemed to get everything she wanted and then some. Beautiful Maggie, who was taking Simon away from her without even trying.

She decided to focus all of her pent-up aggression on something positive—convincing Simon that he had made the right choice, that *she* was the one for him. And she was determined to show him that she was.

"What's all this?" Simon entered his apartment and dropped his camera bag on the floor after a long day of shooting.

The place was spotless. She spent all day cleaning his apartment from top to bottom. The carpets were vacuumed, floors mopped, shelves dusted, windows washed. The glow of two tapered candles lit the dining room table, which was set for two.

He walked into the kitchen, where Michelle was stirring chunks of chicken, vegetables, and rice around in a skillet.

"I'm making you dinner." She smiled at him over her shoulder. Something was wrong. She could tell by the look on his face.

"I'm not very hungry, but thanks." He gave her a quick kiss on the cheek.

"What's the matter?"

"I'm just tired."

"Are you sure? Did something happen at the wedding?"

He shook his head and ran his fingers through his hair. It was his telltale sign of frustration.

"Simon. What happened?"

"Nothing, Chelle! Just drop it!" He stomped off to the bathroom in a huff.

Whatever had happened that day most certainly had to do with Maggie. She was the main photographer for the wedding, but Simon had also been hired to take fashion formal portraits for the bride, which had become his signature style. Michelle didn't like that they were working together, and she couldn't shake the feeling that something more might be going on between them.

Michelle turned the burner off and dumped the half-cooked meal in the garbage. She blew out the candles, and put the plates and silverware away. Just as she grabbed her purse from the counter, Simon emerged from the bathroom.

"Are you leaving?"

"I think I should. You're clearly not in the mood for company."

Simon took her purse and set it down. He pulled her into a tight hug and kissed the top of her head. "I'm sorry I snapped. It wasn't a great day, that's all."

"Do you wanna talk about it?"

"Not really. Can we just watch some *X-Files* or something? Like old times?"

She smiled up at him. "That sounds perfect."

"The apartment looks amazing, by the way. You didn't have to do this."

She grinned, proud of her accomplishment. "I wanted to do something special for you." *Because I love you.* She wanted to say those three little words, but she held her tongue, afraid he wouldn't return the sentiment.

Simon's mood did not improve much after that night. In fact, it seemed to swing in every direction during the busy wedding season. If only he would open up to her about what was really going on.

They sat in her apartment quietly eating dinner together for the first time in two weeks.

She glanced over at him and noticed dark circles under his eyes. "You look tired. Maybe you need to take a vacation." She was trying to be helpful, but he looked at her like she was insane.

"This is my busiest time of year."

"I know, but we never see each other." She pouted. He owned his own company. Couldn't he take some time off now and then?

He reached across the table and took her hand. "I'm sorry, Chelle. It will get better."

She tried to smile, but couldn't even manage to fake one.

"In fact, I have the next two Saturdays off."

Her eyes lit up. "You do? No weddings?"

"Well, I have Friday and Sunday weddings, but we should do something this Saturday. What do you wanna do?"

She jumped up from her seat and climbed into his lap, hugging him with all her might. "It doesn't matter. Whatever you want. I just wanna be with you."

He pulled back and looked at her. "It's a date."

She beamed at him and softly touched her lips to his over and over. He returned the favor, until his arms tightened around her, and their kisses became more intense.

The food on their plates was cold by the time they came up for air.

Picnicking at the beach in Grand Haven, walking the pier, and strolling along the boardwalk was the plan. Michelle had been looking forward to this all week. A whole day together. The perfect date with Simon. It sounded like a dream.

Just as she was packing a towel and sunscreen into her bag, her phone rang. "Hey! Are you on your way?"

Simon cleared his throat. "I'm so sorry to do this, Chelle, but I can't go."

She dropped hard onto the kitchen bar stool. "What? Why not?"

"I have to work."

She should have known it was too good to be true. But she was confused. "You don't have a wedding today."

His end of the line was quiet for a few beats. "Sarah's sick, and Maggie had nobody else to fill in for her today."

She gritted her teeth together, so angry she could barely see straight.

"Chelle, I'm so sorry. Rain check?"

She didn't respond.

"I know you're upset. Why don't I stop by after the wedding."

"Fine." That made her feel a tad better.

"It might be kinda late."

"I don't care if it's three in the morning. You better get your butt over here."

He chuckled at that.

One thing was for sure, if she didn't see his face before morning, things were going to get ugly.

⚬⚬ ♡ ⚬⚬

The clock had not yet struck twelve. Michelle was watching the Tonight Show while she waited. Well, she wasn't really watching. Her eyes were fixed on the clock. The more minutes that ticked by, the more anxious she became. Her crazed mind concocted all sorts of scenarios. All of them ended with Simon kissing Maggie again. She was relieved when the click of the key in the lock announced Simon's arrival just after midnight.

He strolled in happily and dropped his bags just inside her door. "You waited up for me."

"Yeah. I wanted to see you. Why would I go to sleep?"

He shrugged and walked to her kitchen. He returned to the living room with a glass of water and sat down close beside her on the couch.

"How was the wedding?" She was afraid to ask.

"It went well." He took a sip of water and smiled a little. "Really well." It spread wider across his face and turned into a full-blown smile.

She looked at him curiously. "What is with you?"

"What? It was just a really fun wedding." He set the glass on the coffee table.

"Tell me about it." She wanted all the details, but she knew she would probably get the abridged version.

"It was at the Public Museum downtown. Really fun group. Poor Maggie took the bridal party outside for pictures and ended up getting drenched in a downpour." He laughed.

Michelle didn't find it very funny, but she gave him a fake laugh to humor him. She was secretly glad things hadn't gone perfectly for Maggie for once.

"They had the carousel running for all the guests," he continued, "which made for some fun pictures." She noticed the corner of his mouth turn up a little, like he had left out an important piece of the story. It annoyed her immensely, and she wanted to slap that look right off of his face. "And, boy, did they like to dance."

The wedding was fun. I get it.

She reached for the television remote and clicked "off".

"Are you tired? Do you want me to go?"

She shook her head and wrapped her arms around his waist, leaning her head against his chest.

He rubbed his hands up and down her back. "I'm sorry about today. I'll make it up to you. I'll come over for dinner a couple nights this week if I can. Maybe we can go out to dinner and a movie one night. We haven't done that in a while. Next Saturday is the bonfire at Pete's for the Fourth."

She heard him speaking, but his voice started fading out as his soft caresses soothed her into a deep slumber.

Simon said he wouldn't be too late, that he was just stopping over for a couple quick card games with Tom and Uncle Pete after work. Once again, Michelle sat alone in her apartment watching the clock.

At nine, she tried his cell phone and got no answer. The hours crawled by. When the hour hand hit eleven, she dialed his phone again. Still no answer.

Groaning, she grabbed a pile of unopened mail from the counter and stomped into her bedroom. She angrily tossed the mail across the room, scattering it about the floor. Climbing under her comforter, she pulled the covers tight around her face and drifted off into a fitful sleep.

In her groggy, half-asleep state, she felt the covers lift and the bed dip as a warm body climbed in next to her. She pretended to be asleep, and slowly inhaled the familiar scent of Simon.

He brushed the hair back from her forehead and planted a kiss there.

She didn't move.

He snuggled up to her and draped his arm over her hip. "Chelle," he whispered.

She wished he didn't have a key to her apartment.

He planted a soft kiss on her lips and shook her lightly.

Her eyes slowly opened and met his.

"I'm sorry I'm late." He softly stroked her back.

She said nothing.

He kissed her again.

No response.

He leaned over her, and his lips found her earlobe—her weakness. When he did that, she could almost forgive him anything.

She rolled away onto her back and looked up at him. "Why didn't you call?"

"We lost track of time."

She eyed him. "Was Maggie there?"

He opened his mouth to speak, then pressed his lips together, as if he was deciding something. "Yes," he replied, not looking her in the eye.

"What happened?" She glanced over at the clock. It was well past midnight.

"We played cards."

"With Maggie?"

"No, with the guys."

"What about Maggie?"

"We just talked."

Michelle swiftly sat up, pushing his arm away.

Simon rolled onto his back and began softly running his fingers up and down her arm. It was very distracting.

She didn't look at him. "Can you please stop that?"

His hand stilled.

"What did you talk about?" Michelle had a feeling there was more to the story.

"She was really upset. She went to a meeting tonight with a couple who wanted to hire her for their wedding, and it turned out to be Ben."

"No." Michelle felt sick to her stomach.

"Yeah, it was pretty messed up."

"Is she OK?"

"Why don't you call her, Chelle?"

The room was silent for several eternal minutes. It broke her heart that Maggie had seen Ben so unexpectedly with his new fiancée. She knew how devastating that must have been, but she wasn't ready to talk yet.

"I can't," Michelle finally said.

"You don't have to go to Fourth of July if you don't want to."

"Why would I not go?"

"Well, you're mad at Maggie, and she and her family will be there. You might not have any fun."

Her eyes narrowed. "Are you trying to get rid of me?"

He sat up next to her then. "Stop saying stuff like that."

She swallowed hard.

"Michelle." He searched her face. He only called her Michelle when he wanted her to take him very seriously. "I'm sorry. I really am. Please don't be angry with me."

"Do you wanna end this, Simon?" She wasn't afraid to ask the tough questions.

He closed the distance between them and replied with a sweet kiss. "Does that answer your question?"

She wanted to believe him. More than anything, she wanted them to work. She wanted happily ever after with Simon.

But what she wanted and what God wanted for her were two very different things.

❦ 18 ❦

$\mathcal{M}$ichelle sat next to Simon on top of Uncle Pete's picnic table and watched the boats motoring about on the lake. The colors of the sunset reflecting across the water reminded her of graduation night. That seemed like a lifetime ago.

Simon put his arm around her and kissed her on the cheek. "What are you thinking about?"

"That night you threw me into the freezing cold lake."

He laughed aloud. "It wasn't *that* cold."

"Not when I was in your arms."

A look of remembrance crossed his face, and he grinned.

"Hey, buddy!" Tom waved at Simon as he and Sarah rounded the corner of the house. "Hi, Michelle."

"Hey, Tom." She greeted him with a smile. "How are you?"

"I'm very well, and you?"

"Super."

The lovely girl standing next to him held her hand out to Michelle. "Hi, I'm Sarah. We haven't been formally introduced." She flashed a look of disapproval at Tom.

"Oh, sorry. This is my fiancée, Sarah." Tom grabbed Sarah's left hand and shoved it in Michelle's face.

Sarah pulled her arm away and elbowed him. "Sorry. We just got engaged, and we're very excited about it."

Michelle laughed. They were cute together.

The guests took their seats on lawn chairs and blankets that were scattered about the yard. Pete sat with his neighbors chatting and smoking cigars. Maggie's parents and their best friends, Dave and Vi, were seated around the bonfire circle, while Tom and Sarah sat in lawn chairs closer to the dock.

154

Simon kept glancing toward the side of the house. Michelle didn't have to ask why. There was still no sign of Maggie.

He hopped down and went to get them drinks. When he returned, he leaned in close and nipped her earlobe. "I'm glad you're here," he whispered.

She grinned and playfully grabbed his knee in that way of theirs, then kissed him.

"Mags!" Sarah suddenly shrieked and came running across the lawn.

Simon ripped his lips away and trained his eyes on Maggie, who was standing across the yard watching them.

Maggie gave them a weak smile, then took a sparkler from Sarah and followed her across the lawn toward Tom.

Michelle glared at Simon until she caught his eye. "Seriously?"

He had no reply.

Despite Simon's earlier behavior, they cozied up on a blanket when it came time for the show. The fireworks were breathtaking, bursting in brilliant flashes of red, white, and blue against the starry night sky.

Michelle rolled over, draped her leg over Simon's, and rested her head against his arm.

"It's hot," he whispered, then abruptly shifted so he was propped up on his elbows.

She laid back and stared over at him. There was no doubt in her mind that his eyes were not fixed on the sky above, but on the pretty girl seated across the lawn.

Tears burned her eyes, and she did her best to fight them off.

I'm losing him.

After the fireworks, the guys worked on starting the bonfire, while the ladies congregated around the picnic table. Maggie seated herself across from Michelle.

"How are you, Chelle?" she asked.

"Fine."

"How's it going with you and Simon?"

"Great." She couldn't talk to Maggie right now. If she did, she would lose it, and that was not something she wanted to do. She just wanted to get through this night and go home.

Maggie didn't push her for more conversation. She started talking to Sarah about wedding plans, chitchatting with her mother and Vi, and joking about the guys fire-making skills.

"Good job, honey," called Sarah.

Tom gave her a thumbs-up and jumped back suddenly when a large flame licked up at him. "*Ah!*"

The girls laughed. Even Michelle smiled at that.

"Aren't they so strong and manly?" teased Maggie. "We made fire." She mocked them in her manliest voice.

"Let us see you do it better, Canon," Simon called across the yard.

Maggie strolled across the lawn toward him, and Michelle could feel the jealousy start to burn inside her.

One at a time, Simon took her hands and put the gloves he'd been wearing on her.

Michelle thought she might lose it right then and there. Seeing him touch Maggie nearly pushed her over the edge.

Simon patted Maggie on the back. "Go for it."

Maggie glanced over at Simon, who was poking at the fire with a stick. "What is it with guys and fire?" she asked. "Pyro."

"It's a bonfire. You're supposed to burn stuff," he replied.

"Go roast a wiener or something," Maggie commanded. "Make yourself useful."

He laughed at Maggie's comment, and Michelle's heart ached. That laugh was supposed to be all for her. She glared at him when he walked over and grabbed a hot dog and went about roasting it on a stick. He didn't seem to notice she was still sitting there. And the looks he and Maggie were giving each other were unacceptable.

Michelle could stand it no more. She walked over and wrapped her hands around Simon's bicep. "Simon, can you take me home now?"

He continued to roast the hot dog.

"We should have coffee next week." Maggie smiled at her, so clueless, as usual.

Michelle clung tighter to Simon's arm and kept her thoughts to herself. She could barely control her anger. It was all-consuming.

Simon finished the hot dog and walked across the yard to get a bun.

Michelle watched Maggie's eyes follow him. If she didn't leave now, she would definitely say some things she would later regret.

She glared at Maggie, then swiftly turned and walked away.

"For you, Canon. Enjoy," Michelle heard Simon say.

She glanced over her shoulder and saw Simon hand the hot dog to Maggie as he passed by.

Maggie grinned at him. "I'm a vegetarian." She tossed the dog into the fire.

Michelle rolled her eyes and walked as fast as she could to Simon's car and waited.

Simon clicked the button on his keychain to unlock the doors, and they climbed in.

"Everything OK?" he asked.

Michelle looked over at him and shook her head. A little burst of air escaped her nose in disgust.

"Chelle?"

"That was humiliating."

He looked down in shame.

"Just take me home."

When she arrived at the office on Monday, there was a large bouquet of roses waiting for her with a sweet card that read:

Michelle,
I'm so sorry for everything. You are my best friend in the world. Please don't give up on us.
Love always,
Simon

She so wanted to believe that they could make their relationship work. But, more and more, she felt him slipping through her fingers, and she didn't know what to do about it.

"Put on your best dress, Chelle. I'm taking you out tonight."

She grinned into the phone. "What's the occasion?"

"Remember how I was up for that big wedding?"

She gasped. "The governor's daughter? Oh, Simon! You got it?"

"I got it!"

She could hear the excitement in his voice, and she pictured him standing there holding the phone with a huge smile on his face. "I'm so happy for you."

"Thank you. Can you meet me at my place at six?"

"I'll be there."

Michelle put on her red halter dress with the wispy skirt that fell just above her knees. She always felt beautiful in that dress. She curled her hair for once rather than twisting it up in a messy bun and even applied some makeup. She stared at her reflection. Her walnut brown eyes really popped with a little eyeshadow and mascara. Deep red lipstick completed the look.

She arrived early to Simon's apartment and let herself in. She helped herself to a glass of iced tea and noticed a card tucked just under the edge of Simon's laptop, which sat open on the counter. She tugged the card out. It was an invitation from Tom and Sarah to attend a surprise birthday party for Maggie at State Grounds a few nights before. He hadn't mentioned it, and they had been together that night, so she knew he hadn't gone. Maybe he truly wanted to make this work.

She jiggled the mousepad on his laptop to pass the time on Facebook. The screen lit up to reveal Simon's email inbox. There were many unopened messages. She was pleased not to see Maggie's name among them. But when she scrolled further, there was, in fact, a previously read message from Maggie dated the same day as her birthday party. Her heart began to race as she read.

Simon,
Thank you for the pictures. Best gift ever!
You were missed tonight.
Maggie

Michelle noticed that the message was in reply to one that Simon had sent to Maggie that same day. She scrolled down to see the content of the original message, which read:

Happy Birthday, Canon!
Click this link for your gift.
- S

Curiosity got the better of her, and she clicked the link, which took her to an online folder of images from the photography conference in Vegas—the same conference where Simon and Maggie had kissed.

There were several photos of girls hanging on Simon, posing, and laughing. She recognized a couple of them from the photographer dinner they had attended. Maggie was in the photos, but she was standing off to the side, not participating in their silliness.

The last photo, however, made Michelle's breath catch.

Simon was dipping Maggie back. His nose was close to hers, their faces only inches apart, and they were smiling, while the other girls laughed behind them. The way Simon was looking at Maggie in the photo was so different than the way he looked at her.

She paced the apartment in a panic. *If I don't do something fast, I'm gonna lose him.*

Simon arrived half an hour later. He greeted her with a grin. "Hey, beautiful."

She smiled back at him from her spot on the couch, but was inwardly cringing.

"Let me get cleaned up and changed real quick, and we'll go."

Michelle let out a sigh when he disappeared into the bathroom. She heard the water run and the squeak of the towel ring as he wiped his hands. He moved from the bathroom to his bedroom.

She took a deep breath, stood, and walked to his room.

He looked over his shoulder as she entered, standing there with a few buttons open on his dress shirt. His gaze moved from her head to her toes and back again. "You look nice."

She raised an eyebrow at him as her eyes took him in. "So do you."

He chuckled.

She walked slowly toward him, and he grabbed her hands and pulled her to him.

The feel of being in his arms was so comforting, but she didn't want comfort tonight. She wanted more.

Her fingers caressed the small section of bared chest and went to work on the next button.

He took in a quick, unsteady breath.

She leaned in and kissed the spot she had revealed behind the button, then undid the next button and kissed that spot, then the next and the next, repeating the pattern.

He grabbed her arms and pulled her up to him, kissing her deeply.

She smiled against his mouth, knowing that her plan was working. Her fingers traced a path down his bare chest again and unbuttoned the last two pesky buttons. She pushed the shirt over his muscular shoulders and off his arms.

He shook the shirt off, letting it fall to the floor, and dragged her to him, finding her lips once more.

Her hands moved down over the muscles of his back to the top edge of his pants. She slid her fingertips around to the front and popped open the button there.

He jerked back away from her. "Michelle!"

She moved against him again. "I want you, Simon," she breathed into his ear.

He groaned.

She reached for his pants again, for the zipper this time.

He grabbed her wrists and practically jumped back. "Stop!" He dropped her arms like hotcakes and ran his fingers through his hair.

She stared at him in disbelief.

"What were you thinking?" He looked completely panicked.

"I was thinking we should take our relationship to the next level," she blurted.

His eyes shifted about the room, anywhere but at her.

She stepped toward him. "I know you want me, too."

He backed away from her and shook his head. "Not like this."

"Not like what?"

"We're not doing this." He grabbed his crumpled shirt from the floor.
"Why not?"

He looked her straight in the eyes. "I'm not having sex before I'm married."

She was sure her face was as red as her dress. Her cheeks were on fire, but not from the heat of their kisses. She was embarrassed and ashamed for what she had tried to get him to do. She backed up against the nearest wall, covering her face with her hands as she sank to the floor. Tears sprung to her eyes. And her mind suddenly flashed on Sean, whose entire life she had derailed for one night of sex. How could she have tried to use that very thing to keep Simon in a relationship with her? How could she do that? She had been so desperate to keep them together, when she knew deep down that it wasn't working. She had been so willing to stoop to this level, when she knew it was a sin. And she realized that something was very wrong, something within her was still broken, and sex would never fix it.

Simon sat on the foot of his bed. "Michelle?"

She couldn't look at him.

"I love you very much," he said.

She glanced up at him then, tears streaming down her cheeks.

"But I don't think we're meant to be."

A sob escaped before she could stop it.

He moved to sit next to her on the floor and took her right hand between both of his.

Her head fell onto his shoulder. "I'm so sorry," she whimpered. "I don't know what I was thinking. I wasn't, really." She spoke between sobs. "I was just trying to hold onto you any way I could. It was so wrong to do this to you. So wrong, Simon. Can you ever forgive me?"

His forehead met hers. "Only if you forgive me."

She leaned away and looked at him questioningly.

"I don't wanna hurt you, Chelle, OK? I never wanted to hurt you. But I have to be honest with you."

She knew what he was going to say even before he put it into words.

He looked out across his bedroom. "I have feelings for Maggie."

A brief flash of jealousy hit her, but it faded quickly away and was replaced with relief at the truth she had long suspected.

"Whether I want them or not, they're there," he continued. "They have been for a very long time. And I can't stay with you when I feel this way about her. It wouldn't be right."

She didn't know what to say, but something about his honest confession freed her.

"You are one of the most important people in my life, Michelle. I hope you can forgive me for breaking your heart and ruining our friendship."

The room was uncomfortably silent for far too long. The entire night seemed like a very bad dream. But it was real. All of it. And if she spoke, it would be the end for them.

"Please say something." Tears had formed in his eyes, too.

"You haven't." Michelle paused. "Ruined our friendship, I mean."

He looked at her hopefully.

"You could never lose my friendship. Not ever."

He kissed the back of her hand, and she felt lighter somehow. The weight of wondering was replaced with the freedom of knowing.

When she arrived home, she sat for hours against the wall in her bedroom, trying to figure out how things had gone so wrong. Not just in her relationship with Simon, but in all of her relationships. The hours of thoughts and tears exhausted her, and she finally changed out of her dress and climbed into her bed for much needed rest.

In the middle of the night, she awoke in a panic. She couldn't remember what she had dreamed or if it had been a nightmare, but her chest felt tight. She was sure she was having an actual panic attack. It was difficult to breathe, her brow was covered in sweat, and she trembled.

She was suddenly overwhelmed by all that had happened in her life—her crappy childhood, the things she had done, and the many secrets she held inside for so long. Her thoughts raced as she pictured her father walking to his car and driving away. It played like a movie on repeat. She stood at the door over and over staring after him, crying for him, wanting her daddy. But he didn't want her. He left her. Everyone always left her.

Memories flashed by of all the high school partying, the guys she had been with, temporarily filling a void left by her father.

Then she saw the faces of the ones she loved. Simon. Maggie. Sean. She had wronged them all with her jealousy and promiscuity. And it suddenly occurred to her that, although she had asked Jesus into her heart all those years ago, she had never truly given all of her past over to God. She had held onto sinful habits and let them carry into her new life.

The slideshow in her mind paused on one particular moment—the day the invitation to Sean's wedding had arrived in Simon's mailbox. There was a wall of bitterness built up surrounding that day, and though she thought she had let it go long ago, she had not. She was angry with God for taking Sean away from her, and she realized *that* was it. *That* was the moment she had let come between her and God for all these years. From that day on, she had tried to find happiness on her own, rather than trusting God, and she had failed miserably.

She sat up, whipped the covers off, and slid to her knees on the floor. She didn't know where to start or what to say. As she began to lower her forehead down to the carpet, her eyes caught sight of an envelope lying under her bed. She retrieved it from among the dust bunnies.

It was from Janice, postmarked nearly a month before, and she remembered the night that she had tossed the mail across the room when Simon stood her up. She opened the envelope and removed a simple notecard with a verse from Hebrews that read "I will never leave thee nor forsake thee."

Inside, Janice had written, "I don't know what kinds of things you've been dealing with lately, but I felt God very strongly telling me to write you today. So I am. Sweetie, God loves you so much. He is your loving Father, who wants you with Him always. He wants you to give Him all of the burdens of your past and live for Him from this moment on. And maybe you feel like you aren't good enough because of things you've done, but let me tell you right now … YOU ARE. You are worthy of love. No matter what your past looks like. God will never leave you nor forsake you. Believe it, 'cause it's the truth!"

A sob ripped through her at the phrase "never leave you".

"Oh, Lord," she prayed aloud as she rested her forehead on the floor. "I'm so sorry for holding all of this bitterness inside for all of these years about my dad and about Sean. Please help me to forgive my dad for leaving me, for not loving me like he should have. Help me to let go of everything that happened with Sean and forgive myself for it. I'm sorry for the horrible things I've done. Please forgive me. I don't want to do them anymore. Please give me the strength to overcome these sins that keep creeping back into my life. Please help me to let go of my past. All of it. Because I don't want it to define me or have any part in the choices I make in the future. You made me a new creation, and it's about time I start living like one."

The carpet grew damp from all of her tears, but she didn't remove her forehead from that spot. She lay there crying until her knees started to ache and her legs tingled from lack of circulation. She pulled them out from under her and lay flat on her face on the floor. The panic that woke her began to subside, and she relaxed. More than she had in a very long time.

The tears returned when she thought about all the time she had wasted searching for her place in the world without really asking God what it was He wanted her to do. "I want to live for you now, God," she whispered. "I do. You are the strength of my heart and my portion forever. Show me what to do next."

And she thought she heard God softly whisper, "Go and sin no more."

❧ **19** ❧

$\mathcal{I}$t felt strange to be back on campus again for the first time in a decade, but it also felt like home. Especially since the counseling center was housed in the same building that used to be her dorm. There had been a lot of updates to the college since she graduated, including the change in name to Cornerstone University.

After her breakup with Simon and her talk with God, she prayed daily for guidance, and her prayers were answered in the form of a job opportunity. Janice informed her of an opening for an administrative assistant in Cornerstone's counseling department. It wasn't her dream job, but it was far better than the boring office manager job and much closer to her psychology degree. She applied and got the job.

It was nice going to work every day, being part of a place that was so helpful to the students at Cornerstone. She wished she had sought out the kind of help the counseling center offered back when she was a freshman and dealing with so many changes in her new Christian life. She could have used someone to talk to, someone qualified to help. Maybe she would have figured out the error of her ways much sooner and not made so many mistakes along the way.

Day in and day out, she answered calls from students wanting to talk about problems in their families, couples dealing with marital troubles, girls dealing with sexual pressures in their relationships. She could relate to so many of these issues, and although her job was simply to set the counseling appointments, she believed what she did genuinely mattered.

After work one February evening, she strolled along the sidewalk toward the athletic center to attend a basketball game. The team was doing well this season, but it didn't matter to her whether they were winning or not, she just missed the game. She missed cheering them on. She missed being a part of the student body, and being on campus made her feel connected again. Cornerstone was so important to her. Not only was it her alma mater, it was the place she had accepted Jesus into her heart, and she knew it was exactly where she was supposed to be.

She walked past Quincer and glanced at the bench she and Sean sat on so often freshman year. She could still remember the way he looked at her with those intense blue eyes. How could she still so vividly remember his face after all these years?

A group of students wandered by her, talking and laughing, and it made her miss her friends. As much as it pained her, she and Simon had agreed to take some time apart in the hopes that one day they could be best friends again. She missed his friendship more than she thought possible. And she often wondered if she and Maggie would ever be friends again.

Michelle arrived at the game and took a seat low on the bleachers to watch. Cornerstone scored several baskets in a row, and the crowd roared.

Her eyes wandered the room. There were familiar faculty members there, a whole section of rowdy, cheering students, and cheerleaders on the sidelines. People filtered in and out of the entrance. She looked closer at a small group of people just outside the doors. There were two dark-haired men standing with a teenaged boy and girl. One of the men looked very familiar to her. He stepped through the door into the room, holding the teenaged girl's hand.

Michelle squinted. *No! It couldn't be!*

They walked toward her. The man was speaking to the girl as they passed by. He looked a little older, and his hair was shorter, but she would recognize those eyes anywhere. *Sean!*

She watched them walk toward the far end of the gym, closer to the rowdy students, where they found a seat near the top. She couldn't believe he was actually there. Her heart raced, and her palms began to sweat. Her nerves kept her from jumping up and running to their end of the gym. It had been more than fourteen years, after all. Maybe he wouldn't recognize her.

She glanced in their direction again. He seemed to be looking her way, but she couldn't tell at that distance. He could have been watching the action in the game. She turned back to watch a foul shot and played with a loose thread on her sweater.

Oh, Lord, what should I do? He's here. He's actually here. Should I go talk to him? Or should I just let the past stay in the past?

"Michelle?"

Her prayer was interrupted, and she looked up into those blue eyes she remembered so well. "Sean."

"Oh my gosh, I thought that was you." He shook his head back and forth and blinked a few times, like he couldn't believe what he was seeing.

She stood and awkwardly held her hand out to shake his.

He let out a little nervous laugh and hugged her instead.

Oh, man, he smells good.

The noise of the crowd around them grew louder. He turned his head and spoke into her ear. "It's so good to see you."

She smiled.

He pulled back, keeping a grip on her forearms. "You look great."

"So do you," she managed.

He motioned toward the bleacher behind her, and she gave him a shy smile as they sat down together.

He kept shaking his head, another nervous laugh escaping his lips. "I'm sorry, I just … I can't believe it's you. You're here. I thought about you when we got here today. I wondered if you still lived around here or if you ever went back to Chicago."

"I'm still here."

"I think I was secretly hoping I might run into you, but I thought that was pretty much impossible. I'm … I don't know. I have no words." The smile never left his face.

"I actually saw you come in, and I thought my eyes were playing tricks on me or something."

They sat in silence for a few moments, his attention turned to the game. He made a few comments on the game play, but she wasn't listening. She was distracted by his presence, by how good he still looked, and by the glint of gold on his left ring finger. She knew he was married. Simon had told her so years ago.

"I'm here with my family. Do you wanna come sit with us?"

"Oh, I wouldn't want to intrude."

He stood and motioned for her to follow. "Don't be silly. Come on."

They walked across the gym, his hand resting against her lower back as he guided her along. It felt so good, so natural. But a surge of guilt overcame her for the things she was thinking about a married man.

He led her up the bleachers to where his family was seated. "Guys, this is my friend, Michelle, from back when I went to college here. Michelle, this is my brother, Scott, his son, Alex, and my daughter, Ashley."

"It's nice to meet you," Michelle responded politely.

"Nice to meet you, Michelle." Scott gave his brother a look. Maybe it was an unspoken brother language that only they could understand, but she took it to mean that Scott did not approve of his brother hanging out with a woman other than his wife.

"Hey," Alex greeted her casually.

Ashley flipped her long, golden blonde hair over her shoulder and said nothing. She was a beautiful girl, probably no more than thirteen, and she had that new teen attitude to prove it.

Sean made space for Michelle, and she joined them.

"So, what brings you to Grand Rapids?" she asked.

"Alex is here for a college visit," Scott replied. "He's been offered a basketball scholarship."

Michelle locked eyes with Sean, and he looked back at her knowingly.

The group of students next to them cheered loudly. They tried to talk throughout the game, but it was difficult to carry on a conversation.

"I really wanna catch up without all this distraction. Are you busy tomorrow night?"

She shook her head no with a little too much enthusiasm, unintentionally revealing how eager she was to spend more time with him.

"Great!" He looked pretty eager himself.

They swapped phones and entered each other's numbers into their contact lists. When she handed his back, their fingers brushed, and she felt it deep down inside.

He smiled, and she wondered if he had felt it, too.

He turned his attention back to the court below for the last minutes of the game.

Michelle glanced over at Ashley and smiled, which got her a dismissive eye roll.

When the game was over, they all walked out together.

Sean held back from his family and hugged Michelle once more. "I'll see you tomorrow."

"OK." She grinned happily.

He started to walk away, but suddenly stopped and turned around. A huge smile spread across his face, and his eyes lit up. "Until then."

She could not contain her smile. "Until then."

He lifted his hand in a wave and went to catch up with his family.

As she walked to her car, she tried to breathe slowly to calm her rapidly beating heart. She couldn't believe he remembered that. She was so happy he remembered. But she tried not to get too excited about dinner with a married man.

꙳ ♡ ꙳

It didn't work—her plan to stay calm about dinner. She was giddy. All day long. Giddy as a school girl. Sean was picking her up at six-thirty at her apartment, and she hadn't been able to think of anything else all day long. She kept trying to check herself. He was married, and they were just two old friends getting together to catch up.

When six-twenty arrived and he came knocking, she practically jumped out of the living room chair. She breathed slowly in and out, smoothed her shirt, and opened the door.

He wore a smile and held a small bouquet of flowers for her.

"They're so pretty. Thank you. Come in, while I put them in some water."

"OK." He looked around the small space.

"It's not much, I know, but it's mine."

He stepped further inside, taking in the simple decor. "No, it's nice. It feels like you."

She grinned. She liked Sean in her apartment.

While she searched her cupboards for a vase, he wandered around the living room looking at the photos she had displayed.

"Oh my gosh." He leaned in closer to look at the frames on top of the bookcase. "This is so great."

"What is?" She closed the cupboard door, vase in hand.

"This picture of all of us at Celebration On The Grand."

"Oh, yeah." She had forgotten that was there.

"I love it. We look like babies."

"I know."

"So, you and Maggie and Simon are still friends?" He pointed at two other photos—one of her with Maggie at graduation, and one of her and Simon when they were dating.

"Not really," she replied.

He looked over at her.

She shrugged her shoulders. "It's a long story." She snipped the ends off the flowers and placed them in a vase.

He walked over to where she stood in the kitchen. "Well, you can tell me all about it over dinner."

And she did. Over chicken parmigiana at The Olive Garden, she filled him in on Maggie and Ben's engagement and breakup, minus the horrible thing she had done. She told him about her long friendship and relationship with Simon, and how Maggie was part of the reason for their breakup. She didn't tell him the whole story there either, but she gave him enough information to understand why her friendships with Simon and Maggie were damaged.

Sean was as easy to talk to as ever. They talked about work, and her recent job change. He told her he never finished his college degree, but dropped out after his wife got pregnant with Ashley.

"But a degree seemed so important to you."

"I don't regret it. I went to work for my father-in-law's construction company and worked my way to upper management. It's a great job, and I actually love being part of a team that creates something out of nothing. Seeing projects from the design phase all the way through to completion is really rewarding."

She liked how passionate he was about his work.

When dinner was over, she took a sip of her bellini tea and sighed. "I'm sorry. I feel like I've talked your ear off the whole time."

"I loved hearing all of it."

"But we're done eating, and I haven't heard much of anything about your life." What she really meant was the topic of his wife and kids.

"The night's not over yet."

Sean drove to the Cornerstone campus next.

"What are we doing here?" she asked.

"I thought it would be fun to revisit all the places I remember from our time here. We already went to the gym last night. I think The Skillet is next."

She laughed. "It's not called The Skillet anymore."

"It will always be The Skillet."

Along with Cornerstone's upgrade from college to university came many improvements around campus, including an update to what they had known as The Skillet. The look and name had been changed, but the spirit of the place remained the same. It was busy on this Friday evening. They grabbed some greasy food and pop and found an open table in the corner.

"So, your nephew got a scholarship here, huh?"

Sean nodded proudly. "He's good. Better than I ever was. He's gonna do great." A shadow crossed over his face for an instant. "I just pray he doesn't mess things up like I did."

Michelle gulped her pop.

"That kid is gonna go places. I know it."

"Your daughter's very pretty." Michelle felt the need to change the subject. "I see a lot of you in her."

"Really? That's nice to hear. Most people say she looks just like her mom."

Her mom. They had yet to speak of her.

Sean took a sip of his pop. "I've been having kind of a hard time with Ashley lately."

"Teenagers, right?"

He nodded, then paused like he was going to finish a thought, but he didn't. Instead, he spent a while bragging about his brilliant, tech-savvy, soccer-loving, eight-year-old son, Aaron.

"He sounds like a great kid."

Sean nodded. "He really is."

"So …" Michelle decided it was time to broach the subject. "Tell me about your wife."

Sean took another sip of his pop and stared at the table. The shadow fell over him again, and there was a long silence between them.

"I'm sorry. Did I say something wrong? Should I not have asked about her?"

He let out a sad sigh. "My wife died in a car accident two years ago."

Michelle covered her mouth with her hand. She didn't know what to say.

Though the room was noisy with students, the silence at their table seemed endless.

He looked at her and shook his head. "I knew I shouldn't have said anything. I didn't wanna put a damper on our night."

"Of course you should have said something. You can tell me anything, Sean." She reached across the table and took his hand. "I'm sorry I got all quiet. I was just surprised."

"You don't have to say anything. It was awful and sad and it happened. It's our reality, and we're doing our best to move on."

"I'm so sorry."

He pressed his lips together.

She released his hand and leaned back in her chair. "You said you've been having trouble with Ashley. Is it about her mom?"

He nodded. "She's acting out in ways I can't understand or control."

"Like?"

"These kids she's been spending time with are bad news. Some are older than her. I've got these teenaged boys calling her all the time. They're the partiers, the kind who get into trouble. I'm worried. Really worried."

"I know that type." Michelle cleared her throat. "I *was* that type."

He covered his face with his hands and rubbed his forehead. "I'm sorry, Michelle. I didn't think."

"I'm not offended. It's who I was then. Am I proud of it? No. But I can't change it."

"I keep thinking maybe I should leave Chicago. Get her out of there."

Michelle thought about that day in the kitchen when her family did the same to her. "She'll fight you. Every step of the way."

He let out a deep breath.

"That's what I did," she continued. "But coming here to Cornerstone was the best thing that ever happened to me."

"Because you met me, right?" He grinned.

"Right." She smiled.

He leaned back in his chair and looked at her.

"Ashley's gonna be OK, Sean. I can tell she has a great dad, who loves her more than anything. A dad who's there for her and won't let her go down the same path I did."

His eyes softened.

"That's how I know she'll be OK."

He shook his head in disbelief like he had at the basketball game. "I can't believe you're sitting across from me right now."

"I know what you mean."

"Thank you," he spoke softly.

"I didn't do anything."

"Yeah, you did."

৽৵ ♡ ৵ఴ

When they had finished an order of cheese fries, they walked along the sidewalk together, and he took her hand.

She smiled at him as a tingling sensation made its way up her arm.

"Deja vu," he said as they walked past Miller—formerly her dorm, now her place of employment.

"Well, if we're making the rounds to all the places of the past ..." She tugged him toward the entrance of the building and stopped near where they had stood all those years ago after their talk on the beach.

She could almost hear Jill and Darcy yelling "Three second rule!" out their dorm room window.

He faced her and took both of her hands. "This is surreal."

She nodded.

He let go with one hand and pushed a hair back from her face. "You're still just as beautiful as you were back then." His thumb trailed along the curve of her jaw. His eyes met hers, and he stared as if in a trance.

Her pulse picked up, and a breath caught in her throat.

His gaze found her lips.

She squeezed his hand, which seemed to bring him out of it.

He grinned at her and turned back toward the parking lot, leading her by the hand.

"Surreal," she agreed.

20

It seemed like a dream. In the morning, she awoke and actually believed for a moment that it had been. But when she walked out of her bedroom and spotted the flowers he gave her, she knew it was real.

In all the years since Sean left school, she never imagined they would run into each other again or that he would be a widower. She couldn't fathom suffering that kind of loss, grieving the death of a spouse, all while trying to raise two children.

At her desk on Monday morning, she heard the muffled ring of her cell phone in her purse. She retrieved it quickly and answered.

"This is Michelle."

"You miss me, don't you?"

A huge smile spread across her face at the sound of Sean's voice. "You know the answer to that."

A soft laugh came as his reply.

She closed her eyes, remembering those same greetings spoken to each other years ago.

"I just wanted to thank you again for the other night."

"You don't have to keep thanking me, Sean."

"I don't think you realize how much you helped me."

She didn't know what to say.

The phone at her desk rang. "Hold on a second." She answered the work phone and forwarded it to the proper extension. "I'm back."

"Sorry. You're working. Can I call you again later?"

"You can call me any time you want." It came out more flirty than intended.

"OK. Three a.m. it is then."

He made her laugh. She needed more laughter in her life.

They talked on the phone every night after that. Long, easy conversations about life, memories, his children, even his wife sometimes. Short, quick recaps if they'd had a long day. Though they grew closer over the phone, there had been no discussion of making their friendship into anything more than that. With each conversation, she liked him more and more, and she grew to despise the physical distance between them. She wanted to see him again, but she wanted him to bring it up first.

"I hate not being able to see you when we talk," Sean said during one Thursday evening phone call.

"We could Skype."

"I don't even know what that is," he admitted.

She laughed at his lack of technical know-how. "I think your kids know more about computers than you do."

"That's a fact."

"Aaron can set it up for you." She was sure Sean's son could get the job done.

"I'd rather have you here."

"Oh, yeah?" She literally crossed her fingers, hoping he would ask to see her.

"Will you come visit us?"

Yes! She was ecstatic, but did her best to sound calm. "I might be able to arrange that."

"Good."

"I'll call my mom and let her know I'm coming."

"I want you to stay with us."

This filled her with unease. "Are you sure? What about your kids? Will they really want some strange lady staying in their house?"

"Well, you are kind of strange," he teased.

"Hey!"

"It'll be fine. If you get here and you're not comfortable with it, you can stay at my brother's or go to your mom's."

She hesitated a moment longer, then gave the reply she already knew she would give. "OK. When?"

"The sooner the better."

The tone in his voice brought a flush to her cheeks. "I'm on my way." She tried to sound sexy, but she was sure it came off as silly instead.

He gifted her with that great laugh of his. "See you in a few hours then."

If it wasn't for her job, she would have been out the door and in her car in ten seconds flat. Instead, they planned for her to visit over Easter weekend.

💖 ♡ 💖

"I'm not so sure about this," Michelle told Janice at church on Sunday.

"Why are you so worried?" Janice's forehead crinkled with concern.

"I mean, it's Sean, for one thing. I've thought about him so many times over the years, and now he's back in my life. But he lost his wife, and he's grieving … and he's got kids." Although she was excited to see Sean again, she was very nervous about spending time with his kids. She didn't want them to feel like she was trying to step in and take their mother's place or steal their father's attention away.

"And?"

"Kids!"

Janice grinned at her. "What is your point?"

"Here I am, this stranger from their dad's past coming into their home, messing up their life." She was overreacting and she knew it, but the whole thing was freaking her out more than she had anticipated.

Janice put her arm around Michelle. "That's how it goes sometimes. Whether it's because of a death or a divorce, people move on and find new love in their life, and the kids have to deal with that. And there is no way you are gonna mess up their life. You could only make it better, because you're you, and you're special and wonderful."

Michelle grinned at her friend, but it quickly faded. "What if they don't like me?"

"They will," Janice assured her.

"But what if they don't?"

"Michelle, I've never seen you like this before."

"Like what?"

"So unsure of yourself. Like your whole life's happiness all comes down to whether or not these kids like you."

"Maybe it does."

Janice shook her head. "Only God can bring you happiness. Don't worry. It will all work out."

Michelle nodded, but she wasn't so sure.

"Sean inviting you into their home is a big deal. I get that. But he wants you there, and I have a feeling you're gonna win those kids over."

"I hope you're right." She wished she had Janice's confidence.

"You know I'm always right." Janice gave her a wink.

The sermon went in one ear and out the other. Michelle couldn't focus on the pastor's words. All she could think about was what in the world she would have in common with a couple of kids. She pictured terrible scenarios, where they both hated her and made the trip miserable. If she didn't get along with them, would Sean still want her in his life? How could that possibly work if the kids didn't like her?

Before she left the church, Janice gave her a hug and a knowing glance. "Stop worrying."

If only she could.

❦ 21 ❧

*T*he closer she got to the suburbs, the more nervous she became. Was it too soon for her to be visiting him? They hadn't talked about their relationship status yet. But why would he invite her if he didn't think this was going somewhere? Their time together in college had been brief, but neither of them could deny that there was still something between them. Nervousness mingled with excitement. She couldn't wait to spend more time with him. She cared about him so much. She always had.

In the weeks since they had reconnected, she caught herself smiling often. She couldn't help it. For so long, she thought Simon was the one she was supposed to be with, but when that didn't work out, she feared God might want her to be alone. Deep down in her heart, she desired to find love. But she also desired to please God and was prepared to accept singleness if that was what He wanted for her. So when Sean came back into her life, she couldn't help but smile at the way God worked things out sometimes. She didn't know for certain if Sean was the one God meant for her. Not yet. But she was filled with hope for the future.

She turned onto Sean's street, scanning the house numbers, and caught sight of him and Aaron. They were playing basketball at the hoop set up in their driveway, and a smidgen of her anxiety disappeared.

Sean waved as she pulled in, and Aaron dropped the ball and jogged over to greet her.

"Hi, Michelle." Aaron grinned at her. He was a dark blond version of his dad, with those same bright blue eyes.

"Hi, Aaron."

Michelle popped the trunk and climbed out of her car.

The guys had her bags before she had a chance to close her door.

She glanced around at the lovely two-story brick home. It seemed Sean had done very well for himself.

Sudden movement in a first-floor window caught her eye. The curtain flipped closed. *Ashley.*

Sean headed toward a side door with her bags. "Let me show you where you'll be staying."

"Oh, don't let me interrupt your game." She dropped her purse by the door and grabbed the basketball from the grass, where it had landed. She dribbled toward the basket and shot from a good distance away. *Nothin' but net!*

"Pretty good," Sean noted.

"Pretty good?" She gave him a smug look. "Show me what you got, Davis." She tossed the ball at him as hard as she could, and it hit him in the chest with a loud *thud.*

He grunted, then took a shot from where he stood. It swooshed silently through the net. He glanced over at her and grinned.

"My turn!" Aaron ran to retrieve the ball. He stood back almost as far as Michelle and took a shot. *Swoosh!*

Her eyes widened. "Aaron, that was awesome!" She and Sean both clapped for him.

Aaron shrugged his shoulders. "No big deal."

Sean grinned at Michelle again.

A shuffle in the doorway signaled Ashley's arrival.

"I'm starving. Can we eat already?"

Sean shot his daughter a look of disapproval, and she turned and walked back into the house.

Aaron walked over and grabbed Michelle's bag. "Come on. I'll show you your room."

She looked at Sean, then followed his little gentleman of a son into the house.

It was as nice inside as it was out. They walked through the mud room, which held their washer and dryer, and into the kitchen with its large center island, dark granite countertops, white cupboards, and stainless steel appliances. It looked like something she had seen on an HGTV makeover show.

They led her through to the open staircase that led to the second floor.

Sean pointed past the dining area to a hallway. "My room's down there. There's a bathroom just over there."

They continued upstairs. There was a bathroom at the top of the stairs, Aaron's bedroom was on the right, and two bedrooms were to the left. "This is where you'll stay. Ashley's right next door."

Ashley walked past them and closed the door to her room. "My room is off limits."

"Ashley," Sean scolded.

"It's OK," Michelle assured him. "I understand. A girl's gotta have her own space."

Ashley rolled her eyes and walked back downstairs.

"Aaron, will you please go help your sister get dinner started?"

"OK." Aaron hopped down the stairs two at a time.

Sean carried the bags into the guest room, and Michelle followed.

He placed them at the end of the bed, then turned and enveloped her in his arms. "I'm so happy you're here."

She gave him a quick hug, then stepped back. "Are you sure this isn't weird? I mean, we're just getting to know each other again. And this ..." She motioned around the room, feeling suddenly uncomfortable.

He looked at her searchingly. "This what?"

"This was your home with your wife." It was blunt, but it was what she was thinking.

He laid a hand on her shoulder. "I know. But that doesn't mean we can't have happiness here again. Lindsay was the kind of person who made the most out of life. She wouldn't want me moping around here all alone for the next eighty years."

"Eighty years, huh?" She grinned. "So, you're planning to live past a hundred then?"

"Seventy. Eighty. Whatever. I was never good at math."

Michelle chuckled.

He looked her in the eye. "I want you here, OK? Let's just make the most of it."

She smiled. "OK."

❦

The kids made spaghetti for dinner. Ashley had most certainly been forced to help. She poked at her food the whole time and refused to take part in the conversation. Aaron baked garlic toast in the oven all by himself and lit candles on the table to set the mood, which was very thoughtful.

"You'll love our church," Sean told Michelle. "Great people there. We're having an Easter sunrise breakfast Sunday, so we can go if my sleepyhead kids get out of bed in time."

"That sounds nice." Michelle glanced over at Aaron, then Ashley.

Ashley stood and picked up her mostly full plate.

"Where do you think you're going?" Sean asked.

"I'm not hungry." She certainly fit the stereotype of the snotty teenager.

"Sit! You are not leaving this table until your plate is clean."

"Da-ad," she whined.

"And we have company."

"She's *your* company." Ashley glared at him.

"It doesn't matter who she's here to see. We do not treat people like that."

"Whatever." Ashley rolled her eyes and plopped down in her seat, dropping the plate onto the table.

"Hey!" Sean raised his voice. "You're lucky that didn't break."

"I wish it had."

Sean's fist met the table. "Enough!"

Michelle looked down at her plate. She felt very out of place and had an overwhelming urge to cover her ears like she had as a child during her parents' fights.

Sean seemed to realize how uncomfortable she was. "I'm so sorry, Michelle."

She shook her head. "It's OK."

They finished the rest of the meal in silence, then Ashley bolted up the stairs to her room and slammed the door.

Aaron walked over and took Michelle's plate.

"Thanks, Aaron. Can I help you clean up?"

"Nah." He patted her on the arm. "You're our guest."

Her heart warmed. He was the nicest kid.

Sean looked over at her when Aaron left the room, and his shoulders slumped. "I'm so sorry. Sometimes I just lose my patience with her, and I get a little crazy."

Michelle nodded. "I get it. I was the same way at her age, and I did everything I could to push my parents' buttons." She noticed Sean's weariness, and it reminded her of her mother of all people. He had the same look on his face that her mother had so often worn—the exact same look her rebellion had put there time and time again.

"Why did you do it?" he asked.

"I thought I didn't need them, and I didn't want them telling me what to do or how to live my life."

He rubbed his tired eyes. "I just don't know what to do anymore."

"Have you thought about counseling? It could help her deal with the grief in a more positive way. And I'm sure it's hard for her not having her mom to talk to about all the changes she's going through right now. It can be a tough time for a teenage girl."

He shook his head. "I've thought about it, but I don't want her to feel like I'm sending her off to a shrink because something's wrong with her."

"It wouldn't have to be like that. There are a lot of great Christian counselors out there that could help her so much. I see things like this every day at Cornerstone."

He leaned his elbows on the table and rested his forehead in his hands. "I'm just not very good at being both the dad *and* the mom, ya' know?"

She reached across the table and touched his arm. "Maybe you need to talk to someone, too. It might be good for all of you."

He nodded. "Maybe."

"I'll pray for you."

That seemed to calm him.

Long after midnight, Michelle jolted awake. She glanced over at the alarm clock on the nightstand, which read 2:36 a.m. Her head met the pillow again, and she let out a calming breath. Something had woken her, but she wasn't sure what. Had it been a bad dream? She couldn't remember dreaming about anything. In fact, she had drifted off rather quickly last night and slept quite comfortably. Maybe it was just being in Sean's home, so close to him, knowing he was lying in his bed in the room beneath hers.

Just then, she heard a faint sound coming from the room next door. She quietly moved to the wall that separated her room from Ashley's and leaned her ear there to listen. What she heard broke her heart.

It was the sound of a young girl crying.

An hour passed as she lay awake staring at the ceiling. Everything in her wanted to go to Ashley's room to comfort her, but she fought the instinct.

When the crying stopped and all was quiet, she tiptoed down the stairs to the kitchen for a drink of water. One of the cupboards squeaked when she went searching for a glass, and she winced. She slowly opened another, but found bowls instead.

Strong hands suddenly grasped her waist, and she jumped and let out a loud yelp.

Sean chuckled and wrapped his arms around her to calm her. His bare chest met her back. "*Shhh!* The kids," he whispered.

She was hyper aware that she was wearing a tank top without a bra, and she wished she had wrapped up in a blanket or thrown on a sweatshirt before she left her room.

"Don't scare me like that," she whispered back.

He laughed into her neck. The rough feel of his stubble against her shoulder sent a shiver down her spine, and she tilted her head a little to the side, giving him more access if he wanted it. The heat of his breath there made her warm all over.

They stood like that for long minutes, breathing together, his chin resting on her shoulder.

She waited for him to move. It had been her who took the lead in the past, but things were different now. She was different. She would never pressure him into doing anything ever again. He had suffered a great loss, and his life had been turned upside down. She wanted him to be ready.

"Sean?" she whispered his name.

"*Hmmm?*" His lips brushed her earlobe, and her eyes slid shut. *Stupid earlobe.*

"You can let go of me now," she breathed.

She felt him nod, but he didn't move for several long, exhilarating minutes. She could feel the pulse in his neck beating rapidly against hers.

"I don't want to," he finally replied. "I let you go once, and I don't ever wanna do it again."

She smiled. How wonderful it was to hear that.

He turned her around to face him. "I never forgot about you, Michelle."

Her arms wrapped instinctively around his back. She wound her fingers together, and her hands came to rest against the elastic waistband of his plaid pajama pants.

His hands rubbed softly up and down her arms, as if to warm her, and settled on her shoulders. "I never stopped wondering what might've happened if I had stayed." His expression turned serious then, and he sought permission with his eyes, which appeared even deeper in the dimly lit kitchen.

Staring into the depths of blue, she knew she was a goner.

His fingertips trailed along either side of her neck, his thumbs gently brushing her cheeks, as he leaned forward and pressed his lips to hers.

She was surprised at how familiar his kisses felt, yet so new at the same time. It seemed so strange to be kissing this man, whom she had kissed so long ago, when he was just a boy, and she just a girl. But they weren't eighteen anymore, and he was no longer a boy. He was a man—a strong, mature, passionate man. A man who knew how to kiss a woman.

He pulled back and rested his forehead against hers. "I've wanted to kiss you since that night at the basketball game."

She couldn't contain her smile.

He leaned in and kissed her again, softly caressing the back of her neck, playing with the wispy hairs that had fallen from her messy bun. His kisses were as tender and perfect as she remembered. Goosebumps spread over her entire body, as he led them into a wonderful fog of sensation and longing. She never wanted it to stop.

She slowly slid her hands up his back, relishing in the feel of his skin beneath her fingertips. His mouth left hers and moved along her jaw, his breath hot against her neck. When his lower lip brushed her earlobe, she buried her fingers in his hair and tilted his head, kissing him deeply.

A little moan sounded in the back of his throat, and he swiftly turned them, until she was pinned between him and the kitchen island. With one hand flat against her back, one behind her neck, he leaned into the kiss. She snaked her arms around his neck and arched her back, wanting to be closer.

"Dad?" a small voice came from the stairway behind them.

Sean stepped away immediately.

Aaron stood bleary-eyed, staring at the two of them. "I can't sleep."

"Maybe some warm milk will help, bud," Sean stuttered.

"OK," Aaron replied.

Sean went about preparing the milk for his son.

Michelle stepped out of the way and crossed her arms. Her hands were shaking, both from being caught and from the blood pounding through her veins.

Sean looked over at her and mouthed, "Wow!"

She grinned and held in a giggle.

Once Aaron had finished his milk, he gave Sean a hug goodnight, then shuffled over to Michelle and hugged her, too.

"Goodnight, Michelle."

"Goodnight." She placed a hand over her heart and looked over at Sean, who was wearing the biggest smile on his face.

They watched Aaron walk back up the stairs to his room, and their eyes met.

"Should we talk about what just happened?" She wanted it to happen again. Right now.

He walked slowly toward her with a look that said he, too, wanted to pick up where they left off.

She took a step backwards, flirting with her eyes.

He caught her and slid his arms around her waist, resting his forehead against hers. "I really wanna take you down that little hallway right there." He nodded toward his bedroom.

She swallowed hard, and that old familiar tingling took over her body. "Sean."

His lips pressed feathery soft kisses on her cheek, her neck, her ear. He spoke in a whisper. "I never wanna stop kissing you."

Butterflies. So many butterflies. She needed to gather what little control she had left, before this went too far. She didn't trust herself with Sean, because she wanted him more than she'd ever wanted another man—even Simon.

"Why did you stop writing me?" she blurted out. It was the only thing she could think of to stop his advances.

He pulled back and looked at her.

"I sent you letter after letter, and you just stopped."

"I don't know," he answered sheepishly. "It was a long time ago."

She looked down sadly.

"Life happened, I guess."

Her eyes met his again. She was disappointed in that answer. "Life happened? That's it?"

"I don't know what else to say."

What she wanted was for him to admit that Lindsay was the real reason he had stopped writing her.

He shrugged. "I'm not much of a letter writer."

"I'm not either, but I wrote you every week, even when your letters weren't coming."

"I know." His eyes fell away from hers.

"And you wouldn't return my calls."

"I'm sorry." He hugged her comfortingly. "You have no idea how sorry I am for all of it."

The old pain resurfaced without warning, and she fought back tears. "You broke my heart, Sean."

His shoulders slumped. "I never meant to hurt you, but I had to do the right thing."

She leaned back, her brow furrowed, and looked into his eyes.

He opened his mouth to speak, then closed it. "I got Lindsay pregnant," he admitted hesitantly.

"Oh." It was all she could think to say. This was not what she had expected. If she had done the math, she probably could have figured out that Ashley was born less than nine months after Sean's wedding, but it never crossed her mind. She didn't know what to say. She stepped out of his arms and moved toward the window, staring at her own reflection against the darkness of night.

"When I came home from Cornerstone, I was feeling really down. My parents tried to be supportive, but I could feel how disappointed they were in me. I tried to throw myself into classes and basketball and not think about how much I wanted to just drop out and move back to Michigan to be with you."

She looked over at him then.

"Lindsay was in my study group. She was nice to me, and she encouraged me when I was at my lowest. And one night, it just happened."

She chewed the inside of her lip to keep from crying. It hurt to hear the truth, even after fourteen years. She was overcome with sadness. If not for Sean's one night with Lindsay, they might have stayed together. And if not for her one night with Sean, none of it would have happened in the first place.

"Please say something." His voice held an edge of panic. "What are you thinking?"

"Thank you for telling me the truth." The war she was waging against her tears was becoming a losing battle. Her chin began to quiver. Her throat ached. She closed her eyes to fight them off.

He came up behind her and wrapped his arms around her waist. His lips met the back of her neck and pressed softly over and over. "I need you to forgive me, Michelle." He spoke in between kisses. "Please." One of his hands slid slowly back and forth across her stomach. "I need you."

She turned into him, a few tears escaping, and fierce lips met hers. These kisses were different, desperate. His hands held her firmly to him, like he was afraid she might slip away. The intensity scared her, and she tore her lips from his.

He let go and took her hands, leading her out of the kitchen toward his bedroom hallway.

Her feet stopped moving, and she froze. "Wait, Sean. We can't."

He stopped her protests with another deep kiss and walked backwards, pulling her with him along the hallway.

Something about his sudden desperation felt wrong. She got a nervous feeling in the pit of her stomach, and that little voice in her head told her this was going way too fast. She stepped away to catch her breath, but he reached for her again and pressed her against the nearest wall, kissing her neck, his hands wandering.

Being close to him felt amazing, but the reality of the situation began to sink in. The way he was clinging to her felt like now or never, like everything had to be settled tonight or it never would, and she realized this wasn't as simple as Sean just wanting her. This had much more to do with losing his wife than needing her forgiveness, much more than he probably realized. This was about grief and loss and loneliness, and it was so much bigger than the two of them.

She wiggled from his grip and walked quickly back to the kitchen. He followed close behind, and she spun around to face him.

"Is this why you asked me to come here?" She nodded toward his bedroom.

"What? No." His eyes widened.

She pressed her lips together and shook her head sadly. "You're lonely. You're lonely, and you miss your wife."

"Michelle." He moved toward her again, but she held up her hands to stop him.

"You're not ready for this." She took a deep breath in and released it shakily. "You're still grieving, and I refuse to be just a warm body to fill the empty place she left behind."

His mouth dropped open.

"The truth is, we don't know each other all that well. We barely dated fourteen years ago, and we've had some nice phone conversations."

"It's more than that, and you know it."

The tears threatened to fall again. "We never said we were a couple. We're just friends."

He shook his head. "No."

"Maybe it's best for both of us if we keep it that way." She walked toward the stairs.

"Michelle." He grabbed her arm, his expression pained. "I don't wanna be just your friend."

Her heart ached. How many times had she longed for someone to say those exact words? "I think I should go."

"No, please. Please don't leave like this," he begged. "Please. Let's talk about this."

She bit her lip to hold back the tears. "I'm really tired. Let's just talk in the morning." Her feet moved quickly up the stairs to her room. She closed the door and threw herself onto the bed, burying her sobs in the pillow.

❧ 22 ❧

The sun shining through the window and the sound of birds chirping roused her. The pillowcase beneath her head was tear-stained, and her arms hurt from squeezing it so tightly. She sat up and stretched her arms above her head. Memories of the night before came rushing back. She was more than a little disappointed—especially in herself for hinging all of her happiness on a lonely widower.

She climbed out of bed and quickly dressed, brushed her hair up into her usual messy bun, and went to work packing her things. This was not how she thought the weekend would go.

The smell of coffee and sizzling sausage wafted under the door and made her stomach growl. She took a deep breath, blew it out, and hesitantly headed down to the kitchen.

Aaron met her at the foot of the stairs. "We made you breakfast." He led her to the head of the table, where there was a pretty place setting, a linen napkin, and a tall vase filled with red and yellow tulips and purple hyacinths. She took her seat and admired the flowers, while Aaron brought her a plate of pancakes, sausage, and scrambled eggs, and a glass of orange juice.

"Thank you, Aaron. This is so sweet of you."

"Dad helped," he replied.

She glanced over at Sean, who was standing over a griddle, flipping pancakes. He smiled sweetly at her, which caused her heart to flutter.

Aaron got a plate of food for himself, sat down next to her, and bowed his head to give thanks for his food before he dug in.

She couldn't help but love this kid already. He seemed incredibly mature for his age.

"Where's Ashley?" Michelle asked.

"She sleeps 'til noon," Aaron replied.

Michelle nodded and took a bite of pancake.

Sean finished in the kitchen and brought his plate over to sit on the other side of the table next to Michelle. "Morning."

She noticed his eyes were bloodshot, and she wondered if he had lost sleep, too.

"Morning." She was embarrassed and unsure what to say to him. "Looks like a nice day." It was all she could think of.

"Perfect for some soccer," Aaron announced.

Sean looked at Michelle. "He's got a soccer tournament today."

"Oh." She smiled at Aaron. "Good luck. I hope you have fun and your team wins."

"Wait, you're not coming?"

"Oh, no, Aaron. I'm going home today."

The sad look on his face broke her heart.

"Aw, I thought you were staying 'til tomorrow."

She glanced over at Sean, then back at Aaron. "I don't think I can."

Sean looked down at his plate.

"Pleeease," Aaron begged. "After the game, we're going out for pizza."

That face. That sweet little face. How could she refuse him?

She sighed. "Maybe just until tonight."

"Yeah!" Aaron threw his hands in the air in celebration.

Sean smiled at her. His blue eyes lit up.

And how could she refuse Aaron's dad?

So this is what it's like to be a soccer mom. Sean drove his minivan from house to house, picking up Aaron's teammates for the game. The vehicle was bursting at the seams with soccer players, their gear, and a cooler loaded with water and Gatorade. Michelle glanced over her shoulder at the boys, who were talking incessantly about how they were going to kick the other team's butts and how good their victory pizza was going to taste.

She glanced over at Sean, who looked so handsome in a team

jersey. His father-in-law's company had sponsored Aaron's team and paid for their uniforms. Michelle found herself wondering what it would be like to be a part of their life for real. She imagined herself driving Aaron to games, taking Ashley to the mall, going places together as a ... family. She pushed the thought out of her mind as fast as it came. Maybe she wasn't meant to have a happy family life. Maybe it wasn't in God's will for her.

The boys scrambled out of the van the second Sean shifted into park and ran across the field toward their coach. They flew out the door so fast, Michelle almost got whiplash.

"Wow! They are really excited about soccer. Are they always like this?"

"Pretty much." Sean suddenly jumped out of the van and hollered after them. "Hey! Grab the cooler!"

Aaron and a couple of the boys returned, grumbling as they carried the heavy cooler to the sidelines.

Michelle couldn't help but giggle at how slowly they were moving, compared to how fast they had been just moments before.

Sean walked to the back of the van and retrieved a couple of camp chairs.

As they walked toward the soccer field, Sean reached for her hand, his fingertips brushing her palm.

She moved her hand away.

He didn't respond to her snub, but she could tell he wasn't happy about it.

The soccer tournament was a great success for Aaron and his team, but not so for Michelle and Sean. They sat in silence most of the time, except when they were cheering Aaron on or commenting on the game. It wasn't the ideal place to have a serious conversation.

Aaron's team won all their games and took home a trophy. Even more exciting, Aaron scored the winning goal in their final game.

"He's really good," Michelle commented.

"He wants to keep playing on into high school. He loves it."

"Maybe he'll get a scholarship like his dad."

Sean didn't reply. She wasn't sure if the sad look on his face was because he had lost that scholarship or because of how things were between them at the moment.

The pizza celebration was loud and rambunctious. The place was filled with several teams, parents, and siblings. It was noisy, to say the least.

Afterwards, they went from house to house again, dropping the boys off. Sean's van should have had a taxi sign on top.

When they arrived home, the house was completely dark. It should not have been.

"Ashley!" Sean cried as they ran through the mud room. "Ashley!"

Aaron ran upstairs and looked in all the rooms. Sean ran downstairs to the family room. Michelle stood helplessly in the kitchen while they looked.

Ashley had stayed home from the soccer game with plans to go to her aunt and uncle's house in the afternoon. Alex wanted her to come over and help his younger siblings color Easter eggs, or so she had said. Sean had agreed to it, but she was supposed to be home right after dinner.

The house was silent. No Ashley.

Sean called his brother in a panic. "Is Ashley there?"

Michelle prayed for her, that she was safe, wherever she was. And she prayed that Ashley hadn't done any number of stupid things she herself had done at thirteen.

"OK. If you hear from her, call me on my cell." He hung up and ran his fingers through his hair.

"Maybe she's with Brandon," Aaron said.

"She better not be with that punk," he snapped loudly.

Aaron winced.

Sean sadly lowered his head and wrapped his arms around his son. "I'm sorry, bud. I'm just worried."

"Does she have her cell phone on her?" Michelle asked.

Sean nodded. "She never goes anywhere without it."

"You could call it," Michelle suggested.

Sean pulled his phone out.

Michelle laid her hand on his. "Wait! That might spook her."

"Hold on!" Aaron suddenly declared, and he ran upstairs to Ashley's room.

They followed close behind.

Aaron seated himself at Ashley's desk, opened her laptop, and started scrolling through the posts on her Facebook wall.

Sean hovered over him.

"Somebody tagged her in some photos," Aaron announced. "See." He clicked on one that showed Ashley with a couple of her friends at a party, then scrolled through several others, including one of her kissing a guy. His face was not clearly visible in the photo.

"That's gotta be Brandon," Sean stated with gritted teeth.

Michelle pointed at the screen. "It looks like they were just posted an hour ago."

Aaron clicked through a few more.

"Look," Michelle grabbed Sean's arm. "That one says 'Party at Brandon's'."

Sean was out the door before she finished her sentence. He called his brother, and they dropped Aaron off at his house on the way.

As they drove across town, Sean was seething.

"You need to calm down and have a level head when you go in there," Michelle told him.

He gripped the steering wheel so hard his fingers turned white. "I'm not gonna calm down. My daughter is somewhere she knows she's not supposed to be."

Michelle said nothing more.

Brandon's house was old and run-down and not in a very nice neighborhood. The yard was overflowing with cars, and there was loud, thumping music coming from within.

Michelle followed behind Sean as he entered through the front door.

There were lots of underage kids drinking, smoking pot, and making out. A strong feeling of deja vu hit Michelle. She had been at parties just like this when she was Ashley's age. She had been the girl getting high and making out with older guys.

They walked from room to room, scanning the crowd for Ashley. Sean started calling out her name, which drew strange looks from the kids. As they reached the back of the house, they finally found her curled up in a ball in the corner of a dark stairway. The expression on Sean's face at the sight of his daughter broke Michelle's heart.

"Ashley."

Ashley's face was tear-streaked, her eyes wide with horror. "Dad? What are you doing here? How did you find me?"

"Let's go."

She broke down sobbing, and he scooped her up in his arms and carried her out of the house.

Michelle slid open the side door of the van, and Sean lowered Ashley onto the seat.

"Are you OK? Are you hurt?" he asked.

Michelle reached into her purse, pulled out a tissue, and started to wipe Ashley's tears.

Ashley slapped her hand away. "Don't! You're not my mom."

She was close enough to smell alcohol on Ashley's breath.

Sean paced back and forth beside the van. She could tell he was doing everything he could to keep control.

"Tell me," he demanded. "Did someone hurt you?"

"Brandon," she whimpered.

Sean spun around and covered his face with his hands. He was very close to losing it.

"What did he do to you?" Michelle asked.

"I found him in bed with my friend, Ari." She spoke through more tears.

Sean turned and looked at her. "He didn't touch you?"

"Nobody touched me, Dad."

He let out a relieved sigh. "You are so lucky, young lady. Do you know what could have happened to you tonight?"

Ashley didn't reply, and he slid the van door closed between them and climbed behind the steering wheel.

Michelle returned to the passenger seat and looked over at him.

He took a few deep breaths in and out, then started the van.

"Do you want me to drive home?" Michelle asked.

"I'm fine," he cried.

He was far from fine. And neither was his daughter.

Back at the house, there was a lot of yelling and slamming of doors. Michelle sat at the kitchen table and prayed for them. She wished she could help. As she sat there, the image of her screaming at her mother, slamming her bedroom door, then sneaking out later that night popped into her mind. And she suddenly saw the entire situation from her mother's perspective. She suddenly understood that helpless feeling a parent gets when their child is out of control and they have no idea what to do about it.

Sean came stomping down the stairs after Ashley locked herself in the bathroom to get cleaned up from the party. He plopped down at the table next to Michelle and rested his head in his hands. "Bet you're glad you came to visit, huh?"

"I am, actually. I think I can help you."

He looked up at her, exhausted and at a loss. "How?"

"When we walked into that party tonight, it was like stepping back in time. That was my life. Exactly my life."

He listened intently as she shared about her partying ways, losing her virginity at Ashley's age, thinking she had to put out for guys to like her.

"I've been where she is right now. Maybe I did it for different reasons, but we're the same."

"But how can you help?"

"I don't know. Maybe I can just tell her my story. See if she'll at least listen to me. It's worth a try."

"I'm open to anything at this point." His head sank back into his hands.

Michelle took a seat at Ashley's desk and waited for her to return to her room. She had no idea how this conversation would go, but she had to try. Her stomach was tied up in knots. She wanted to help, so much. She wanted to make things better for Ashley. But if this didn't go well, she would have to walk down those stairs and see the disappointment in a father's eyes.

Lord, please help me. Give me the right words to get through to her.

"Get out of my room!" Ashley cried when she spotted Michelle.

Michelle held her hands up. "I come in peace."

"Whatever! Just get out!" Ashley picked up some clothes from the floor and threw them into her hamper.

"I thought you might wanna talk to someone other than your dad."

"Well, you thought wrong," Ashley snapped. She walked over and sat down at her vanity.

Michelle was quiet for a few minutes, while Ashley combed through her wet locks.

"You can go now." Ashley stared at Michelle's reflection in the mirror.

"I grew up in Chicago, too. Did you know that? I lived in the city with my mom in a crappy little apartment."

"Who cares."

Michelle ignored her and continued. "My parents weren't around very much, so I could pretty much do whatever I wanted and get away with it."

Ashley grabbed her cell phone and started checking her messages, but still Michelle talked.

"And I did for the most part. I went all over town with my friends. We went to parties, got drunk, smoked pot. We thought we were so cool."

Ashley glanced at her, then back at her phone.

"I used to be so in love with this guy, Tyler. He was sixteen, a couple years older than me, and I thought he was everything."

Ashley rolled her eyes.

"But he was a lot more experienced than me, and I thought the only way to get him to like me was to put out. So we got really drunk at a party one night, and I lost my virginity to him on some kid's parents' bed." Michelle paused. She was surprised how raw the emotions were, and she fought back tears. "I've never told anyone but your dad about that."

Ashley looked over at her and set down her phone. She reached for a tissue and held it out to Michelle.

"Thanks." Michelle dabbed her eyes.

"Did he like you?" Ashley asked.

Michelle was surprised to hear her voice.

"Was he your boyfriend after that?"

Michelle shook her head sadly.

"What a jerk."

"Can I ask about your friend, Brandon?"

"Brandon's not like that Tyler guy." Ashley's defenses went up. "He's the sweetest. He would never hurt me."

"Have you forgotten what happened at the party? If he really cared about you, he wouldn't have had sex with your friend."

Ashley's chin fell.

Michelle had to ask. "Have you had sex with him?"

"That's none of your business," Ashley snapped, her attention returning to her phone.

Michelle closed her eyes and prayed silently for guidance. When her eyes opened, she noticed a tear slip down Ashley's cheek.

"You can talk to me. Nothing you say will leave this room."

Ashley brushed the tear from her cheek, but said nothing.

Michelle didn't push. She stood and walked to Ashley's bookcase and looked at the pictures of her with her mom, with her dad, some of the whole family together. There were photos of her with friends and one with a boy, who might have been Brandon, but she thought it best not to ask. She looked back to the photo of Ashley with her mother. Lindsay was an attractive woman with a vibrant smile and bright eyes. Sean had been right—the resemblance between Ashley and her mom was unmistakable.

"You're so lucky," Michelle said. "Such a beautiful family. My family was a mess. My dad was never around. I barely knew him. And my mom worked all the time."

"At least you have a mom," Ashley blurted. Large tears fell from her eyes, and her shoulders began to shake. She threw herself down and cried into her comforter.

Michelle wasn't sure what to do next. This was all new to her. She slowly walked to the bed, sat down, and laid her hand on Ashley's back. When Ashley didn't jerk or slap her hand away, Michelle took that as a good sign.

She began to run her fingers softly through Ashley's damp hair. She had very few memories of bonding moments with her mother, but one thing she remembered was how much she loved Mom playing with her hair when she was little.

"Your dad went crazy looking for your tonight, because he was so worried something might've happened to you. He loves you more than anything in this world. You know that, right?"

Ashley's head moved a little, and she took that as a nod.

"I wish I'd had that when I was your age. I wish I had it now."

Ashley turned her head a little and rested her cheek on the bed. "Your dad doesn't love you?"

"I don't know. If he does, he's never showed it."

They were quiet while Michelle continued playing with Ashley's hair. Her thoughts returned to the party, to Brandon sleeping with Ashley's friend.

"I'm sorry about what you saw at the party tonight. I had the same thing happen to me with Tyler more than once, and it hurts to see the guy you like with someone else."

Ashley propped herself up on her elbow and looked at Michelle.

"But now you know what he's really like. And Ashley ..." She reached over and cupped her cheek. "You deserve better."

Giant tears filled Ashley's eyes.

"I wish someone had told me that when I was your age." She went back to playing with Ashley's hair. "I can't go back and change the things I did. I can't ever get my virginity back." She choked up for a minute, thinking of what had happened between her and Sean, what she had taken from him. "It's a precious gift, and I wish I'd saved myself until God brought me the right guy to marry."

A single tear slipped down Ashley's cheek.

Michelle shifted and looked her straight in the eyes. "Have you had sex with Brandon? You can tell me."

"No, I've never had sex before," Ashley mumbled.

Oh, thank God.

"Then you have a choice. You can choose to save that part of you for your future husband—for him and only him."

Ashley wiped the tear away.

"And I know you think these people are your real friends. I thought the same thing about mine. But they aren't. They'll use you, and then they'll leave you with nothing. I guarantee you God has wonderful people out there that are meant to be your true friends—supportive, encouraging friends, who really love you. You deserve all the blessings God has planned for you, Ashley."

The tears spilled from Ashley's pretty blue eyes then, and she reached for Michelle.

Michelle wrapped her up in her arms, and Ashley began to weep into her neck.

"I miss my Mom," she murmured. "I need her."

Michelle closed her eyes and let out a sigh. "I know you do."

"Why did God take her away?"

"I don't know, Ashley." Her heart broke for this sweet girl. "I'm so sorry about your mom." She held onto her for a long time and let her cry it out.

When Ashley's tears subsided, she seemed more comfortable with Michelle. "I'm mad at God."

Michelle nodded knowingly. "I get that. It's OK to feel that way. I've had moments like that, too."

"About what?"

"Well, it's nothing as serious as losing a parent, but back in college, I liked your dad. A lot. And when he left school and came back to Chicago, I was really sad. Then he met your mom, and I was angry with God for taking him away from me. I let it get in the way of my relationship with God for a long time. But now I can see all that as His plan. If your dad hadn't left, he might not have met your mom, and you might not be sitting here with me right now. I can't be angry with God for that."

Ashley smiled at her—a real, honest-to-goodness smile. It was a little breakthrough, and Michelle wanted to shout for joy. *Thank you, Lord.*

"We don't always understand why things happen. But one day, after some time has passed, we might look back and see things differently. It's OK to be upset, though."

Ashley glanced down for a moment, then back at Michelle. "Are you still sad?"

"About what? About your dad leaving college?" Michelle asked.

Ashley nodded in reply.

"Sometimes. Sometimes I wonder if we would have stayed together if he hadn't left." She shrugged. "What might have been."

"But you're together now. You found each other again. That's a good thing, right?"

Michelle couldn't have put it better herself. "Do *you* think it's a good thing?"

Ashley's mouth twisted a little to the side, like she was pondering the situation.

"You don't have to say yes if you don't want me to be with your dad."

"I think I'm OK with it."

When Michelle emerged, Sean was pacing back and forth in the kitchen. She stopped at the top of the stairs, and her presence caught his eye.

He walked over and looked up at her. "How'd it go?"

Michelle tilted her head in the direction of Ashley's room. "You should go talk to her."

"Are you sure?"

Michelle nodded.

He raced up the stairs past Michelle to his daughter's room.

She heard Ashley say, "I'm so sorry, Daddy", and she knew it was a step in the right direction. They had a long road ahead of them, but she felt like she had broken through to Ashley—enough that she was willing to open up a little. There were a lot of things they would need to work through, but she believed her words had made an impact.

Michelle was exhausted and decided to turn in for the night. She collapsed onto the bed and thought about all that had happened since she arrived. In sharing her story with Ashley, she realized that she still had a lot of her own issues over what she had done as a young teen and the ways she had let guys use her. That had carried over into her betrayal with Ben, her relationship with Simon, and into the kitchen with Sean last night.

Lord, thank you for helping me through the conversation with Ashley. Thank you that you kept her from harm tonight, that you led us to her, and that she is home safe and sound. Be with Sean and the kids as they continue to grieve. And, Lord, about my issues—show me how to deal with them and make things right that need to be. I miss Maggie and Simon. Help me figure out how to fix things and ...

She drifted off to sleep mid-prayer.

A pressure on Michelle's hip and a gentle jostle woke her suddenly.

"What is it?" She sat up to Sean's handsome face illuminated by the moonlight through her window. "Is it Ashley?" She was groggy, unsure if this was a dream.

His hand remained on her hip. "She's gonna be fine."

"Oh," she rubbed her eyes. "Are you OK?"

He nodded, and suddenly wrapped his arms tightly around her. His fingers gripped the back of her shirt, and warm tears soon dripped onto her shoulder.

She pulled back and looked at him. Tears filled his eyes, some plopping down his cheeks. The sight of a man crying got her every time. She gently brushed his tears away.

He closed his eyes at her touch.

She traced his cheek and along his jawline.

When he looked at her again, her stomach flipped. Such tenderness behind those eyes, and that same look of adoration he had given her the day he left Cornerstone for good. "Thank you, Michelle."

"You're welcome. I just shared my own story with her. I wish I could have done more."

"You've done so much already. And you were right about a counselor. I think she needs to keep talking."

Michelle nodded. "She does."

"I think we all do." He sat back and wiped the remaining tears from his face, then took a deep breath and looked at her again. "I'm sorry to wake you. I didn't know if you were planning to stay for church tomorrow morning or not, and I thought we should talk before you go."

"We should."

"I'm not sure how to say this to make you understand. I'm not always clear about my feelings, and sometimes things come out wrong. Like last night."

She listened intently.

"You were right. I *am* lonely. It's been two long years taking care of these kids by myself, sleeping in my bed alone. And I won't lie. I wanted to take you to my room last night." He shook his head. "I'm kind of a mess right now. But I wasn't trying to use you to replace Lindsay. I didn't plan to get you into my bed. That's not why I asked you here at all. I just ... I wanted to be close to you." He took her hand in his. "I wasn't lying when I said I never forgot about you. Your letters meant everything to me, but when I found out Lindsay was pregnant, they were like torture. Every hope I had about you and me and a future together was ruined by one stupid mistake. I had to face the consequences, and that's why I stopped writing. My future was with Lindsay, whether I wanted it or not, and I couldn't open another letter from you telling me how much you missed me." His eyes were brimming over with tears again. "I'm sorry if I came on too strong last night and made you think—"

Michelle stopped him with a soft, tender kiss.

He smiled against her mouth and breathed a sigh of relief.

"It's OK. I understand. Let's just forget about last night," she declared.

He shook his head. "I could never forget kissing you."

Her cheeks flushed. That charm of his was hard to resist.

He took both of her hands in his then. "I hope we can keep talking and get to know each other better."

"Me, too."

"But not as friends, as a couple. That's what I want."

She smiled at him, happy he made his intentions clear. "I want that, too."

"You do?"

She nodded with a shy smile.

He reached up and held her face in his hands. "I'm so crazy about you," he whispered, and softly pressed his lips to hers.

She wasn't sure what she had done to deserve this wonderful man's affection, but she knew for sure who to thank.

❧ 23 ❧

When she arrived home from the long, emotional weekend in Chicago, the light on her answering machine was blinking.

"Hey, Chelle, it's Simon. We haven't talked in a while, and I thought maybe we could get together and catch up. If you're ready to see me, that is. Call me if you are."

Over the past nine months since their breakup, they had spoken a handful of times, but only on the phone. She hadn't been ready to face him after what she had done. But now that things were moving forward with Sean, she knew a phone conversation was not enough. She needed to see her best friend. It was time.

They agreed to meet at Panera Bread for dinner on a Tuesday. She thought she might be nervous to see him, but she realized she was just excited. She missed him and wanted to share what had been happening in her life.

As she walked across the parking lot toward the entrance, she heard her favorite nickname.

"Chelle!"

She turned to see Simon jogging across the lot toward her, and she walked quickly to meet him.

He wrapped his arms around her and lifted her up.

It felt good. It felt right to let all that relationship stuff fall away and just be his friend again.

"How are you?" she asked as they walked into the restaurant together.

He held the inner door open for her. "I'm good. You?"

"Great, actually."

"Great? Really? Well, you're better than I am then."

They ordered and found a seat off in a quiet corner.

"So, how's everything? How's work?" she asked.

"Not so fast. I wanna hear why you're so great."

She grinned and blushed a little.

"Is this about a guy? Do I want to know this?"

"Well, if we are, in fact, friends, then yes, you should want to know this and be happy for me."

He nodded. "OK then."

"I'm kinda seeing Sean now."

"Sean? Sean who? Sean Davis?" His eyes widened. "How did *this* happen? Wait ... I thought he was married with children."

She shared everything and got him all caught up to date.

"This is unbelievable. So, is this something serious then?"

She shrugged. "I don't know. It's still really new. We're in the getting to know each other again phase. But I'm hopeful."

He smiled at her. "You look happy, Chelle. I don't think I ever saw that look on your face when we were together. I don't think I ever have. It looks good on you."

She waved him off. "Now tell me about you. What's been happening?"

"I'm moving to California," he announced.

Her mouth dropped open in surprise. "Wow!"

"Yeah."

"Moving back in with your parents, are ya'?" she teased.

"Funny."

"Simon." Her tone turned serious. "What happened with you and Maggie?"

He avoided eye contact. "What do you mean?"

"I know how much you liked her. I kinda thought something might happen after we broke up."

"No. There's nothing there."

She was confused by this, but pressed him no further.

"So, what made you wanna move?"

"I don't know. I was thinking about it before Pete asked me to help with his studio, and I sorta put it outta my mind. But I think it's time for a fresh start. There's nothing here for me anymore."

"Hey! I could take offense at that."

"Besides you, of course. But you have Sean now." He gave her that cute smirk of his.

She smacked his arm playfully.

"I've also realized some things about the way I've been living my life." It was Simon's turn to be serious, which was so not like him.

Michelle was very curious to hear this.

"I grew up in a Christian home. I've been saved since I was a kid. I prayed a prayer I don't even really remember praying. I knew the truth, and I believed it, but I never really lived it, ya' know? I kept doing whatever I wanted without focusing much on my relationship with God. It's like I knew He was there, but I never knew how to let Him be a part of my life. And I sure didn't do anything to show the world there was something different about me."

Michelle nodded. She didn't grow up a Christian, but she understood the struggle.

"But being around Maggie and Tom's family this past year, getting to know them, seeing the faith they have, has changed my point of view. They pray for each other, even for the little things. Like Maggie's business—she lost some wedding clients last year, and they were all there praying her through it. They were so sure God was gonna work things out. I've always been pretty independent. I always felt like I could take care of myself. I never knew what it felt like to let go of things and really trust God to show me what to do next."

They were alike in so many ways.

"Until now," he said.

"And this is part of your whole moving to California decision?"

He nodded. "I feel like it's the right thing to do."

"And it has absolutely nothing to do with Maggie?" Michelle asked.

Simon was quiet for a few beats. "Yes."

"Yes, it does, or yes, it doesn't?"

"You worded that weird."

She laughed and rephrased the question. "Does it have anything to do with Maggie?"

"Yes," he answered, not making eye contact with her.

"I thought so."

A look of doubt crossed his face. "You did not."

"I know you, Simon Walker."

He grinned at her.

She looked him straight in the eyes. "What happened with Maggie?"

His shoulders sank a little. "She didn't want me."

Michelle didn't believe that. "I saw how you were looking at each other at Fourth of July. Something was there."

"Maybe so, but she made it very clear that I'm not the right guy for her. She's still not over what Ben did to her, and I don't know if she'll ever get over it. And because of that and something that happened last summer, she thinks she can't trust me."

Michelle raised an eyebrow. "What happened last summer?"

Simon cleared his throat. "She thinks I slept with my assistant, Anna, and I just let her believe it was true."

Michelle's mouth dropped open again. "Why? Simon, why would you do that?"

"I was angry. She has such a low opinion of me sometimes. She threw my breakup with Emma in my face. I couldn't believe she was still holding onto that after all these years."

"First impressions can be hard to recover from."

"Well, it doesn't matter anymore."

"Simon." She could see the pain in his eyes.

"I prayed about it, and I felt God telling me to walk away and let her be. So I did."

"OK. Are you sure that was the right decision?"

He nodded resolutely. "Yes."

"I'm so sorry, Simon."

"Thanks, Chelle." His smile was weak.

"I'll miss living in the same town as you."

He reached across the table and squeezed her hand. "I'll miss you, too."

❧ 24 ❧

*R*ain pelted the windows of the car as Sean drove through the streets of Chicago toward Michelle's mother's apartment. This trip was a first for Michelle and Sean. Not only was it their first as a couple, but it was the first trip with the kids in tow. School was out now, and it was the perfect way to kick off summer.

Michelle glanced into the back seat as Sean turned into the parking garage. Aaron was staring out the window, curious about everything. Ashley was on her phone, not paying attention to anything but the text messages she was sending and receiving.

"Ash, put your phone away," Sean demanded. "We're here."

She rolled her eyes, but did as she was told.

Michelle looked over at Sean, and his gaze met hers. She loved the way he looked at her. It made her feel warm all over. But it didn't stop the nerves that were causing a ruckus in her stomach.

This three days would be the most time she had spent at her mom's in years. She had been there for the occasional holiday, but usually quick trips—arrive in the evening, stay one night, visit in the morning, then home. Never long enough to truly connect.

But this trip was different. This trip felt more important than those brief visits. She wanted the kids to bond with her mom, because if things progressed, she might just be their grandmother someday.

When they had parked and gathered their bags, they made their way up the elevator to the apartment. Louise was waiting at the door when they arrived.

"Well, hello there," Louise greeted them. "Hello, Sean. Welcome to our home."

"Thank you, Louise," he said as he hugged her.

She pulled back abruptly from the hug. "Oh, you can call me Lou."

"OK, Lou."

She turned toward the kids. "You must be Ashley and Aaron."

"Yes, ma'am," Aaron replied.

Ashley managed a half-smile.

Louise put her hand on Aaron's arm and led him into the living room. "Come on in."

Michelle was happy that her mom, who didn't usually take much to strangers, was so welcoming to Sean and the kids.

Louise showed them the guest room, where she had made the bed and set up a small air mattress on the floor. "I hope this is OK for you, Aaron."

Aaron plopped down on the mattress and bounced a little. "It's great!"

"I thought maybe you girls could have the bed and Sean the couch, but you can decide."

Ashley looked at her dad and made a face, obviously unhappy with the sleeping arrangements.

Michelle noticed him subtly shake his head at her as if to say, "Now is not the time."

They left their bags in the guest room and moved to the kitchen table, where they had snacks and chatted about the drive over. Louise asked the kids lots of questions about school. Aaron was very forthcoming, especially when it came to the topic of soccer. Ashley wasn't as willing to share, but she wasn't rude either, which was a relief.

Since the weather was not conducive to any of the outdoor activities they had talked about, they decided to hang out at the apartment for the evening.

Michelle helped her mom prepare dinner while the others played some Yahtzee and Boggle. Mom began to ask questions about her and Sean and their relationship. Was it serious? Were they going to get married? Was she ready to be a stepmom to these kids?

"Keep it down, Mom," Michelle whispered. "It's a little early to be talking about that stuff."

"It's never too early to figure out what you want. I made that mistake when I married your father. I jumped blindly into it, and look where it got me."

"Well, that's not me. My eyes are wide open right now, and what I want is Sean."

"Does he know you were a wild child?"

She shot her mom a look. "Did you really have to bring that up? Can't you see that I've changed."

"I can see that," Mom replied. "I just think honesty is the best policy."

"He knows, Mom."

"Well, good."

A little gnawing started in her stomach then. Sean knew about the things she had done before she became a Christian, but the rest of it—her night with Ben, her attempted seduction of Simon—she had not admitted to him. She feared that it would change things between them, and everything was going so well. Why bring that up and risk ruining it?

"It *is* good," she said, more to herself than to her mom. "Sean's one of the good ones."

Sean wandered into the kitchen at that moment. "Did I hear my name?" He came up behind Michelle and rested his hands on her hips and his chin on her shoulder.

Michelle turned her head, brushing her cheek against his. "You might have."

"Can I help with anything?" he asked.

She shook her head. "We've got it covered."

"OK." He kissed her earlobe, which he knew drove her crazy.

She gave him a warning look, and he walked away laughing.

Mom looked over at her with a grin on her face.

"What?" Michelle went back to chopping lettuce for the salad.

"You sure are cute together. It's too bad it didn't work out back in college."

"I know." Michelle thought the same thing. "But I really think it's gonna work this time."

Her mom nodded. "I'm rooting for you two."

"Thanks, Mom." It was probably the first time she ever felt like they were really bonding like a mother and daughter should.

Marv arrived home from work just as they finished placing the food on the table.

"It's raining cats and dogs out there," he stated. "Looks like a pretty big thunderstorm tonight, probably tomorrow, too."

"Not surprising with how hot and humid it is out there today," Louise replied.

They chatted about the weather throughout dinner. It was supposed to rain on Saturday, but clear up for Sunday. This was the type of conversation Michelle was used to when it came to visits with Mom and Marv. They liked to discuss the weather and the mundane details of life, never anything too serious.

The kids were bored stiff, but they ate quietly while the adults talked.

Michelle and Sean exchanged smiles throughout dinner. She had warned him the conversation might be like this, and she could tell he was trying not to laugh at how right she had been.

After dinner, the kids settled in front of the television, and Mom insisted on doing the dishes herself. Marvin sat in his favorite chair and split his attention between the newspaper and whatever television show the kids were watching.

Michelle and Sean disappeared into the guest room to discuss the sleeping arrangements.

"If Ashley doesn't mind, she and I can sleep in the bed," Michelle suggested as she walked into the room.

Sean clicked the door closed behind them.

She raised an eyebrow at him as he approached. "Or maybe you'd rather I take the couch."

He shook his head and slid his arms around her waist, his hands flat against her back, pulling her closer.

"You and Aaron could take the bed, and Ashley could sleep on the air mattress." She gave a little chuckle at that.

"Oh, she'd love that." He was cute when he was sarcastic.

She moved her hands over his shoulders, up the back of his neck, and lost her fingers in his dark, wavy hair.

"Or we could just kick the kids out of the room altogether," he teased.

She felt the full meaning of his words. *Oh boy, he was going to be difficult to resist.*

He slid his hands up her back, burying them in her hair, as his lips met hers.

When he kissed her like this, she knew without a doubt that he was the only man she wanted to kiss for the rest of her life.

His hands slid down her back again and gripped the back of her shirt as he kissed her deeply.

She returned the kiss with just as much passion, until her phone suddenly rang.

Sean groaned against her mouth.

She placed a finger against his lips. "Hold that thought," she breathed.

He kissed her finger.

She retrieved her phone from her purse, but didn't recognize the number. "Hello?"

A small, soft voice spoke on the other end of the line. "Is this Michelle?"

"It is."

There was no response.

"May I ask who's calling?"

The girl cleared her throat. "This is Ava."

Ava? My sister, Ava?

"Ava? Is everything OK?"

Once again, silence.

"Hello? Can you hear me? Did the call get dropped?"

"I can hear you," Ava replied.

"Are you all right?"

"Can I come to Michigan to see you?"

"Ava, I'm not in Michigan right now. I'm visiting my mom in the city."

"That's perfect!" The level of Ava's voice raised. "I'll be in the city tomorrow. Can I meet you somewhere?"

"You're coming to the city? With Dad?" Michelle did not want to see him.

"No. With my mom."

Michelle had never met Ava's mom, Betsy. She wasn't sure she wanted to meet her now. Sean came up behind her just then and rested his hands on her waist, and it gave her strength. "All right. We're going to the aquarium in the morning. Could you meet at Millennium Park after lunch? Say two o'clock?"

"Yeah. I'll be there."

Something in her sister's voice sounded shaky and uncertain. "Are you sure you're OK, Ava?"

"I will be when I see you."

When they hung up, she turned to Sean with a look of confusion on her face.

"What was that all about?" he asked.

She shrugged her shoulders. "I guess I'm gonna see my little sister tomorrow for the second time ever."

"How old is she now?"

Michelle thought about it for a minute. "I think she's twelve." She was shaking a little.

"Hey," Sean took her in his arms. "Are you OK?"

Michelle moved to sit on the bed. "You know, I was always so mad at my dad for getting a new family and for never letting me be part of Ava's life, but I never made an effort to know her. I didn't even try. And I never really stopped to think about how that must have made her feel. I just couldn't bring myself to reach out to her. It never occurred to me that one day she might want to reach out to me."

Sean sat close to her and wrapped his arm around behind her, resting his hand on her waist.

She leaned into his side.

"Your sister's growing up, and she's starting to make decisions about her own life now. If she wants you to be a part of it, then that's a huge blessing. For both of you."

"You're right." She turned and took his face in her hands and kissed him softly. "Thank you."

"*Mmm.* You are more than welcome."

With sticky humidity, rain, and thunderstorms off and on, it wasn't the best day to wander about the city. It was, however, the perfect day for a visit to Shedd Aquarium.

"I should've invited Ava to come along with us this morning." Michelle regretted not asking, but everything had happened so quickly that it hadn't crossed her mind until they hung up.

"Who's Ava?" Ashley looked at her curiously.

"Oh," Michelle glanced her way. "Ava's my little sister."

"I didn't know you had a sister."

"I do. She's my half sister. And she's close to your age, actually."

Ashley perked up a little at this. "Do I get to meet her?"

Michelle nodded. "We're meeting her after lunch."

Aaron tugged Ashley's arm and led her to some brightly colored fish that he was enamored by.

Sean's fingers threaded through Michelle's. "I haven't been here since Ashley was five and Aaron was just a baby."

"I was probably five the last time I was here. We went with school, I think." She could barely remember that day.

Michelle watched as Aaron and Ashley caught up with her mom and Marv to see what they were looking at. She was surprised when Mom said they wanted to join them on this outing. She had never done anything like this with her mom—not when she was a child, not when she was a teenager. Louise doted on Aaron and Ashley, as if they were part of the family, and Michelle got a glimpse of how it might be if she ever gave her mother a grandchild.

This thought made her glance over at Sean, who was also watching the kids. He really was a handsome man, and she imagined the adorable brown-haired, blue-eyed babies they would have together. Or maybe they would have brown eyes like her. No doubt they would be tall, maybe basketball players. She smiled to herself. Her thoughts were taking her to places she had never visited before, and she liked it.

She let go of Sean's hand and wound her arms around his waist, leaning into him as they walked. He wrapped his arms around her and kissed her temple.

"Can we see the dolphins now?" Aaron cried.

Michelle chuckled at his enthusiasm.

"Of course," Sean replied, and off they went.

215

૭૭૦ ♡ ୯૯

On their way out the aquarium doors, Michelle thought she heard someone call her name.

A young girl with the same brown eyes as hers and a thin nose like their dad's scurried up the steps. Her dark, chestnut hair was dripping wet from the drizzle.

Ava.

"You're Michelle, right?" She nervously tucked a loose hair behind her ear. In her grip was a damp, folded piece of paper with Michelle's Facebook profile picture printed on it. It was sad that her own sister had to look her up online to see what she looked like now.

"Hi, Ava."

Ava sighed with relief and gave her big sister an awkward hug.

Michelle squeezed her extra tight and held on longer than a casual hug would be, but Ava didn't seem to mind.

Sean held the umbrella over their heads to keep them dry.

When they let go, Michelle glanced at her watch. "We were supposed to meet at Millennium Park. Where's your mom?"

"She couldn't come," Ava answered. "She told me to go ahead on my own."

"Your mom let you come into the city alone?" Michelle found this a little peculiar. Not that she didn't wander all over the city when she was Ava's age, but as far as she knew, Ava had never lived in the city.

"I took the train."

"You took the train from Naperville? Have you taken the train by yourself before?"

"All the time."

Michelle didn't know whether to believe her or not, but she was there. She was safe. How she got there didn't matter.

"This is my mom, Louise, and her boyfriend, Marv. And this is my boyfriend, Sean, and his kids, Ashley and Aaron."

Ava looked uncomfortable. "I didn't know you were here with a bunch of people. I'm sorry to interrupt your trip."

"It's all right. I'm happy to see you."

Ava's face lit up. "So am I."

The group traveled by taxi to The Cheesecake Factory for lunch. The wind whipped between the buildings causing the vehicle to sway. Rain came down in sheets, and they could barely see out the windows. Lightning flashed immediately followed by a loud clap of thunder, and the younger girls both screamed at the same time.

Everyone got a good laugh at that, and the girls began chattering and instantly bonded as girls their age often do.

The conversation over lunch was light. The adults talked about the weather. What else? Ashley and Ava were fast friends, and they spent lunch showing each other photos, games, and apps on their phones. Aaron couldn't stop talking about the dolphins and his other favorite, the frogs.

After lunch, they all headed back to the apartment.

The kids settled in the living room with games, television, and their phones.

Michelle stood in the doorway to the kitchen. "Ava, do you have to head home soon? I thought maybe we could talk before we get you to the train."

Her sister looked over at her. "Oh, I don't have to be back tonight. Mom said if it was OK with you, I could stay here."

Michelle glanced over her shoulder at her mother, who had been listening from her seat at the table.

"It's fine with me," Louise said.

"OK, that's fine. Call your mom and let her know we'd like you to spend the day with us tomorrow. We can take you to the train on our way home."

Ava smiled at her. "OK. Thanks."

A little past midnight, Michelle heard the apartment phone ringing in the other room, then shuffling of feet from Mom and Marv's room.

"Hello?" Marv's voice was groggy from sleep. "Who? Yeah, she's here." There was a pause. "What? She did no such thing. Your daughter's safe in our apartment. You have nothing to worry about." His voice was louder and more firm.

Michelle climbed from the bed, careful not to wake the girls, and walked into the dark living room. "Marv?" she whispered. "What's going on?"

"Well, you're gonna have to take that up with her." Marv looked grumpy.

Louise joined them and clicked on the table lamp. "Who is it?"

Marv shoved the phone in her direction. "It's your ex-husband." He marched back to the bedroom and shut the door.

"What's going on, Robert?" She looked over at Michelle with concern as she listened. "Ava's here. She's sleeping right now, but she's fine."

"What's he saying?" Michelle whispered.

"Michelle did not plan this. It was all Ava's doing."

Michelle got a nervous feeling then, and she knew that Ava was there without permission. She had taken the train to Chicago, to her, without anyone knowing. *Oh, Ava.*

"No, we are not gonna wake her right now. We will get her home safely tomorrow."

Michelle could hear her dad yelling on the other end. His go-to reaction to everything.

"That's completely idiotic. Let her sleep. She's not going anywhere." Another long pause while Louise listened to her overreacting ex. "Fine. I'll tell her." She pulled the phone away from her ear suddenly.

Michelle could hear the dial tone from where she stood. Dad had hung up on her.

Louise rolled her eyes as she returned the cordless phone to the charger. "Your father is coming into the city tomorrow to collect his runaway daughter."

Michelle sank into the nearby chair. Her Mom turned off the lamp and shuffled back to the bedroom, leaving her sitting in the dark.

"Hey." Sean's voice came from the direction of the couch, his makeshift bed. "Are you OK?"

Michelle shrugged.

He motioned for her to join him, so she stood and walked quietly to the couch. He pulled her onto his lap and wrapped her up in his arms.

"I can't believe she did this. It's the sort of thing I would've done when I was her age. I just pray she's not turning out like I did."

"Don't be so hard on yourself. You turned out just fine." He pressed his lips to her temple and tightened his arms around her.

She settled into him and closed her eyes, relaxing with every rise and fall of his chest.

He leaned against the back of the couch and flipped the blanket over the both of them. "We can sort it all out in the morning," he whispered.

"*Mhmm.*" She vaguely remembered making that sound before she drifted off to sleep in his arms.

⅋ ♡ ⅌

It was still dark outside the window when her eyes opened. Sean's breath was hot against her face. They had shifted from their seated position to lying down at some point in the night. He was still asleep and peacefully so. One arm was under his head while the other rested across her hip. Their legs were intertwined, which was probably the only reason she hadn't fallen backwards off the couch during the night.

She leaned back and let her eyes adjust to the darkness. When Sean came into focus, she smiled to herself. His lips were slightly parted, steady breaths flowing in and out, chest pressing against hers with every intake. His five o'clock shadow made him look more attractive than usual, if that was possible.

She relaxed into him again and brushed her lips against his. She really should have let him sleep, but she couldn't help it.

He stirred, wrapping his arm around her as his eyelids lifted. "Good morning," he whispered. He stretched his arm out behind her, then tightened it around her again. His lips found hers for a slow, tender kiss. "*Mmm.* I could get used to this."

"My thoughts exactly," she whispered.

They laughed softly, careful not to wake Aaron, who was sleeping on the floor nearby.

"I should probably get up soon." She brushed her nose against his. "I really wanna talk to Ava before my dad comes to get her."

Sean groaned as he reluctantly released her.

As she walked toward the bathroom, she glanced back over her shoulder at him flirtatiously.

He buried his head in the blanket.

Michelle sat across the table from her little sister, who was devouring scrambled eggs and sausage. "Why would you take off by yourself without telling anyone?"

Ava shrugged and kept eating, like she didn't care if she got in trouble or not.

"Is something going on at home?" Michelle looked at her searchingly.

Ava shook her head and nibbled on a slice of toast.

"Ava, I really need to know. Dad will be here soon, and I want to help you if you need it."

"I can take care of myself," Ava declared.

"I'm sure you can. I wasn't saying that." Ava sounded exactly like she had at that age, and that worried her. "I just need to know if there's a problem."

Ava set her fork down. "I just wanted to see my big sister. Isn't that a good enough reason?"

Michelle smiled at that. "It's a good reason, Ava, but you went about it the wrong way. Don't you know how worried your parents have been? They didn't know where you ran off to. Can you put yourself in their shoes for a minute and think about how they must have felt?"

"I know. But every time I ask about seeing you, they shut me down."

This angered Michelle. "You've asked before?"

"All the time."

"Why won't they let you see me?"

"They don't have a good reason, really. They're just too busy to take me all the way to Michigan, or they have to work, or maybe you don't wanna see me, or some other lame excuse."

"Why would I not wanna see you?" Michelle asked.

"Because of what you said to Dad the last time you saw him."

"You remember that day?"

Ava shook her head. "Not really. I remember meeting you, and I remember crying."

"Why were you crying?"

"Because I thought it was my fault that you left. I thought I did something wrong." Ava picked up her fork then and pushed the remaining bits of egg around on her plate.

"Oh, Ava, that wasn't the reason. It was because of Dad."

Ava looked over at her. "Really? Because I thought you hated me for being Dad's favorite or something."

Michelle let out a breath. "I don't really know our dad, Ava. He left when I was a little girl, and he never looked back."

"Because he didn't love your mom anymore?"

"And because he didn't love me."

"That's not true." Louise shuffled into the room then.

Michelle glanced over at her mom. "Whatever."

Louise stopped next to the table and looked seriously at Michelle. "Your father left because we were never really in love with each other. We jumped into marriage for all the wrong reasons. But he loved you, Michelle. There was no mistaking that."

"How can you even say that? He hated being home, especially being around me. A kid can tell when her own dad doesn't care about her."

"Well, he wasn't the best at showing it, but you were the reason he stuck around as long as he did. If not for you, we probably wouldn't have made it past our first anniversary."

Michelle stared at her mom, her mouth agape. She didn't know what to say. "Why didn't you ever tell me that before?"

"I didn't wanna face it for a long time. It took a while for me to accept the fact that we were doomed from the start. But once I got some distance, I saw the whole thing very clearly. We were already on a rough path by the end of the first year, then I found out I was pregnant. The pregnancy made things better for a while. We were excited about you. And your dad, oh, he was so happy when you were born. You were the light of his life."

Tears burned Michelle's eyes, but she was determined not to cry over her dad. "But he always left. Even when I cried and begged him to stay."

"That was my fault, not yours. He just couldn't stand me anymore. And I think the older you got, the more you reminded him of me and the years he wasted with a woman he didn't love."

"Mom, how can you talk about this so calmly? How are you not breaking down right now?"

"A few decades of distance and perspective, I guess."

"Dad leaves me a lot, too," Ava said quietly.

Michelle glanced over at her sister. "Really?"

Ava nodded. "He works all the time."

"Do he and your mom still get along?"

"Yeah. They don't fight or anything like that, but I can tell she's not happy when he goes away on business trips. And he doesn't really have time for me like he used to."

Michelle could feel herself tensing up, her fists tightening. "I can't believe him. Is that why you ran away?"

"I didn't run away," Ava stated. "Not really. I told you. I wanted to see you. I was sick of not knowing my sister."

There was a knock on the door just then, and Michelle tensed up even more.

Louise went to answer it, and Michelle exchanged glances with her sister.

"You should probably go pack up your things," Michelle told her. "I'll talk to him first."

"OK." Ava skittered off to the guest room, where Ashley was getting ready.

Michelle cleared the plates from the table. She could hear her parents talking in the hallway by the door, which was very strange for her. It had been many years since her parents were in the same place at the same time. At least there was no yelling ... yet.

Robert and Louise walked further into the apartment and joined Michelle in the kitchen.

"Michelle, how are you?" Her father gave her a hint of a polite smile, but it didn't appear sincere.

"Not great, Dad."

"I'm sorry to hear that. I hope your sister hasn't done anything to upset you. She's getting to be a bit of a handful for us." He rubbed his palm against his black hair, which Michelle noticed had quite a bit of grey to it now.

"Well, I guess if she's too much trouble, it must be time to walk away. That's what you're best at, after all."

He looked as though he was going to speak, but he held his tongue. "Is she ready to go?"

"In a minute. I want to know why you haven't let her come to see me before. She said she's asked you several times. Why would you keep her from me?"

He didn't answer at first.

"Why?" Michelle demanded.

"I know what kind of girl you were at her age. I didn't want you to be a bad influence on her."

Michelle began to laugh. She couldn't stop herself. He had no idea what he was talking about, basing a decision on what she was like as a teenager.

"It's not funny," he said.

"No, it isn't. But, honestly, Dad, you don't know me at all. You don't know what I've been through, what I've overcome. You don't know what I've done to fill the void you left in my heart. You don't know that I found a better life, friends who love me for who I am, and faith in God, who forgave me for all those bad things I did because of you. You're far worse for your daughter than I would ever be. You don't know me, so don't pretend that you do."

He stared at her in disbelief. "I didn't know," he stuttered.

"You've never tried to know me, Dad. You didn't care enough about me to try."

"That's where you're wrong." He stepped toward her. "I cared more about what happened to you than anything else in my life."

Her heart skipped a beat.

"Why do you think I got your grandparents to pay for your tuition?"
What?

"I saw my little girl self-destructing right before my eyes. Do you think that was easy for me? Do you think I didn't know that it was my absence that caused it all?"

Michelle was now the speechless one. She had always assumed it was her grandparents and her mother who were behind the plan.

"I'm very happy to hear that getting you out of this city did change your life for the better. That's all I ever wanted for you."

Tears sprang to her eyes.

He took a tentative step toward her, then another. And before she knew it, her dad was hugging her. She stood limp at first, her arms hanging at her sides.

"You may not believe this, Michelle, but I do love you. And I'm very sorry for everything."

Her body began to shake as she cried, and he held her for a long time, before she finally wrapped her arms around him and hugged him back.

"I'm sorry," he whispered.

She swallowed hard and made the decision she knew God wanted her to. "I forgive you."

✿ ♡ ✿

Never in her wildest dreams would Michelle have imagined strolling along Michigan Avenue with her mother *and* her father, but that was the reality of the day. Instead of snatching Ava and heading home right away, Robert gave in to his youngest daughter's pleas after she, Ashley, and Aaron emerged from the guest room holding handmade cards for Father's Day.

With all the chaos, Michelle had forgotten that it was Father's Day. Of all possible days, *this* was the one God chose for her and her father to start the healing process. She was amazed at how God cared about the little details like that.

As they walked along the sidewalk toward Millennium Park on their way to visit Cloud Gate—or The Bean, as it had been nicknamed—Sean took her hand and slowed his step so they were behind the group.

"I'm proud of you." He kissed the back of her hand. "That wasn't an easy conversation to have with your dad, but you held it together."

"My mouth just kind of took off, and I couldn't stop it."

He laughed. "You sounded very confident to me, not at all out of control."

"Well, thanks."

"And you were honest with him about your life. He needed to hear it."

She nodded. This was the second time in as many days that someone had brought up honesty. She was beginning to think God was trying to tell her something, and that terrified her. Because if she told the truth—the whole truth—Sean might not be so quick to shell out the compliments, and he might not offer her the forgiveness she needed him to.

"You're quiet." Sean squeezed her hand. "Is everything OK? Are you OK with your dad being here?"

"I never thought I'd say this, but I'm glad he's here. It's been a good day."

The kids ran ahead as The Bean came into sight. The sculpture looked like a giant silver bean, which was obviously where it got its nickname. It was fun to look at the city skyline reflected and distorted in its surface. The girls immediately began taking photos of their reflections and crawling under it for more pictures. The adults observed from a distance.

Robert walked over and stood next to Michelle and Sean. "Ava seems to have found a friend in your daughter there, Sean."

"I think you're right," Sean replied.

"She could use some friends."

"Why do you say that?" Michelle asked.

"She doesn't have any."

Michelle found this strange. "I'm sure she has friends, Dad. Just because you don't know them, doesn't mean they don't exist. She doesn't talk about anyone from school?"

"She's home schooled," he admitted.

"Oh."

Robert shook his head in dismay. "I think because of how you were at Ava's age, I overcompensated with her. I wanted to protect her from the same kind of bad friends, so we kept her home. She hasn't had a lot of social interaction with other kids."

"Well, I'm happy she and Ashley found each other then," Michelle replied.

Robert nodded. "And I think it will be very good for her to have you in her life."

"Thank you for saying that, Dad."

He nodded and looked toward The Bean. "Your mom seems happy."

Michelle glanced over at Louise and Marv, who had joined the kids for some selfie-taking in front of the sculpture. "She is." Her attention turned back to her dad. "How about you? Are you happy with Betsy?"

"I'm not an easy man to live with, Michelle."

"Don't I know it." The sarcastic comment slipped out of her mouth before she caught it. "I'm sorry I said that."

"At least I'm man enough to admit it now. Betsy puts up with a lot, and she loves me in spite of everything. She's a good woman, and I'm lucky to have her."

"But are you happy?"

He looked at her seriously for a few moments. "I don't think I am."

The creases between her eyebrows revealed her concern.

"Don't get me wrong, I'm happy with Betsy and Ava, but I don't think I've found the kind of joy in life that you have. Not yet anyway."

"Jesus is the reason, Dad. He changed my life. You can have that kind of joy, too. It's there for the taking, all you have to do is believe and accept salvation through Him."

"I'll keep that in mind."

She smiled at her father, and he smiled back. She wanted nothing more in that moment than for him to come to know Christ.

"Michelle!" Ava's cry interrupted her thoughts.

"Dad!" Ashley and Aaron yelled simultaneously.

The kids motioned for them to come take some pictures.

Michelle looked over at her dad.

"Go on," he told them.

She grinned and walked with Sean to join the kids.

"I want one of just the two of us in front of The Bean," Ava told her.

Ashley took the phone from Ava, who positioned Michelle in just the right spot, wrapped her arms around her, and smiled for the camera.

Michelle hugged her and smiled for the dozen pictures that Ashley took of them together.

"I'll send you the best one," Ava said as she took her phone back from Ashley.

Michelle put her arm around her little sister. "I'd love one."

Robert walked over to them then.

Ava glanced at their dad. "Is it time to go already?"

He nodded.

Ava's shoulders dropped. "No, it's too early. Can't we just stay a couple more hours?"

He gave her a stern look. "We need to get home, Ava. Your mom will worry."

"Just an hour then?"

Michelle turned to her. "Don't worry. We'll see each other again soon."

"Really?"

"Of course."

"Can I text you?"

"Whenever you need to." Michelle hugged her tightly. "I'm here for you whenever you need me."

🌿25🌿

After the successful Chicago trip, the strains of a long distance relationship began to wear on Michelle. Sean's schedule grew busy with the kids' summer activities, church camp, and a vacation with his in-laws. Over the course of the next two months, their communication consisted of a series of phone calls and many hours on Skype, which he finally figured out with a little help from Aaron. Even on nights when they weren't able to talk until midnight, they still made time. It was not ideal, but they did their best.

In late August, the day after Michelle's birthday, Sean and the kids came to Grand Rapids with his brother's family to move Alex into the dorm. Michelle was giddy at work that Friday waiting for Sean to call. She stared at the phone for the last twenty minutes of her work day willing it to ring.

"Excuse me, miss."

She would know that voice anywhere. Her office chair spun around as she leapt up and ran around the desk to greet him. She wished their long-awaited reunion could have happened somewhere a little more private, but she kissed him anyway, and he returned the favor.

"Oh my gosh! I missed you so much." She wrapped her arms around him and held him as tightly as she could.

He did the same.

After dinner with the whole family, the kids returned to the hotel with their aunt, uncle, and cousins to do a little swimming, while Sean and Michelle went to her apartment for some alone time.

She couldn't get the key into the lock fast enough, and she fumbled with it even more when he brushed her hair to the side and pressed his lips to the nape of her neck. Her eyes closed, making it impossible to unlock the darn door. His hands rested on her hips, and he moved his mouth to her earlobe. She dropped her keys and turned into him, finding his lips. They kissed slowly for long minutes leaning against her apartment door, until they were both breathless.

"Oh, I've missed you," he whispered against her mouth.

"I've missed you, too."

"But maybe I shouldn't come in." He let out a slow, shaky breath. Her look was a question.

"I mean, look at us. We can't even get through the door."

She raised an eyebrow at him and grinned.

"Besides, we won't be here long."

"Oh, really?" Her eyebrow remained raised.

"I wanna take you somewhere special for your birthday."

That brought a smile to her face. She retrieved the keys from the ground and opened the door. "I just wanna change first. Are you really gonna stand out here?"

He smiled. "I'll behave. I promise."

Once inside, he kept his word. They chatted about his trip over and how excited Alex was for his freshman year. She mentioned her job, which bridged to the topic of the counselor that Sean and the kids had been seeing for the past couple months. He shared about their latest session. It was helping. They were talking, letting their feelings out about the accident, finally dealing with it all.

This pleased Michelle. She had been thinking a lot about counseling lately and about her job. She wanted to do more. Ever since the night at Sean's when Ashley snuck off to that party and the day Ava hopped the train into the city by herself, she had an overwhelming urge to help them. It was like an instinct within her. And the possibility of helping other girls their age filled her heart with joy.

Michelle wanted to have a serious conversation with Sean about this. She really hoped that they could discuss their relationship and where things were going. She had been thinking and praying about the next step in her life, and if Sean was going to be a part of it, she needed his input.

She changed from her work clothes into something more casual, and they headed to the mystery location.

"I need to talk to you about something," she blurted as he drove along the highway. "Something big. I'm very excited about it, but I wanted to talk to you first, before I make any plans."

He looked sideways at her. "What is it?"

"I've decided to go back to school to get my masters in counseling."

His eyes widened. "Michelle, that's amazing. You will be so great at that."

"I just haven't been able to stop thinking about that first conversation I had with Ashley and how much I wanted to help her. I've been praying about it so much lately, and I really believe this is what God wants me to do. I feel like I've finally found my purpose."

"I'm so happy for you." He was beaming. "I've been praying for you."

"You have?" This made her heart ache in a good way.

"Of course. I always do."

Sean turned the car into the drive of Frederik Meijer Gardens.

Michelle smiled at him. "You know, I haven't been back here since our first date."

"Really? But it's so close to the college."

"I know." She shrugged. "I just couldn't bring myself to come back without you."

They bought tickets and walked out along the path. There were many new sculptures that weren't there fifteen years before, including the twenty-four-foot tall horse sculpture, built to Leonardo DaVinci's original design.

Michelle walked over and stood beneath the giant horse. "It's huge!" She stared up at it.

Sean laughed and joined her next to the horse's uplifted front leg.

They walked around and under the sculpture, admiring the detail of the horse's head, the lines of its muscles, and the curls in its mane.

"Hey, take my picture." Sean lay down under the horse's right hind leg, which was lifted a foot off the ground, and pretended he was being trampled.

Michelle laughed so hard, she could barely hold her phone steady to take the picture.

They walked on along the sculpture path and stopped when they reached the waterfall pond they had sat by all those years before.

"I love this spot." She walked over and looked down into the water, watching the koi swim along under the surface.

They took a seat on the bench, and he took her hand in his, then leaned over and placed a soft kiss on her lips.

She sighed. "So, should I stay here and go to Cornerstone for my masters or should I find a school in Chicago?" Her question was abrupt and pointed, but she thought it might lead to a more serious conversation.

He looked over at her, but said nothing. He looked like he was mulling things over, but as the seconds stretched on silently, she thought it might be too soon to include him in a major life decision like this. She swallowed hard, feeling a little foolish.

Suddenly, Sean stood and got down on one knee in front of her. "Answer me one question first." He reached into his pocket and retrieved a little velvet box from within.

The pace of her heart increased, until it was beating wildly with panic. "Sean, what are you doing?"

"I have loved you since the first moment you walked into the gym freshman year. And now that you're back in my life, I want to make things more permanent." He opened the box to reveal a sparkling princess-cut diamond ring.

She gasped.

"Michelle, will you—"

"Wait!" Michelle laid her hand over the ring and looked at him.

His bright blue eyes were filled with confusion and a look of dread.

"Before you finish that question, there are some things I have to tell you." She grabbed for his hand and pulled him back to the bench beside her, pausing to look at the ring. "Oh my goodness. It's so beautiful." She looked into his eyes, which were now filled with uncertainty.

He bounced his knee nervously. "What things?"

She swallowed hard again and chewed on the inside of her lip, willing her heart to return to a normal rhythm.

"Michelle, please. You're killing me here."

"I don't know how to tell you this." She never wanted him to know the horrible things she had done, but a powerful force within was pushing her to confess. "If we're going to move forward ... together ... I have to be honest with you about my past."

"You can tell me anything. You know that. I know you didn't have an easy childhood, and I know you regret what you did when you were younger."

"Yes, but I've done other things since I became a Christian that I have no excuse for."

His forehead creased with worry, and he looked like he was struggling to find words, as he was apt to do. "What things have you done?" He spoke so quietly, she could barely hear him.

Her breath caught in her throat as she tried to speak. This was much harder than she thought it was going to be.

"Back when Maggie was engaged to Ben ..." She could barely get it out. She had never admitted it before, and saying the words out loud was more difficult than she ever imagined.

He waited patiently.

"We got into a fight. I got really stupid mad and jealous of her, so I went to Ben's apartment, and we ..." She couldn't say it.

A look of horror crossed his face. "You didn't."

She was so ashamed. She wanted to hide. "It gets worse."

"Worse than that?" He was staring at the ground now, obviously affected by what she had revealed.

"I made him call off their wedding."

He sank against the back of the bench. "So you could be with him?"

"No! I didn't wanna be with him at all. I slept with him that one night just to make myself feel better, which, of course, I didn't. But when I made him break up with her, I didn't do that for me. I did it for Maggie. He was cheating on her, and I couldn't let him ruin her life."

"Does she know about this?"

Michelle shook her head sadly and sniffled. "I've never told anyone about this."

Sean didn't speak.

"There's more."

She felt his shoulders sag deeper.

"When Simon and I were together and I thought I was losing him, I tried to seduce him to get him to stay." She glanced over at Sean. The disappointment was written all over his face.

"So, you and Simon ... you didn't ...?" He was fidgeting now.

"No!" She shook her head vehemently.

Sean sat forward and leaned his elbows on his knees.

"I knew it was wrong. I was just so jealous, I couldn't see straight. I hurt Maggie and Simon, and I failed God and myself."

"I'm no expert, but I'd say you could use a little counseling yourself."

She hung her head.

"I didn't mean that the way it sounded." He wouldn't look at her. "But there are reasons why you did those things. Reasons that probably have a lot to do with your childhood. You need to work through that. Counseling really has helped me and the kids. You should take your own advice and try it."

She nodded weakly. "I'm so sorry I didn't tell you all of this sooner. I was afraid it would change things between us."

He was quiet.

"Has it?"

He shifted on the bench, clearly uncomfortable.

All she wanted was for him to tell her they were going to be OK, but his silence spoke volumes. "It has, hasn't it? I ruined this."

There were several long minutes of silence before Sean spoke again.

"I think you need to make things right with Maggie. It seems like you've been carrying the burden of that secret around with you all these years, and you need to deal with it before you can move forward."

She wished he had said *we* rather than *you*. The tears began to burn her eyes, and her throat felt like it was closing up.

"And I need some time ... to process all of this."

Unexpected sobs suddenly hit her.

Sean wrapped his arms around her, and she buried her head in his chest. He held her while she cried. And, oh, how she cried. Sob after sob ripped through her body uncontrollably as she released all the tension over secrets held too long, disappointment in the night's unexpected turn of events, and fear that she had lost Sean once again.

When the crying subsided, he kissed the top of her head and let her go.

She turned away from him and wiped at her wet cheeks.

He clicked the velvet ring box closed, and she startled at the sound.

A weak laugh escaped him. "Not exactly how I saw this night playing out."

She turned to look at him just as he tucked the box back into his pocket. It felt like the end of more than just the perfect proposal.

"I should take you home."

She stood when he did and walked with him along the sidewalk to the park exit. He didn't take her hand, and the space between them felt like more than mere inches.

The drive home was silent. When they reached her apartment, he walked her to the door. "We'll talk soon, OK?"

"OK." She wasn't sure how she managed to reply.

He started to walk away, but suddenly turned and pulled her into his embrace.

She wrapped her arms around his back and locked them together, burying her head in his chest. When he started to pull away, she squeezed tighter. If this was it, she wanted to hold onto him for as long as she possibly could.

His arms loosened. "Goodbye, Michelle."

The air rushed out of her lungs. She dropped her arms and backed away, staring at him in disbelief. It was the worst possible thing he could have said to her.

His expression changed as realization came over him, and his shoulders sank. "Michelle." His voice pleaded for forgiveness.

Crocodile tears slid down her cheeks. "You know how I feel about goodbyes."

She quickly unlocked her door and escaped inside.

"I'm sorry." His words muffled through the door.

She threw herself down on the couch cushions and sobbed until she fell asleep from exhaustion.

The entire weekend was miserable. She spent all of Saturday in the same place she had fallen asleep. Sunday, she dragged herself into the shower, but didn't make it to church. She lay on her bed for much of the day staring at her ceiling, praying for God to give her the strength to make it through this. On Monday, she called in sick to work. She was physically and emotionally spent, but she knew this was the day she needed to drive to Hastings to talk to Maggie. Sean was right. She had hidden the truth for far too long. It was time.

When she parked in an empty space in front of Maggie's shop, her stomach churned nervously. She didn't want to get out of her car. She stared up at the Magnolia Photography sign. *Please help me, Lord.* She took a deep breath and went inside.

Sarah glanced up from behind her desk. A look of surprise crossed her face. "Hi, Michelle. How are you?"

"I'm fine. Is Maggie in?"

"She's on a call with a bride right now. Do you have time to wait?"

Michelle held her purse in a death grip. "Sure." She wandered over to the seating area toward the front of the shop and sat in a wingback chair to wait. This was the first time she had been in Maggie's shop since her almost wedding to Ben. Had it really been that long? The space had changed a lot since she first moved in. The walls were now lined with photos of gorgeous flowers and wedding cakes and happy couples. She stared at a candid photo of one of the couples sitting together on the steps of The Grand Hotel on Mackinac Island. They looked perfectly happy and in love, and it made her heart ache. She had blown any chance she had of a moment like that with Sean.

Sarah stood then and peeked through the french doors that led into Maggie's office. "Michelle is here."

Maggie came out with a big smile on her face. "Michelle! I'm so happy to see you."

"Me, too," Michelle managed as she stood.

"What brings you to town?"

Michelle didn't answer at first.

"I don't even care." Maggie suddenly hugged her. "I'm just so glad you're here."

Michelle held onto her dear friend, more afraid than ever to say what she came to say. "I just ... wanted to talk to you about something."

"I need to talk to you about something, too." Maggie motioned to the seating area.

"Um ..." Michelle glanced over at Sarah. "Maybe we could talk somewhere more private."

Maggie's forehead scrunched up. "OK. We can talk in my office if you want."

Michelle nodded.

"Do you want something to drink?"

"No, I'm fine. Thanks."

They walked into the office, and Maggie turned to Sarah. "Can you take a message if anyone calls?" She closed the doors behind them.

Maggie plopped down in her office chair. "I was afraid we would never talk again. And I want you to know how sorry I am about what happened with me and Simon when you two were together."

"I know." Michelle's eye was suddenly drawn to the sizable diamond on Maggie's left ring finger. "What is *that*?" She stared at the rock.

Maggie hesitantly held her hand out to Michelle. "That's what I wanted to talk to you about."

"Wow! You're engaged? I didn't know you were dating anyone. Who's the lucky guy?"

"Simon," Maggie revealed.

Michelle was dumbfounded. "Simon? I thought he moved to California."

"Well, he was going to, but I asked him not to go." She could barely contain her smile.

"So, he was wrong," Michelle said.

"Wrong?"

"Last time I talked to him, I asked about you. He told me that you didn't want him."

Maggie glanced down at her ring. "I did tell him that. I was so afraid of being hurt again. I just wanted someone who would be faithful to me, but I thought I couldn't trust him. I thought he slept with his assistant, so I pushed him away. But I was wrong."

"Simon wouldn't do that." The memory of the night she tried to get him into bed rushed back.

"I know that now. He really does love me."

"I know he does."

"And I love him." She paused. "I hope this isn't too uncomfortable for you to talk about."

"Not at all. I'm very happy for you both."

"We're getting married in March," Maggie announced with a deliriously happy look on her face.

"That's fast." She thought of her six-month, long-distance relationship with Sean and the near proposal, and her heart ached.

"I know, but I refuse to go through another five-year engagement."

Michelle's throat went dry. "Right. Five years. That's sort of what I wanted to talk to you about."

Maggie sat back a little in her chair with a look of confusion.

Michelle clung to her purse and fiddled with the zipper. "This is really hard. I don't know where to start."

"What is it, Chelle?"

Tears burned behind her eyes, and it hurt to swallow. "I've done a lot of things in my life that I regret. You know about some of the things I did when I was younger."

Maggie nodded.

"But if there's one thing I regret most, it's this." A tear slid down her cheek, and she quickly brushed it away.

Maggie reached across the desk and laid her hand on Michelle's. "Just tell me. It can't be that bad."

"Oh, but it is."

Maggie continued to look at her with the tender look of a true friend, and Michelle almost changed her mind. She tried to think up a quick excuse, but a little voice whispered. *Tell her.*

"Do you remember how upset I was the day of your bridal shower? It was after that terrible weekend seeing my dad, and you and I were still upset with each other."

"Yeah, I remember that."

"Remember how I took off that night? I was so ticked off, and I yelled at you and stormed out?"

Maggie nodded. "I remember that, too."

"I left because I was jealous."

"Jealous? Of what? Of me?"

"I was always jealous of you and your relationship with your family. Your life seemed so perfect, and everything always seemed to go your way."

"Oh, Michelle."

"And I was jealous because I was in love with Simon, and I knew deep down that he was in love with you."

Maggie pressed her lips together.

"It's always been you, Maggie, ever since college. And that was the day I finally got him to admit that he cared about you. It made me crazy jealous and so angry."

"It's OK, Chelle. I understand. We all get jealous sometimes." Maggie squeezed Michelle's hand.

"When I left the apartment that night, I went to the one person I knew I shouldn't. The one person I knew would hurt you the most." She paused.

Say it.

I can't.

Just say it.

She closed her eyes. "I went to Ben's."

Maggie let go of her hand.

"And we slept together." Michelle opened her eyes to see Maggie's face turn white as a sheet. "And then I made him call off your wedding." Her hands were shaking now.

"Wh ... what? What are you talking about?"

"He had been cheating on you, not just with me. I was trying to save you from more pain."

Maggie struggled to keep her composure. "So, was this like an ongoing thing with you two?"

"No. It was just the once."

Tears filled Maggie's eyes. "And that's supposed to make it all right?"

"No, Maggie. It's *not* all right. That's why I'm telling you. I did a terrible thing, and I'm so sorry. You have no idea how much." Her chin began to quiver. "I've been holding this in for all these years, and I should have told you the truth a long time ago, but I was scared."

"Get out," Maggie ordered.

"I came here to ask for your forgiveness. I know it was a horrible, unforgivable thing that I did, but it happened so long ago, and now you have Simon, and—"

"Get out!" Maggie yelled. She had lost her usual kind demeanor.

Michelle had never seen that look in Maggie's eyes before. It was anger, hurt, and betrayal all rolled into one. It was like she was looking at a whole different person.

"Maggie, please."

"Get out of here! Get out of my life!"

Tears streaked down Michelle's cheeks as she bolted out of the building. She had done what she knew God wanted her to do. She had told the truth, but her worst fears were realized. She had lost Maggie in the process. And she didn't blame her one bit.

When she arrived home, the pesky light on the answering machine was blinking.

"Michelle." Simon used her full name, and she knew it wasn't going to be good. "How could you? How could you do that? Why did you have to ruin what's supposed to be a really happy time for us? I will never forgive you for this."

Michelle sank onto her couch. The pain in her chest was almost too much to bear.

Oh, this hurts so much, Lord. I pray one day they will find it in their hearts to forgive me.

26

$\mathcal{A}$lone.

The three most important people in her life were no longer a part of it, and she felt lost again. Only this time, it wasn't about her career. She had great plans to begin studying for her masters degree, but she had no one to share her excitement with. It put a serious damper on her plans.

She had been honest with Sean about her past, and everything had fallen apart. He said they would talk soon, but he hadn't called. As three months passed slowly by, it became more and more obvious that he wasn't coming back into her life. She wished there was something she could do, something she could say to change his mind. But if he couldn't forgive her for what she had done, especially considering what he had done with Lindsay, then he wasn't the man God had for her. That wasn't easy to accept, but she trusted God, and she believed His plan for her life was far greater than anything she could dream up for herself.

Pastor preached a wonderful sermon the Sunday before the Thanksgiving holiday all about counting your blessings. She thought seriously about that. She had her health, a place to live, and food to eat. She had a job she enjoyed and plans to get more involved in counseling through her education. And she had Jesus, the greatest blessing of all. He was more than enough to meet all of her needs. Even so, she was sad.

Her attempt to make things right with Maggie had lost her both of her best friends in one fell swoop. She couldn't imagine going through life without them. How could she embark on this new career path without their encouragement and support? She needed them.

Lord, you see straight into my heart and you know exactly how I feel. I'm missing my friends so much, and I could use a little encouragement right now.

On Thanksgiving day, she drove to Lake Michigan and sat on the beach in her winter coat, all wrapped up in a blanket. She stared out at the waves lapping against the shore. The steady, cool breeze turned her nose red, but she didn't care. In her quiet apartment, she felt alone. Sitting next to this massive body of water, she felt closer to the one who made it, the one who made her.

Something wet suddenly touched her cheek, and she turned to see a golden retriever's nose sniffing at her.

"Sammy!" his owner cried. He ran over and grabbed the dog's leash. "I'm so sorry."

Michelle petted the dog's shiny coat. "That's OK. He's cute."

The dog circled around her and sat at her feet, warming her legs.

"And friendly," Michelle said with a laugh.

"He is that," the owner replied. "I'm Mike." He was an older gentleman with salt-and-pepper hair and warm brown eyes.

"Nice to meet you." She felt a little wary of this stranger, but there was something about him, a calming presence.

"May I?" he asked, pointing at the spot next to the dog.

"Sure."

Mike sat down and petted Sammy's back. "It's a little cold for a day at the beach, isn't it?"

She nodded and laughed. "I just had to come out here to clear my head."

"Yeah, fresh lake air will do that for ya'."

"Sammy doesn't seem to mind the cold." She rubbed her fingers on the top of his head, and the dog looked at her with an understanding that surprised her. "Wow. I feel like he sees right into me. Like he knows me. Does that sound weird?"

Mike shook his head. "He's always felt like a wise old soul to me, too."

"Do you live around here?" she asked.

Mike nodded. "Just up the beach."

"How nice. I would love to live on the lake someday."

Sammy barked at some people that walked by, and they laughed.

"I hope you don't mind me saying this, but you seem troubled," Mike said.

She looked over at him, and like Sammy, she felt as if he already knew her.

"Maybe I can be of assistance. Sometimes a listening ear and a fresh perspective can be helpful."

She was hesitant, but almost without knowing, she started spilling her guts about everything—her family situation and rebellious teen years, her time at Cornerstone, the horrible betrayal, and on until the present day.

Mike listened intently to every word.

When she had finished, it was like a gigantic weight had been lifted from her.

"I can't believe I just told you all of that. I don't even know you."

Mike laughed. "People always tell me I'm a good listener. It's my gift."

She smiled.

"I have but one piece of advice for you. The Bible says 'Trust in the Lord with all thine heart, and lean not unto thine own understanding. In all thy ways acknowledge him, and he shall direct thy paths.' The book of Proverbs. I believe you *are* trusting God, young lady. He has guided you to this career in counseling, where you will do so much good for others in His name. Do not lose faith. All the rest will fall into place."

"Thank you for saying that, Mike."

He reached over and patted Sammy. "Well, we better get back. It was nice meeting you."

"You, too." She hugged Sammy and got another lick on the cheek. "Bye, Sammy."

As they were walking away, he turned back to her and said, "Keep trusting the Lord, Michelle. He loves you, and He will give you the desires of your heart."

She waved at them, then turned to face the water. *Thank you, Lord, for letting me meet them tonight. It was just what I needed, and I know you brought them to me. I'm so thankful ...*

Suddenly, she realized what Mike had said. *Keep trusting the Lord, Michelle.*

Her head whipped around to where they were walking, but they were gone. She should have still been able to see them, but they were nowhere in sight.

She started to laugh.

I never told him my name.

When she returned to her apartment, she let herself in and nearly jumped sky high when she saw Simon and Maggie seated on her couch. "Oh my gosh!" She laid her hand on her chest. It took half a minute for her heart to return to its normal rhythm.

"Sorry to scare you. I still have a key," Simon explained with a shrug.

Michelle closed the door and set her things on the kitchen table. "That's OK," she replied quietly. "What are you guys doing here?"

Maggie's eyes looked slightly puffy, like she had been crying. "We've been talking." She squeezed Simon's hand and looked into his eyes. "A lot."

He nodded at her reassuringly.

"I wanted to come here and tell you that ..." Maggie struggled to find her words.

Michelle's chin began to quiver in anticipation of what Maggie might say, what she hoped her friend would say.

"The past few months have been really hard for me. I was furious at first. Then I felt hurt and betrayed. I wanted to be angry at Ben and blame him for everything. That would have been so much easier. But you were the one that went to his place, and that was the hardest thing for me to understand. You knew how much I loved him and how much I wanted to marry him, but it was you who broke us up."

"Maggie ..." Michelle started to speak, but Maggie held her hand up.

"But the more I thought about it, the more I realized that you saved me from making a huge mistake. Ben wasn't a good guy. He was selfish and unfaithful, and I know you saw that in him long before I ever let myself see the truth."

Michelle's shoulders relaxed slightly.

"I've been talking to my mom and Vi about everything, and they both encouraged me to forgive you as God has forgiven me. I know you're sorry that you did it. And ... I forgive you, Michelle."

Michelle covered her face and wept.

Maggie stood and went to her, wrapping her arms around her friend.

"I'm so sorry, Maggie," Michelle cried.

"I know."

"If I could take it back, I would."

"I know that. But if you hadn't done it, I probably would've married him. And then where would I be today?"

Simon wrapped his arms around both of the girls then. "And where would I be? Probably still single, living in my parents' basement in California."

Their laughter broke through the tears.

Simon looked Michelle in the eyes. "Hey, I'm really sorry for what I said to you on that phone message, Michelle."

"It's OK. I deserved it."

"No, you didn't." He kissed her cheek, then released the girls from his hug.

The three of them moved to sit on the couch.

Maggie began to talk. "I've been having these weird dreams the past few weeks. Maybe they're suppressed memories or something. I don't know. But it's like I'm at the engagement party, and you're standing on the patio watching Ben. At first, I feel really jealous because you're staring at my fiancé, but then I see what you see—Ben sneaking around the side of the house into some dark corner with another girl."

"Yeah, that wasn't just a dream," Michelle interjected.

Maggie nodded sadly. "I thought so."

"You're so special, Maggie, and I always believed God had someone better for you. Someone really wonderful like you." Michelle glanced over at Simon. "But He brought you this guy instead."

"Hey!" Simon playfully smacked her arm.

She winked at him.

"I think I'll keep him." Maggie's eyes twinkled as she looked at Simon.

The three old friends sat for hours, talking and catching up. It was as if no time had passed, as if there had never been a rift between them, and the heavy burden Michelle had been carrying around for so long had lifted. She felt lighter and happier than she had in years.

The love in her friends' eyes as they looked at each other was unmistakeable, and Michelle was so happy for them and the love they had found together.

But the happiest moment came at the end of the night.

"Michelle, I have something very important to ask you." Maggie's tone was serious as she and Simon readied to leave.

"OK. Shoot."

"I was wondering ... would you be a bridesmaid in our wedding?"

Michelle's mouth dropped open. "Are you serious? After everything that happened, you would still want that?"

Maggie nodded. "Yeah, but ... I mean, would you even want to? Or is it too weird to have you stand up in your ex-boyfriend's wedding?"

Michelle looked over at Simon, her best friend.

He smiled sweetly. "What do ya' say, Chelle?"

The fact that he called her that again melted her heart. "If Simon's OK with it, I'm OK with it."

"Maybe you should be my best man." He winked at her.

She laughed at that. "Maybe." She was suddenly overwhelmed with emotion, and couldn't find her words.

"Chelle?" Simon squeezed her arm. "We want you there with us. It wouldn't be right without you."

"But I hurt you. Both of you."

"We're putting that in the past," Maggie assured her. "Say yes."

Michelle smiled. "Yes."

❧ 27 ❧

$\mathcal{H}$aving her best friends back in her life and seeing them together over the months leading up to their March wedding filled Michelle's heart with happiness. She could not imagine two people who were more perfect for each other. They were her heroes. Not only were they planning the wedding, they were remodeling Maggie's shop and merging their wedding photography businesses into one. It was inspiring. And seeing the love in Simon's eyes when he looked at Maggie made her long for that kind of love. She wasn't jealous of the fact that he had chosen Maggie. It was the opposite, in fact. She was overjoyed for them.

But being around them reminded her of what she had lost with Sean. She still thought about him, more than she should, and she wondered what he was doing. She wondered how the kids were and if they missed her. She wondered if he missed her.

On the morning of Maggie and Simon's wedding, the girls had breakfast at the James' residence. Patty and Vi made a glorious spread—bacon and eggs and pancakes and sausage. And there were waffles covered with fresh strawberries and whipped cream, made especially for the bride.

"Hey, you didn't make special waffles for me when Tom and I got married," Sarah whined.

"You didn't ask for them," Patty replied with wink.

Sarah pouted, then winced. "Ouch!" She poked at her protruding pregnant belly. "Quit kickin' me."

Maggie turned to Sarah and placed a hand on the spot Sarah had touched. "Now, you stay in there, little lady. At least until after the ceremony."

Sarah giggled. "She's staying put for at least two more weeks."

Michelle hoped she looked half as beautiful as Sarah if she one day had a baby. She really did have that pregnant glow people were always talking about.

Maggie's phone rang, and her lips turned up in a happy grin as she looked at the screen. She hit "talk" and practically cooed. "Hey, baby." Maggie's eyes swiftly focused on Michelle, and she suddenly looked giddy. "Uh-huh. OK. I'll tell her."

"What?" Michelle was curious. "Tell me what?"

Maggie held up her index finger. "Are you kickin' Tom's butt?"

The guys were at the church playing basketball. Michelle knew without asking that Simon probably hadn't scored a single point all morning. But she didn't care how his game was going, she wanted to know what they were talking about and what was behind the look on Maggie's face.

"I love you," Maggie declared. "I'll see you at the end of the aisle."

When she hung up, she looked at Michelle with a sly grin.

"What?"

Maggie could barely contain her smile.

"Maggie, what?"

"Sean's here."

Michelle's heart skipped a beat, and she nearly choked on a bite of pancake.

"He called Simon last night to let him know he made it to town, and Simon invited him to play basketball with them today."

Michelle didn't know what to say. She knew Sean had been invited to the wedding, but last she knew, he had sent an RSVP marked "will not attend".

"I thought you said he wasn't coming."

Maggie grinned and tilted her head to the side. "Surprise."

"Well, he's not here to see me, so ..."

Maggie touched Michelle's hand. "But he's here."

Michelle smoothed the skirt of her golden yellow bridesmaid dress and gripped her small bouquet of white hydrangeas and yellow ranunculus. She walked slowly down the aisle of the church to Pachelbel's "Canon in D", fighting the urge to scan the crowd for Sean. Knowing he was in attendance was nerve wracking.

Instead, she focused on Simon, smiling at her from the front of the church. It suddenly struck her as funny that, all those years ago, she had hoped Simon would one day be waiting for her at the end of the aisle, and now it was happening, though not in the way she thought it would. He looked so handsome in his tuxedo. She smiled back at him, and he pressed his lips together. She could tell he was fighting back tears, which caused her to fight tears of her own. They had been through so much together and had come out on the other side with their friendship still intact. He reached out and squeezed her arm as she passed by. There was nowhere in the world she would rather be at that moment.

Tom stood to the other side of Simon along with Uncle Pete. It was the sweetest thing in the world for him to ask his uncle to stand up with him.

Michelle took her place, followed by Sarah, the matron of honor. Sarah glanced back at her, and they both grinned and looked toward the entrance in anticipation.

The bridal march began, and Maggie made her way down the aisle on her father's arm. A sheer veil hung over her face and rested just past the edge of her strapless neckline. The silky organza of Maggie's gown angled and flowed softly around her legs as they walked. She looked like an angel.

It was hard to believe that fifteen years had passed since she first met this lovely girl in their dorm room. She never would have imagined that Maggie would one day marry Simon or that she would stand by their side.

Maggie's father lifted the veil from her face, kissed her on the cheek, then laid her hand in Simon's.

The smiles on their faces lit up the room. There was so much love in their eyes, and Michelle could not stop a tear from escaping down her cheek.

The happy couple chose to exchange traditional vows, and they smiled their way through them all.

"I, Simon, take you Maggie."

No hesitation.

"I, Maggie, take you Simon."

No sign of nerves at all.

"Til death do us part."

Just happy and very much ready to be married.

"I now pronounce you husband and wife." Pastor Jon smiled at Maggie, then glanced at Simon. "You may kiss the bride."

Simon grinned and shook his head in awe as he looked at Maggie. He took her face in his hands and kissed his wife for the first time.

And Michelle let the happy tears flow.

🤍

After the ceremony and family photos at the church, they were whisked off to downtown Hastings for bridal party photos with the couple's photographer friends, Jamie and Shannon. With temperatures in the forties, the girls wore coats over their dresses and tossed them at Simon's former photography assistant, Anna, when it was time for pictures. They posed by the fountain, on the steps of the old courthouse, and along the quaint streets. The giant mural on the side of the movie theater depicting scenes from movies like *E.T.*, *Forrest Gump*, and *Gone With The Wind* made for a fun backdrop. They took photos of the newlyweds in their new photography shop and at State Grounds. Then it was on to Hastings Country Club for the reception in the clubhouse.

Knowing Sean was somewhere inside made Michelle very nervous. She hoped they would get a chance to talk. If he wanted to talk to her, that is.

DeDe, the wedding coordinator and dear friend of Maggie's, arranged the bridal party just inside the entrance. As they waited, Michelle glanced over at the guest book table, which was decorated with candles, old vintage cameras, and a scrapbook. Anna stood to the side with a Polaroid camera to take photos of the guests, which they could then adhere to a scrapbook page and write their names and a note to the newlyweds. It was perfect for a couple of photographers.

The bridal party was soon announced and took their seats at the head table in front of the big stone fireplace. There were candles and different sized vases of yellow and white flowers along its length. In the center of each guest table were more flowers and candles and engagement photos of Maggie and Simon.

Ron James made his way to their table and took the microphone. "Welcome, friends and family. We're so happy you're all here to celebrate Maggie and Simon's special day with us." He glanced over his shoulder at his daughter. "I'm so proud of this beautiful girl of mine right here. And I'm very happy to officially welcome Simon into our family."

Simon gazed at his wife, whose smile beamed brightly.

Once Ron had prayed for the meal, the waitstaff went to work.

Michelle thought she saw Sean at a table on the far side of the room, but the lights were low, and there were too many guests in her line of sight.

She glanced over at Maggie and Simon, who were staring at each other. He leaned in and whispered something into her ear, then picked up his knife and started clinking it against the side of his glass. As the clinking of glasses filled the room, Maggie's hand lifted to her mouth, hiding her laughter. Simon stood and tugged her up from her seat. The smile on his face was ridiculous. He took her in his arms and leaned toward her slowly, barely moving, teasing her. Maggie gave him a disapproving look, then grabbed him behind the neck and kissed him. He smiled against her lips, then kissed her lovingly.

Michelle and Sarah clapped and cheered along with the guests.

Tom let out a loud, "*Woohoo!* Get a room!"

After the speeches were given, the happy couple danced to the song "Everything" by Michael Bublé. They swayed together, smiling happily, then Simon spun Maggie around a few times, and it was clear they had practiced a little choreography. They laughed their way through it all. Toward the end of the song, he pulled her in close and sang several lines of the song to her. It was a wonderful moment to witness.

Once the guests were invited to the dance floor, Michelle walked to the table for a drink of water. When she turned around to join the bridal party, Sean stood before her. He was wearing a pale blue dress shirt and colorful striped tie, looking handsome as ever, and her heart skipped a beat.

"Hi." He greeted her with a smile.

"Hi. I wondered if I'd see you today." She tried to act nonchalant.

"You look beautiful." Those eyes of his pierced through to her soul.

She smiled shyly and glanced down at the floor.

He didn't say anything else at first. He looked nervous. She wished she could read him, but that was the downside of spending so much of their relationship talking on the phone. She didn't know all of his quirks and tells.

"Would you like to dance?" he asked.

Now *she* was the nervous one. Dancing meant being in his arms again, which was the only place she really wanted to be. Butterflies started flitting around in her stomach. "The song is half over," she managed to say.

He held his hand out to her anyway, and she took it. He wound his fingers through hers and led her to the dance floor.

His hands rested on either side of her waist, and she wrapped her arms around his neck, which felt like the most natural thing in the world to do.

He stared into her eyes, and she was lost.

But he didn't say anything. She wanted him to say something to let her know what he was thinking.

The song ended far too soon, and he lowered his arms. "I should probably get back to my date."

"Oh, OK." Her heart sank. She almost heard it shatter into a million pieces.

As she turned to walk away, his hand clasped her wrist.

She looked back at him.

He grinned. "It's Ashley."

A smile broke out on her face. "Oh." She laughed nervously.

"Come say hello." He let go of her wrist and took her hand again.

She followed cautiously, still unsure of where things stood between them and still hurt that he had walked away when she needed him the most.

Ashley jumped up from the table as soon as she saw Michelle and greeted her with a hug.

Michelle was so happy to see her. "How are you, Ashley?"

"I'm OK. How come you and Dad aren't together anymore?" She got straight to the point.

Sean cleared his throat nervously. "Ash."

"Um." Michelle didn't know quite how to answer that. She changed the subject instead. "How's Aaron? Is he winning all his soccer games?"

Ashley rolled her eyes and took her seat again. "You can ask him yourself."

"Oh, he's here?"

"He found some kids his age. He's running around here somewhere," Sean answered. "Ash, I need to talk to Michelle for a minute. Will you be OK here?"

"I'm not two," she replied sarcastically, and gave her dad a smirk.

Sean started to lead Michelle to a quiet corner to talk, but there was a sudden commotion across the room.

Simon came running toward them and slid across the dance floor, almost knocking her over. "Chelle, Sarah's in labor!"

"What?" Michelle started laughing. "Are you kidding me?"

"Nope! It's happening."

They followed him across the room to the group of family members in panic mode. Sarah was more calm than any of them.

"Guys, we've got time." Sarah cringed at another contraction. "It's not like my water ..." A look of horror crossed her face as a puddle formed on the floor below her. She glanced down and her bottom lip stuck out in a pout. "... broke."

Tom's eyeballs nearly popped out of his head. "I'll go get the car."

Patty and Ron were rushing around letting people know what was happening.

Maggie ran off and returned with all of their things.

"No, Mags," Sarah cried. "Put that stuff down. You guys stay and enjoy your reception."

"Are you kidding me? No way! I'm not missing this. I'm supposed to photograph the birth."

"I know, but it's your wedding day." Sarah began to cry.

Vi piped in. "Maggie, it may be some time before Sarah actually has the baby. I think you and Simon should stay here a while longer, then go to the hospital once we know how far along she is."

Simon stepped up behind his wife and wrapped his arms around her waist. "She's right, baby."

Michelle glanced over at Sean, whose eyes were wide, then back at Maggie. "Is there anything we can do?" she asked.

Maggie noticed them standing together and raised an eyebrow at Michelle. "Can you drive to my shop and get my camera bag? Just in case."

"*Our* shop," Simon corrected her.

Maggie elbowed him.

"Absolutely," Michelle replied.

"Do you want me to come with you?" Sean asked.

She turned to him. "Don't leave the kids alone. I'll be back in like fifteen minutes. You'll still be here, right?"

He nodded. "Of course."

She smiled at him and took off for the shop.

෪ ♡ ෨

Michelle turned into a parking space in front of Walker Wedding Photography, Maggie and Simon's newly-renovated shop. She let herself in and went straight for the office. The camera bag was right where Maggie said it would be.

She glanced around the room. It was bigger than before, the rear wall expanded backward. There was an extra work station across the room for Simon and built-in storage along the walls. She had not been in the shop since that horrible day when she had confessed to Maggie and thought she lost her best friends forever.

She lifted the bag by its handle and started to carry it out when something caught her eye. On a large bulletin board of engagement and wedding announcements were a few photos of Maggie and Simon together and with family. Just beneath those were the picture of Michelle and Maggie in their dorm room on arrival day, a snapshot of Michelle and Simon taken freshman year, and one of the three of them taken this past Christmas. Seeing those captured memories on this special day filled her with joy. They had come full circle.

I don't know if I can possibly express how thankful I am to have these two people in my life, Lord. Thank you.

♡

When Michelle returned to the reception, she delivered the camera bag to the bride.

"Any news?" she asked.

Maggie shook her head. "Not yet. I can't believe she actually went into labor today. With all the teasing we did about it, I never thought it would actually happen."

"I know." Michelle's eyes scanned the room.

"He's over there."

She looked at Maggie, who was grinning as she nodded her head in the direction of the dance floor. Michelle followed her gaze and saw Sean dancing with his daughter.

"Thanks, Mags."

"You bet," Maggie replied. "Go get your man."

As the song came to an end, Michelle strolled across the floor toward them.

"Hey, you made it back."

"That's my cue." Ashley quickly departed the dance floor.

Michelle laughed.

"That was subtle." Sean rolled his eyes. "Can we talk now?"

She nodded.

Sean led her to a quiet, empty table overlooking the golf course, and she sat down beside him. He was quiet.

Knowing his trouble expressing his true feelings, Michelle waited for him to speak.

"I've got so much I wanna say, but I don't know where to start."

She was eager for his thoughts. "Just talk to me."

"I'm so sorry for the way I left things between us, for that thoughtless goodbye. I know that hurt you."

"Yes, it did."

"I'm sorry."

She gave him half a smile. "I'm OK now."

He nodded. "I can see that. You seem happy."

"I am. I'm in grad school now. Loving my job. And I took your advice and told Maggie everything."

"Oh, you did?" He leaned in a little closer. "How did that go?"

"It wasn't pretty, but we came through it OK." She made a motion toward the newlyweds across the room.

Sean smiled. "Obviously. I'm glad it all worked out." He took her hand in his then, and it sent a wave of goosebumps up her arm. "I wish I could say I've been as happy as you. I've been moping around for months. Aaron keeps asking why you haven't come to visit. Ashley rolls her eyes at me whenever I say it's complicated. Both of them want to know why I'm being such an idiot."

Michelle held in a laugh. "So, why *are* you?"

He grinned nervously at that. "All I can say is I was shocked. Hearing what you'd done put all sorts of thoughts in my head, and I was angry that you hadn't told me sooner. But I should've tried to help you work through everything instead of running away. You made some bad choices, but you're human. We all are. We all make mistakes, and you know I've made my share. We're saved, not perfect. That's what I should have told you back in August, but I kinda freaked out about the whole thing. And honestly, I was jealous."

"Of what?" This was unexpected.

He looked her straight in the eye. "Crazy jealous of every other guy that's ever been in your life. Because I wish I had been the only one."

She pressed her lips together to keep from crying and squeezed his hand. "I wish that, too."

"This is probably gonna sound really stupid. I know I wasn't, you know ... your first, but I guess I always assumed that since you became a Christian *after* we were together, that I was your last. I liked the idea that you hadn't been with anyone after me, so I was upset when I found out that wasn't true."

A quick puff of air escaped between her lips. "But you were with Lindsay *after* me."

"I know."

"And I thought if I told you the truth, you'd forgive me. You practically begged me to forgive you for Lindsay."

"I know. It was stupid and selfish, and it had everything to do with—"

"Your ego?"

"I was going to say my pride." Their eyes held for a moment. "I kept praying about it, asking God to help me let it go. By the time I realized what an idiot I had been, months had passed. And the more time that passed, the more I was afraid to pick up the phone. I was afraid it was too late."

She squeezed again, and he glanced down at their joined hands.

"I'm sorry it took me so long to get over myself." He raised her hand to his lips and brushed her knuckles with a soft kiss. "What I've been wanting to say, what I should have said ... what I've been rehearsing over and over in my head since I got in the car to come here is this. It doesn't matter to me what your past looks like, because I believe God has an amazing future planned for us."

Her chin began to quiver, and the tears fought their way out.

He took both her hands in his then. "I love you, Michelle."

Her tears spilled over, and she rapidly pulled her hands from his and wiped them away. She stood and took a few steps toward the window.

"Michelle?" Worry sounded in his voice as he followed.

She turned to face him again. "Are you sure about this? Because I don't think I can go through losing you a third time?"

The look in his eyes was as serious as she'd ever seen him. "Life is short. It can be taken away in a heartbeat. I've already wasted too much time without you." He took her face in his hands. "I want a life with you. I've never been more sure of anything."

She grabbed hold of his tie and tugged him to her, kissing him sweetly.

His fingertips caressed her neck and played with the wispy hairs that had fallen from her up-do, just like that night in his kitchen nearly a year ago.

When she pulled back, he wrapped her up in his arms. "I'm never letting you go again."

She smiled into his neck. "Sean?"

"Yeah?"

Michelle leaned back and looked him in the eye. "I want you to be my last."

The right side of his mouth turned up in the most gorgeous smile she had ever seen on a man.

"Because I love you, too."

The deep blue of his eyes glistened with tears of his own, and a grin spread across his face. His lips met hers again in what was by far the sweetest, most adoring kiss she had ever received in her entire life.

She felt so joyful and light, as though she might float off the floor and up into the clouds.

He pulled her close, his lips brushing against her earlobe.

Her knees were weak at the sensation. She didn't think anything could affect her as much as that, until he whispered a promise into her ear.

"I adore you, Michelle, and I intend to be the first and *only* man to show you what it's like to be truly loved."

Her heart melted right then and there, and she was happier than she ever thought possible. He really did have a way with words sometimes. She wrapped her arms around his neck and held on for dear life. *Thank you, Lord.*

"About time," Ashley cried as she walked toward them.

Aaron ran full speed in their direction and barreled into them.

They let go enough to make room for the kids in their hug.

Aaron squeezed in, then looked up at Michelle. "We've missed you."

Michelle hugged them both tightly. "I've missed you, too."

Sean suddenly began walking the group backward toward the dance floor. "I feel like dancing."

"Daddy!" Ashley nearly tripped over the leg of a nearby chair.

"Sean!" Michelle tried to walk backward as gracefully as she could.

Aaron burst out laughing.

Sean held them all close to him, one arm wrapped around Michelle, the other around the kids, and swayed to the music. "I love my family."

Tears sprung to Michelle's eyes. *Family.* It was what she had longed for, and now that dream was coming true. They were her family, and she was theirs.

Michelle rested her chin on Sean's shoulder as the four of them danced. She spotted Simon and Maggie not too far away. They both looked over at her and smiled. Simon gave her a thumbs-up, and she laughed.

"What?" Sean turned his head toward her.

"Simon and Maggie are happy for us, that's all."

He kissed her cheek softly. "I'm pretty happy for us, too."

"Oh, yeah?" She brushed her lips against his, and he smiled. Even those gorgeous eyes of his seemed to smile.

She was overcome with emotion then. Who would have thought that a girl like her, who'd had such a rough upbringing, would be blessed with such a wonderful man, such a bright future. She never would have dreamed of such a life back then. But now, she was amazed at the way God had orchestrated it all.

Back in college, it wasn't the right time for them. She could see that now. They had to go through life apart for a while, before finding their way back to each other. They had to love others and face the consequences of their choices. They had to struggle with life, with death, with family, with God. They had to wait until God brought them through the hard times, the broken hearts, the many mistakes they would make. They had to lose their way for a while to come back stronger.

Michelle saw it all with fresh eyes now, standing in the arms of the man of her dreams, watching her best friends start their life together. She had longed for Simon because *she* thought he was her perfect match, not because God had told her so. After Simon, she had prayed for her future husband, whoever he might be, that God would draw close to him and prepare his heart. She never dreamed that man would be Sean.

"Is it rude to get engaged at a friend's wedding?" Sean whispered, after Ashley and Aaron scurried off to eat more cake.

Michelle laughed. "Yes."

He smiled against her neck. "Because I have a rather large diamond ring burning a hole in my pocket right now."

Her mouth dropped open as she leaned back and looked at him.

"Not the right time, huh?" he teased.

She clamped her lips together and tried not to smile.

He leaned in close again. "I'm dying to call you my fiancée."

Her hands began to shake as he let go of her and dug into his pocket.

His smile lit up his entire face as he pulled out the ring. "I believe this is yours."

A grin spread across her face. "Yes. I believe it is." Tears filled her brown eyes as he slipped the sparkly ring onto her finger.

His hands trailed up her arms and over her shoulders, cupping her face as he pressed a soft kiss to her lips.

She was in a state of pure bliss as her eyelids slowly lifted. "I love you." She kissed him again and again, quick kisses on the lips, the cheeks, the nose.

He couldn't help but laugh at her sudden enthusiasm. He pulled her into another embrace, and they held each other through the next song.

Michelle's heart was overflowing with contentment and belonging and love for her future husband and his kids—their kids. God had given her the desires of her heart, and she felt whole for the first time in her life.

Sean leaned close once more. "I love you so much, and I can't wait to call you my wife."

She moved her lips close to his ear and smiled as she whispered, "Until then."

It was more than just their farewell phrase. It was a promise—to love each other in the present while they looked forward to every special moment ahead, to every milestone they would reach, to every day of their life together.

Acknowledgments

༄ ♡ ༄

This book would not have come into existence were it not for my Mom's listening ear, letting me ramble on about the idea on our morning walks. I had this crazy idea to turn *Goodbye, Magnolia* into a series by telling Michelle's story, but I only had a glimmer of an idea of who she really was. As we walked and I talked it out, I came up with the initial idea for the story, and it all went from there. Once I had written the first draft, Mom listened during a road trip while I told her the entire story start to finish. Thanks, Mom, for always listening while I talk too fast and too loud about my stories. And for always supporting me and being my #1 fan.

Thanks to my oldest and dearest friend, Jen, who also listened to me babble about a couple of my books on our annual camping trip. I took a little bit of inspiration for the character of Michelle from Jen—she was saved her freshman year of college and got her degree in psychology. Jen also has a niece named Ava, while Michelle's sister's name is Ava. I am so very thankful for her friendship and for her love and support.

Huge thanks to Sandra, who graciously allowed me to use one of her wedding photos for the cover of my book.

I love my Launch Team ladies. Their feedback and support mean the world to me. I'm thankful for connecting with each and every one of them. Special thanks to Heather and Anita for their input on this book. I appreciate them both so much.

All of my books are better because of my husband, Jacob. I wouldn't dream of releasing a book without getting his input first.

The greatest thanks of all go to my Lord and Savior, Jesus Christ. Salvation comes from Him and Him alone.

As always, thank you, lovely reader, from the bottom of my heart. I love telling stories. It brings me more joy than I can ever express in words. My heart is full because I get to share it with you on these pages.

Krista

An excerpt from
Goodbye, Magnolia
Cornerstone Book 1

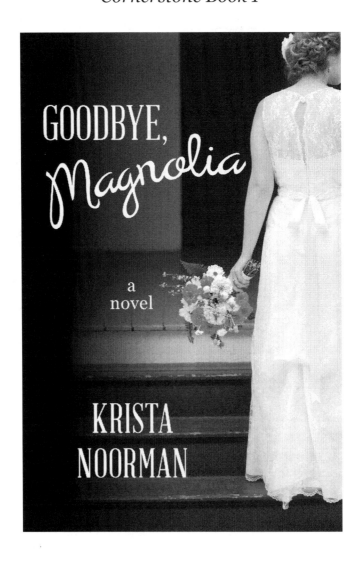

October 31, 1995

———— ⬦⬦⬦ ————

A Beginning

"*C*an I take your picture?"

They were the first words he ever spoke to her.

Maggie stared up into hazel eyes, clearly startled. "Excuse me?"

"For the assignment," he replied with a flirty grin.

The assignment given by Professor Wilkins, the instructor of their photography class, was to pair up and photograph each other using only natural light at a location around campus.

But *he* was the last person she wanted to partner with.

She glanced around the room and realized the other students had already chosen their partners.

"I guess," she reluctantly agreed.

Simon Walker was handsome and charming, immediately catching the eye of her roommate, Emma—the cute, petite one. His easygoing personality made him the friend of many, including her other roommate Michelle—the tall, athletic one. But there was something about him, an arrogance that was off-putting to Maggie. She often wondered if she was the only person on campus who disliked him, because it seemed every girl she knew was infatuated, and every guy wanted to be his best friend.

Maggie and Simon walked together from the Fine Arts building toward their assigned location—Miller Library. The air was brisk as they walked along the sidewalk lined with trees, half of which had already dropped their vibrant yellow and red leaves.

"You're Michelle's roommate," he stated. "Maggie, right?"

"Yeah. Maggie James." She had no idea he even knew who she was. They had been in class for two months, but he had never once acknowledged her existence.

"I'm Simon." He held his hand out to shake hers.

She hesitantly shook it. "I know who you are."

"What's with the Canon?" Simon asked.

"What do you mean?"

He pointed at the camera hanging around her neck. "Your camera."

She looked down at her Canon brand camera. It was new, purchased specifically for the class. Turning it over in her hands, she examined the lens and the camera body. Nothing appeared to be wrong with it.

"Huh?" She was confused.

"Why'd you go with a Canon?" he asked.

She noticed the shiny new Nikon camera with the expensive zoom lens in his hands. "What difference does it make? They both do the same thing, right?"

Simon shook his head, and his nut brown hair fell over his right eye. "Nikon is by far superior to Canon." He ran his fingers through his hair, smoothing it back into place.

Maggie was annoyed. "In what way?"

"Better lenses, faster focus—"

"Says who?" *Know-it-all.*

"My uncle's a photographer," he informed her. "He's done his research."

She rolled her eyes at his condescending tone. "Can we just get this over with?"

"OK." He seemed taken aback, as if no girl had ever been this cold to him before.

They walked into the library and found a bright spot near a wall of windows with light streaming in.

Simon slid a chair into position. "Sit here," he commanded.

She groaned inwardly as she put her camera on a nearby table and sat down in the chair. If she had known she would be the subject of a photograph, she might have worn something nicer than a hooded grey Cornerstone College sweatshirt.

He approached and smoothed a few of her sandy blonde hairs.

It was an awkward moment, and she wished she had chosen to wear her hair back in a clip rather than down.

He touched her chin and turned her head toward the window.

She pulled away from his touch. "What are you doing?"

"Don't move. The light is perfect on your face right now."

Maggie was completely uncomfortable. She hated being in front of the camera, but having Simon photograph her only made it worse. Every muscle in her body felt stiff and unnatural.

Simon crouched down and peeked through his camera. He shook his head, clearly exasperated, and looked up at her. "You need to relax."

"I hate having my picture taken."

"Why?" He looked puzzled.

She shrugged her shoulders. "I'm not very photogenic."

Simon let out a little laugh. "I don't believe that at all." He moved closer, still crouched, and examined her face.

Maggie could tell he wasn't really seeing her as a person, but as the subject of his photograph.

"You're not very good at this," she blurted.

He suddenly looked at Maggie the person. "Not good at what?"

"Making your subject feel comfortable in front of the camera."

His mouth fell open, and he stared at her in disbelief. "Maybe it's just you."

Maggie's eyes narrowed, and she crossed her arms. "Maybe I need a different partner."

He stood and lifted his arms in surrender. "Be my guest."

She shook her head. "It's too late now, and I'm not getting an incomplete on this."

"Fine," he grumbled. "Then relax."

She looked at him stone-faced, her arms still crossed, as he snapped a couple shots.

"Man, you're intense. Don't you ever smile?"

She refused to smile for him and kept her bright green eyes focused on his camera lens.

"I feel like you're about to melt me with laser beams from your eyes or something."

Maggie's face broke into a smile at his ridiculous comment.

Simon pressed the shutter release on the camera. "There it is." He looked over the camera and gave her a cocky grin.

She abruptly stood up. "OK, your turn."

They walked across the library to another wall of windows, and Maggie pointed to one of the large reading chairs.

Simon plopped down, leaned forward, and rested his elbows on his knees with hands clasped together. He was clearly as comfortable in front of the camera as he was behind it, which annoyed her immensely. It also bothered her how great he looked in a simple green henley and jeans. She shoved the thought from her mind. He looked at her with intense hazel eyes, brought out by the color of his shirt. She wished she could force away the warmth in her cheeks. She didn't want him to know he had any effect on her at all.

Maggie breathed in and out slowly as she looked through her camera's viewfinder. She begrudgingly took a few shots, but made a face, not satisfied with what she was seeing.

"What? Is this not intense enough for you?" he teased.

"Don't look at the camera."

He gave her a look of confusion. "Isn't that what we were assigned to do?"

"Yeah, but I like my pictures to be candid. More natural, like you don't know the camera's here."

"But I *do* know the camera's here." He looked thoughtful for a moment. "How do I do candid?"

"You need to relax." She gave him a sarcastic look as she echoed his earlier statement.

He grinned at her and nodded.

"I don't know. Pretend I'm not taking your picture or something." She lifted the camera again.

"Like how?" He shrugged his shoulders.

"Just look around."

"Can I still talk to you?"

"Whatever." She wished this was over already.

"OK." He sat up a little and looked directly at her. "Are you free tonight?"

She looked over the top of her camera in astonishment.

"What? I'm being candid." He had a little twinkle in his eye.

"That's a little *too* candid." She peeked through the viewfinder on her camera once more.

He stared directly into her lens. "We're having a costume party at the dorm. You should come."

Maggie glared up at him. "No, thanks."

All she could think about was Emma, who had been dating Simon since early in the semester. Sweet Emma, who had opened her heart to him. Yet here he was, very obviously flirting with her behind Emma's back. She didn't care if she *was* the only girl on campus who didn't like Simon. Her first impression of him had been dead on. Player, womanizer, heartbreaker—take your pick. They all described Simon Walker to a T.

"Michelle will be there." As if anything he said could convince her to come.

She took another look through the camera. "Well, good. Then you can hit on her instead."

Simon looked out the window as he laughed, a little glint in his eye.

Click!

"There it is," Maggie stated confidently.

He gave her a crooked, amused grin. Even his eyes seemed to smile. "You're good."

Maggie stood and gathered her things.

Simon stepped close and put his arm around her, pulling her against his side. "That was fun. We should do it again sometime."

She wiggled out from under his arm.

He took two steps away, then hesitated. "Hey."

Maggie looked over at him.

"It was nice meeting you, Maggie." That adorable grin of his was back again.

She didn't reply, just watched him stroll away, stopping to talk to—or rather flirt with—two girls before he walked out.

Her mind was made up.

Simon Walker wasn't worth her time—or anyone else's for that matter.

Made in the USA
Columbia, SC
03 May 2018